Skinny Dippin

© 2015

Published by:

Wright Professional Services, Inc.
235 Cash St
Cornelia, GA 30531
tugalophil@gmail.com
(706)201-1092

First Edition

ISBN-13:978-0692494073, ISBN-10:0692494073

Acknowledgements

The support and assistance of Cornelia Walker Bailey were essential to the production of this work. Cornelia's book, <u>God, Dr. Buzzard and the Bolito Man: A Saltwater Geechee Talks About Life on Sapelo Island, Georgia</u>, inspired much of the content. Thank you, Cornelia, for your honesty, kindness, and faith in my efforts. Thanks as well to Frank Bailey for his assistance and hospitality.

The artwork for the project was done by a friend, D. Corey Sisk. Tragically, he took his own life before the book was finished. Corey, I miss you and wish you could have held this book in your talented hands. Your art speaks for itself. I feel your spirit stirring in my life and in these pages.

Dr. Betty Burnett, PhD., retired professor/editor, had to teach me to write. Bless you for your patience and your great talent as a teacher. We should remember not to judge teachers by their students. They must work with what they're given.

Many friends have contributed: Ken Shank, Dudley Sisk, Margie Cheek, Elisa M. Coulter, and Susan Parker. Bill Sheehan and Jennie Alvernaz leap to mind. Others include Sudy Leavy and Jeana Collins. I must also thank Dr. Emerson Brooking and his wife Ginny. Thanks to Wes and Cassie Wright for their skills and support. Darlene, your work with punctuation and the difficult issue of Geechee spellings was crucial. Yes, it took a village.

Of course, special gratitude for Mary Will, my mother, who taught me to love all people and most books. I've tried to make you proud.

Other non-fiction works were important sources of information, including, <u>Incidents in the Life of a Slave Girl</u>, by Harriet Jacobs; <u>Drums and Shadows</u>, by the Georgia Writers Project; <u>Slave Songs of the Georgia Sea Islands</u>, by Lydia Parrish, and the scholarship of Dr. Lorenzo Dow Turner.

Ultimately, <u>A Geechee Homecoming</u> is a work of fiction. Readers should not misinterpret poetic license as fact.

A Geechee Homecoming

By:
Philip Wright
Clarkesville, GA

In consultation with:
Cornelia Walker Bailey
Sapelo Island, GA

All artwork by:
D. Corey Sisk
His art available:
http://www.artistkori.smugmug.com

Spring, 1858. Brunswick, Georgia

CHAPTER 1

Winnie and Etta bolted ahead of everyone down the stairs and out the side door of the church. A few white people were exiting the front as Winnie and Etta walked shoulder to shoulder in the church's side yard, talking quietly.

Winnie laughed. "Dat new boy wuz gettin' his eyes full uh you. Thought he gon fall out'uh de pew tryin' tuh look 'round me."

"Naw." Etta shook her head. "I'm too black for 'im. All de boys over heah like dere girls brown. You know what dey say, 'De lightuh, de bettuh.' He warn't looking at me." Etta stole a glance at the doorway leading to the church balcony.

"Oh, yeah, he wuz, but don't pay 'im no mind. You see dem old man's ragged clothes he wear? And 'sides, he way shorter dan you is."

"He got a handsome face."

Winnie laughed. "Yeah, but lawdy, did you see dem boots? Dat boy hell on ants." She turned and studied the doorway. "Nebuh seen nuttin' like it. You dun put de spell on dat boy. You Saltwater Geechee always puttin' de spell on somebody. Watch now, he gon come obuh heah and try an' talk to you, fuh sho."

1

Etta glanced over Winnie's shoulder as the black churchgoers eased down the steep, irregular steps and into the shaded side yard. Some of the older women moved slowly, hands pressed tightly against opposite walls.

Winnie glanced around as well. "Turn 'round now. I see 'im."

Etta practiced a vacant look.

"What I tell yuh? He's coming dis way. Stand up straight now. Le's see whut he gon say."

Etta stood straighter, took a deep breath and stared into space.

The slim youth walked straight up to them. "How y'all doin'? My name's Dan. T'ought dat preachuh nebuh stop talkin'. Whut yoh names?"

Winnie looked at him and paused. "My name's Winnie. Dis heah is Etta."

She nodded.

"How y'all doin' on dis pretty day?"

Winnie tilted her head and stared back. "We fine."

Etta glanced at him briefly, smiled, and looked back down. With the toe of her shoe, she began pushing rotting acorns into the soft soil.

"Whut y'all doin' dis aftuhnoon?" Dan looked straight at Etta. "Some uh us gon get togeduh and have a ballgame 'hind de church heah. Why don't you gals come on back down heah after dinnah an' watch de game?" He stood with his hands in his pockets, shifting his weight from one foot to the other.

Etta, head still bowed, looked sideways and smiled again. *Dose clothes are bad, and he 'bout de skinniest boy I ever seen, but he got a nice smile and a handsome face.*

2

Winnie turned toward Dan and lifted one eyebrow. "So we gon spend our aftuhnoon down heah watching you play ball?"

Dan's back stiffened, and he turned away slightly but then turned back and held his ground. "We kin do sumpin else if'ns yuh wants to."

Etta turned toward him. "I'd like to go for a walk 'round town."

Winnie gave a soft but audible grunt.

"But my grandma prolly ain't gon let me do dat."

Dan turned his back on Winnie and moved a little closer to Etta. "We could walk obuh to de dry goods sto weh I wurk. We mights could get a col' drink. Dere's a ice box obuh dere."

Winnie frowned at him. "Hmm, sto ain't open today."

"Dat don't mattuh. I's de stock boy dere. I kin get in. Lib' in de back." He smiled at each of them in turn.

Winnie looked Dan up and down. "Well, weh yuh come from, Dan?"

He didn't meet her gaze. "My massuh has a little farm up in Darien." His smile was gone. "Got on hard times an' sold me and my sistahs off." Dan shook his head a little, frowned and took a deep breath. "Needed de cash, I reckon." He pushed his shoulders back and smiled thinly. "I brought top dolluh. Course he ain't my massuh no moh. Don't s'pose I'll ebuh see dat place 'gin, but I wuz sho lucky tuh be bought by Massuh Giles and brought down heah."

"Weh yoh sisters?"

Dan frowned, speaking softly. "Don't rightly know." His voice cracked, then trailed off. "Ain't no tellin'… No tellin' 'bout dat." He took another deep breath. "He jus' bought me." Dan looked off and turned away

3

from them, tightening his fists in his pockets and blinking his eyes. Almost inaudibly he added, "Sho do miss'em. Mama, too."

Etta and Winnie darted startled looks at each other and then moved, putting Dan between them. Etta touched Dan's arm for a moment. "Wish we could do something today Dan, but my grandma never let me do much of nuttin', 'specially talk to boys."

Winnie studied the crowd.

Dan and Etta strolled a few steps away. "You'll get a chance to see your mama 'gin. I been missin' mine, too."

Winnie called out, "Heah she come."

Etta frowned deeply and looked down. "Well, dats, dat, Dan. I... I'd like to go for a walk, but sure as de world, if I mention coming back down heah, she'll have somethin' for me to do."

Winnie spoke, "'Lo, Miss Medina."

Medina, a large woman with very dark skin, didn't respond. She motioned with a sheaf of papers she was carrying. "Etta. Etta, come on now." She paused. "Got tuh get on back tuh de house. Miss Elouise gon drop obuh dis aftuhnoon." She glanced at Winnie and gave Dan a curt nod, then brushed by the group. "Le's go."

Etta looked at her grandmother, opened her mouth, then shook her head and looked down. "Sorry, Dan. Got to go to de house."

"Weh's dat? I'll come dere and see yuh."

"Won't do no good. Grandma ain't gon let you in."

Medina paused, looked back, frowned at Etta but continued walking.

Dan spoke fast as Etta turned away. "Maybe we's could sit togeduh at church nex' Sunday?"

4

Etta lifted her eyes and turned back toward Dan, smiling. "I would like dat. I'll save you a spot."

Medina stopped and called back. "Come on now! Ain't got all day tuh stan' 'round heah!" She turned and walked away again.

Etta looked closely at her grandmother. *Wonduh what dem papers she carryin'.* She and Winnie tagged along several steps behind.

"Sho walks fast fuh a big woman," Winnie observed. "Whut you so quiet 'bout now? Least you kin sit wid de boy nex' week at church. She ain't gon stop dat. While yuh at it, maybe yuh kin fin' him some clothes to weah." She lifted on corner of her mouth and shook her head. "Massuh run de dry good sto' and sen' him to church lookin' like dat? I knows dem people. Dey big in de church. Sho ain't big in takin' care uh nobody. Anyways, whut you stewin' 'bout now?"

"It don't matter. You know I'm goin' back over to Bonita next Monday." Etta jammed her fists down in the little pockets Medina had sewn on her Sunday dress. "Ain't gon be able to see Dan no moh after dat nohow. Whut dif'nce do it make?"

"Yoh grandma de only free black woman I knows, an lawdy if she don't act like uh massuh and you de slave. Hellfire, I get to do lots more dan you do."

"Yeah, I might as well be livin' in a convent."

Winnie stopped briefly and shook her head. "What? In a what?"

"A convent. It's a place where womens who is Catholic go live together, and dey all be married to Jesus."

5

Winnie's eyebrows shot up, and she stopped again. "Dat's de craziest t'ing I ebuh hear'd of in my life. You read dat in one of dem storybooks you always lookin' at? Dem books done made yuh crazy, gal."

Etta laughed to herself, shook her head, and walked along in silence. *Sometimes I think I live in a world all by myself.*

As Winnie turned toward Miss Elouise's, she called back to Etta. "Might be 'long wid Miss Elouise dis aftuhnoon if'n she don't have too much wurk fuh me to do."

Etta looked up and gave a smile and a small wave to her friend. She continued to trudge along several steps behind her grandmother.

Despite her focus on the heels of Medina's worn shoes, Etta noticed a movement out of the corner of her eye. Looking to her right, she saw a slim figure across the street, standing in front of a store window. Dan turned and waved at Etta after Medina passed. As Etta drew even, Dan took his other hand out of the pocket of his ragged pants and blew her a kiss. Etta smiled to herself, but shook her finger at Dan and put a stern look on her face. Then she returned his broad smile, tilting her head back in greeting. Still smiling, she looked down and slowly shook her head, continuing up the street in her grandmother's wake.

A few days ago I sure wouldn'uh wanted to stir Grandma up, but what dif'nce do it make now. Ain't gon be heah but one more week nohow. She glanced back noticing that Dan crossed over to her side of the street.

Betcha he's following us to see where I stay. Wonder what Grandma's gon do when she figure dat out. Nevertheless, Etta felt her mood lift and found a bounce in her step. *Danejus, but le's see what happens. Got to be*

better dan my usual Sunday afternoon sittin' 'round wid ol' folks. All I do is
spend my time reading 'bout how other people live.

Me? I been livin' de dullest story of all times. Shoot, I am almos' 15.
Lot uh girls be done took up wid somebody by de time dey 15. Me? Can't
even talk to nobody. Can't sit in de house or on de porch and talk to a boy
like normal folks. What does she think she is potecting me from? I sure
don't need a house full of babies pullin' on me. Maybe things'll be better
over on Bonita. Maybe after I'm 15, Mama and I can come back over heah
one Sunday and I can see Dan. Go wherever I please.

They walked up the path to the back of the house that served as
Medina's bakery and home. Medina went through the little room that Lonzo
had added to the back. Lonzo was Etta's maternal grandfather. His master
was the owner of the local hardware store. He used Lonzo and a small crew
of men to build houses and other buildings around the community. Lonzo
had a particular talent for building. The room he had built for Medina served
as her pantry and Etta's bedroom. She fell across the bed.

"Change yoh clothes now," Medina called out. "Ain't gon be ironin'
dat dress 'gin next Sunday."

Etta rolled off the bed and made sure her curtains were closed. *Don't*
need Dan thinking I'm puttin' on a show. She took off her Sunday dress and
slipped on a longer, unstarched cotton one her mother had given her the last
time she had come ovuh from Bonita to visit.

While Medina was busy in the kitchen serving up leftover greens,
cornbread, streak-uh-lean meat, and red peas, Etta lay back across the bed,
reached over and picked up a book Miss Elouise had given her. She found
her place and tried to read. *Can't keep my mind on dis story. I know he's out*

7

dere. Wonder what he's doing, how long he'll hang 'round. Etta put her book down on the bed, got up, went over to the window by the outside door and pulled back an edge of the curtain. *Don't see 'im.* She took in a quick breath as it hit he*r. Dem white folks obuh dere gon send for de law if dey sees 'im out dere. Don't like us heah no ways. Maybe he didn't come.* Etta went quickly to the window that looked out the back of the house toward the little woodshed and the chicken coop. *Dere he is. What am I gon do? Look at 'im, all casual-like, leaning up 'ginst de end of dat shed. Winnie's right. He ain't very tall.*

When he saw her movement at the window, Dan jerked his head back as if to say, "Come on."

Etta turned and looked through the doorway leading back into the kitchen. Medina noticed her. "Wash up now. I's puttin' it on de table."

"Yassum." Etta stayed still, watching her grandmother closely. "Be right back, Grandma. I hear something out heah 'round de chicken coop."

Medina looked up, but Etta quickly slipped out the back door and ran to the woodshed. She turned her worried feelings into an angry look. "You better get out of heah. Dem folks over dere gon sen' for de law."

Dan grinned at her. "Cain't 'scape frum me dat easy, can yuh?"

Etta shook her head. "Go on now. Got to eat dinner. You gon get me in trouble."

"Whut she gon do, take de whip to yuh?" Dan smiled, still leaning against the shed.

"Yeah, she got a whip all right. But it's a tongue. Gon give you a lash or two if you don't get out'uh heah."

Dan laughed loudly and crossed his arms over his chest, not moving.

8

"Go on now, dem white neighbors over dere already hates us. Dey see you slinking 'round heah, and dey'll 'ave you 'rested."

Dan reached his hand out to Etta. Suddenly quiet, she responded with her own. He took it, squeezed it gently, and held it to his cheek. He spoke quietly. "Hand's so soft."

She smiled at him. *He 'bout de sweetest boy I ever met.*

He released her hand, smiled, winked and nodded, then turned and headed back down the narrow buggy path toward the dirt street.

Etta hurried to the house. When she reached the back door, they both stopped and looked at each other. Dan smiled broadly. "I'll see yuh nex' Sunday." With that, still grinning, he broke into a lope, clomping loudly down the packed soil of the narrow driveway.

Etta looked down at the hand he had held.

Chapter 2

Medina woke Etta well before daylight. She was busy rolling out pie dough when Etta came in and began making a fire in the large woodburning stove, using the wood she had split and brought in the afternoon before.

"Morning, Grandma."

"Moanin'. I t'inks you kin do it in three trips tuhday. Whut is I gon do w'en yuh ain't heah tuh hep me no moh?"

"Winnie be a big help, Grandma."

Medina grumbled to herself. "Not dis early in de moanin, she won't."

Etta picked up the rolling pin and began rolling out sheets of dough, pressing the sheets into pie pans, then cutting some in strips that would go on top of the fruit.

She glanced over at her grandmother. "I believe you need some more pie pans, Grandma. I can go by de dry goods store an' get you some."

Medina knitted her brow and looked thoughtful. "Hmm, not tuhday, Etta. Look now, aftuh yuh sees yoh mama nex' week, I'd like hit if'n yuh wud go down tuh Grandpa Abraham's, let 'im knows yuh's back, get 'is 'pinion on t'ings."

"Why is dat, Grandma? Opinion on what?"

"Jus' do dat fuh me, Etta. He's in his eighties now an' ain't gon be wid us dat much longuh. 'Sides, he still got some say 'bout de bidness ovuh dere. Mr. Wilson lis'en to 'im some. He kin be a big hep to yuh and yoh mama boff."

"What do we needs hep for?"

Medina frowned at her. "Slabes need all de heps dey kin get!"

Etta stopped working and stood silent for a moment. "You reckon I'll ever be free, Grandma?"

Medina got a small stool and began taking down jars of canned fruit from a high shelf. "I wuz mighty lucky, Honey. Yoh best chance prolly be fuh de whole country tuh go free, but yuh keeps up wid dat stuff moh dan me."

"Yeah. Well, de big thing right now is dat lot uh slaves are 'scapin' up North and ain't bein' sent back, Grandma. From what I'm readin', most places, people jus' let 'em be, don't turn 'em in to de police. Don't pay no 'ttention to de Slave Act. Most black folks up North jus' be free 'long as de bounty hunters don't get 'em."

Etta slid the pie pans she had prepared over toward Medina. "Course way down heah, ain't no way hardly for folks to get up North, 'specially wid me being stuck out on dat island."

11

Medina was focused on adding the canned fruit as pie filling. "Dat 'minds me. Lizbeth gib me some newspapers an' uh magazine b'fo' church. She brought 'em back frum New York City an' ax'd me to gib 'em tuh yuh. You kin hab' 'em w'en yuh gets done wid yoh 'liveries tuhday."

Etta's eyes widened and she smiled broadly. "Thank you, Grandma."

"Yuh needs to write Miss Lizbeth a note an' t'ank her." Medina added strips of dough across the top of each pie.

"Yassum."

Etta's movements became quicker around the kitchen. Her grandmother glanced up at her and frowned. Etta poked at the fire and started to put the first pies in the oven.

"Are yuh sho dat's stove's hot?" Medina slipped around Etta, licked her finger and touched it to the stove. "Awright now, slow down an' watch whut yuh doin'. Stove ain't ready."

"Yassum." Etta took a deep breath, pulled the pies back out of the oven and poked at the fire some more. "I've heard you womens talk 'bout it before, but tell me 'gin, Grandma, 'bout how you got your freedom."

Medina smiled into her bowl and was quiet for a few moments. Etta wasn't sure she was going to respond.

"Should'uh been easy, but den Miss Julia t'ink she gon live fo'ebuh, I reckon. Nebuh got 'round tuh puttin' hit in her will. Makin' a will at all, fuh dat mattuh. She talked 'bout it lots but nebuh done nuttin'."

Medina began cutting out large circles of dough, adding filling, and folding them over. She took a fork and crimped the edges. "Warn't fuh Lizbeth and Elouise, no tellin's where I be or who be ownin' me. Doctuh done tol' Julia dat she had de 'monia. I talked to her mysef. I say, 'Julia, I

12

hates tuh brings dis up, but yuh 15 years older dan I is. If yuh pass b'fo' me, dem boys uh yoh's gon sell me off for sho. Yuh know Lizbeth don't want me. She don' belieb in slabery."

Medina looked over at Etta. "Miss Julia, she promised dat she wuz goin' tuh de lawyuh and gets hit done, but den nebuh done nuttin'. I eben ax'd Lizbeth tuh talk to her mama, but dat didn't turn out no bettuh."

Medina retrieved a large, deep, cast-iron fry pan and put it on top of the stove. "Hand me dat oil dere." She added oil to the fry pan from a gallon tin.

"Yuh 'membuh? She passed back in '53, an' sho 'nuf, Mr. Luke done tol' de lawyuh whut hanlin' de estate, tuh sell de house and auction ebuht'ing else, 'cluding me. Miss Lizbeth fuss wid her bruduhs an' go down dere and raise sand at de lawyuh, but hit don't do no good."

Etta was rolling out one last batch of dough but soon had to move away from the warming stove. "Were you scared, Grandma?"

"Sho I wuz scairt. Been doin' as I please fuh so long, couldn't 'magine bein' back to 'Yassum, No'um.' Lawd, Miss Julia an' I libed togeduh lack sistuhs. Aftuh Dr. Robert died, we gots tuh be de bes' of frien's. I did do fuh her, but she warn't no trubble 'til de bery end. Hadn't uh been fuh Elouise and Lizbeth, I s'pose I could'uh ended up out in de field hoein' cotton in some fah-off place."

Etta opened the oven of the large, cast-iron stove and put in four pies. She looked up at the clock on a high shelf. "It's six o'clock, Grandma. What did Miss Elouise and Miss Lizbeth do?"

"Well, Etta, Honey, heah is how dey pulled hit off. Yuh knows Elouise an' Lizbeth both be smart womens. Dey got dere ways uh gettin'

13

whuts dey want." Medina laughed and shook her head. "Lawdy, you don't wants to be on de uduh side of any dealin's wid dem two.

"Aftuh dey realize dat dey couldn't stop de auction, we all sets down an' gots to wurk. Dey went 'round town and took down all de little 'nouncements dey could find. Had uh big ol' bag uh 'em. Den dat Miss Lizbeth … Lawdy mercy, she so good at actin', she oughtuh be up on de stage."

Etta collected the scraps of dough on the table, rolled them into a ball and then used the rolling pin on this last bit. "What she do, Grandma? She buy yuh?"

Medina took one of the folded, hand-sized pies and touched the edge of it to the hot oil. "Naw. Yuh know how she hate de idee uh buyin' peoples. She don't talk 'bout whut she done, 'cause hit wuz scandalous really." As Medina filled the pan with the small pies, she looked through her eyebrows at Etta and shook her head. "Don't wanna sees yuh actin' like Lizbeth done towards dat slabe traduh."

"Who's dat?"

"He a man whut libes heah in Brunswick. He buys an' sells folks all obuh de coast down heah. Ebuhbody call 'im Cap'n Jack. Head uh de Brunswick paddyrollers, too. He a mean man but makes good money tradin' wid de small slave ownuhs. We'uns knowed Cap'n Jack been 'vited to de auction by de lawyuh. So Lizbeth an' her 'usban' go down tuh de restraunt weh Jack eat ebuh moanin', an' she starts her act. You know dat hotel restraunt dat yuh delivuh tuh down dere on Newcastle."

Etta glanced up and nodded.

14

Medina took down another large fry pan, put it on the stove and added oil. "Her 'usban's special, or he woudn'uh let her do sumpin lack dis. W'en Cap'n Jack go up tuh pay 'is bill, Lizbeth sashay up dere and bend obuh dat case dey got fuh sellin' knick-knacks. She act lack she's lookin' at sumpin. You know dat Lizbeth, she's de one whut usely bein' looked at. Anyways, she up dere givin' Cap'n Jack uh eyeful."

Etta's eyes got big as she picked up a spatula and examined the pies in the first fry pan. "Yassum. I see de mens lookin' at her."

"Anyways, she bend obuh dat case and den twist 'round an' bump her backside into dat nasty man."

Etta put a hand over her open mouth, laughing. "What he do?"

Medina began filling the second fry pan with pies. "Story I heah is dat Lizbeth turn 'round an' batted her big eyes at 'im and says sumpin like, 'Oh, I is soo sorry. Please fohgive me.'

"He say, 'Oh, I'm sho hit wuz my fault, Ma'am.'

"Lizbeth, she smile sweet-like. 'Ain't you dat Captain Jack I've hear'd 'bout?'

"He tipped 'is hat an' say, 'Yes, ma'am,' bowing kinduh deep.

"'Our lawyer wuz telling us dat yuh will be at de auction uh my mother's estate dat we be havin' dis Satday. I be glad to see you dere.' She smile at 'im and bat her eyes 'gin.

"Cap'n Jack nodded and touched his hat. 'My pleasure, Ma'am.'

"Lizbeth ax lack she goin' back tuh de table, den she look back obuh her shoulduh an' spring de trap. 'Oh Jack, we have some kinfolk comin' in frum out uh town, an' we's moved de time uh de auction back frum three tuh five o'clock so dey kin make hit. I 'ope dat don't inconvenience yuh none.'

15

"Cap'n Jack paused and frowned, an' he say, 'Oh, no, ma'am. Dat be fine.' Wid dat, she sashay on back to de table."

Etta began turning the pies in the first fry pan. "So, Grandma, Cap'n Jack wadn't dere for de auction? Miss Elouise was able to buy you den?"

Medina bent over laughing. "Oh, he showed up awright. Miss Lizbeth's spell wurk too good, an' he come early. She had to carry on wid 'im in de kitchen whiles Miss Elouise call out her bid in de livin' room, 'One dolluh!'

Etta laughed, then furrowed her brow. "She bought you for a dollar?"

"Elouise done talked to ebuhbody whut come, mos' uh 'em frien's uh de famly.' She say, 'Yuh knows whut Miss Julia say w'en she wuz alibe. She want Medina tuh go free.' Sho 'nuf den, nobody bid 'ginst Miss Elouise. De auction man start at 300 dollah an' end up at one." Medina laughed. "W'en ol' Cap'n Jack realized dat he 'ad been took, he cussed out de auctioneer an' den stormed out'uh de house. Miss Elouise tell de lawyer tuh draw up the 'mancipation papers, and dat's how I gets my freedom."

Medina began cleaning up, and they were quiet for some time. Finally, she spoke up. "I know I been keepin' yuh close to de house, Etta, Honey. At fus' I didn't want yuh havin' lot uh frien's obuh heah, cause I t'inked you'd be goin' on back to Bonita dat first Fall.

"Den t'ings go frum bad to worser wid Miss Frances an' Mr. Thomas obuh dere. Yoh mama ain't wanted yuh dere wid de fussin' dat wuz goin' on at de Main House. She 'fraid Miss Frances take her craziness out on yuh.

"I ain't knowed whut tuh do 'cept tuh hope dem folks fuhgets 'bout us obuh heah. Ain't wanted peoples talkin' 'bout yuh, who yuh seein', whut yuh doin'. I knowed dat yoh walkin' 'round town, makin' 'liveries wuz bad 'nuf.

Buts yuh knows dat folks lub' tuh gossip 'bout who doin' whut wid whosumebuh. I figured de less said 'bout yuh 'round heah, de bettuh.

Etta sat down at the table. "Aw, Grandma, dat ain't no reason why I can't sit on de porch and talk to a boy."

"If'n yuh 'ad got yohse'f wid chile, dey woulduh snatched yuh back fuh sho tuh claim de baby."

"Dat's crazy, Grandma. I ain't gon carry on like dat. Jus' want some friends to talk to." Etta's mind jumped to an image of Dan holding her hand. She shook her head.

Medina added the last pies to the hot oil. She spoke louder. "Well, yuh headed back now, an' hit's gon be hard on yuh, Honey. Least now yuh ain't got tuh worry 'bout leabin' no boy obuh heah."

Etta frowned, then looked up. "Hard on me? What you talkin' 'bout? Don't worry so much, Grandma. We'll get along awright. You know Mama knows how tuh handle dem folks."

Medina shook her head and looked up at the clock. "Yuh in fuh a change. Lissen up, now." Medina's eyes were focused straight ahead. "Gon be dif'nt obuh dere w'en yuh get back."

"What you mean different? De baby? I don't mind helpin' wid de baby. Me an' Mama get 'long fine, Grandma."

Medina shook her head strongly. "Miss Frances, she ..."

"Dat's my home, Grandma. Don't worry 'bout dat. Dey know me. I did a good job at de Main House. Loved making a pretty table, placing de food just so.

"I know Miss Frances didn't care dat much for me, but she liked de work I done. Liked de way I folded de napkins, set de table and how I waited on folks.

"When I got it jus' right, I could stan' back an' look at dat whole spread. It was almost like my gift. Didn't cook it. Guess it was more like somebody else's present dat I wrapped. Den I go in and 'nounce to Miss Frances dat, 'Dinner is served.' De best part for me was standin' dere whiles dey ate an' listenin' to what dey talk 'bout."

Medina gave a tight smile, still not looking at her granddaughter.

Etta stood back up at the stove, one hand on her hip, the other holding the spatula. She looked around at her grandmother. "Dat Miss Frances didn't care much fuh big parties, but dere was sure a lot of company. Family from up North. Brunswick folks. Some expert on dis or dat from de University. Lawdy, dere wuz some good talk at dat table.

"'Cept for Edward, dey never pay me no mind. Sometimes dey be talkin' 'bout sumpin I was real interested in, and Edward, he look over at me and smile. We could read each other's minds back den. I think dey let me come heah so's you could teach me tuh cook. Dey remember you over dere."

Medina's frown deepened, and she raised her voice again. "Jus' 'membuh hit don't mattuh all dat you knows and unuhstan's. Yuh has tuh keep your mouf shet obuh dere.

"Dis wurl heah, weh you sit 'round wid grown womens, White and Afican, and talk 'bout whut you jus' read, hit's gon be uh dif'nt wurl obuh dere now. Yuh heah me?"

18

Etta frowned and shook her head. "Sure, Grandma. Sure." *What's de bee in her bonnet?*

Medina wiped the workspace with a damp towel. "Yuh knows 'bout play actin'. Yuh gon be playing de part uh a slave obuh dere, but hit be fuh real. Ain't gon be lack hit wuz b'fo'." Medina turned and stared intently at Etta, her words coming in a hiss. "Be keerful, watch yoh mouf and do as yuh tol'."

Etta stopped work and stared back, her mouth open. "Awright. You always worryin' 'bout sumpin, Grandma." *She's more worried 'bout my goin' back dan I is. She sure actin' funny.*

Medina studied her granddaughter for several moments, opened her mouth to speak, then shook her head. She glanced up at the clock again, picked up a thick cloth, walked over, opened the stove and began taking the large pies out of the oven. She placed them on racks to cool.

As the sun cleared the horizon, Etta took the trays full of baked goods and began sliding them into the large, framed knapsack she used for delivery. She laughed to herself. *Grandma don't want people to notice me, but den she send me out to walk all over town wid dis thing on my back.* Etta shook her head. *Wish we 'ad a horse and buggy like normal folks.*

Chapter 3

The next day Etta finished her deliveries and was headed back by the dry goods store. *Wonder if I should go 'round back an' try to see Dan? I could jus' go in de front and get some prices on dere pie pans, see if I can get a chance to talk to 'im. Dey'll sure be watchin' me if I go in de front.*

Etta slipped down the alley, peeked around the corner and down two stores to the back of Giles Dry Goods. There was a wagon loaded with large feed sacks parked behind the store. As Etta paused, Dan came out the back. She started to call out but hesitated, afraid someone was with him. He turned his back and began to wrestle one of the large burlap bags off the wagon. She watched as he staggered inside with it, looking a bit like an ant carrying a leaf. She stepped back. *Lawdy, I don't want to cause him no trouble.*

Etta turned around and went back out to Main Street, stepped up on the little porch in front of the store but hesitated again. *It be better if dey were busy. Need for dat woman who works in dere to be helpin' somebody else.*

Etta stood around out front for several minutes hoping another customer would show. *I bought things for Grandma in dis very store. Go on in dere.* She took her knapsack and put it next to the door.

A little bell rang as she entered. The young white woman who had helped her in the past was nowhere to be seen. The shop owner himself came from the back of the store. *Leave. Now!* Etta's mind screamed, but her feet didn't move.

The shopkeeper stared blankly at her. "What you want?"

Etta paused. "Uh, my grandma wanted me to see what size pie pans you got and how much dey is."

The shopkeeper frowned at her.

As Etta peeked around the shopkeeper, Dan put down a sack, turned around and spied her. Etta quickly looked away and moved in the direction the storekeeper was pointing. "They over there against the wall. Two sizes. I think the small is a nickel, and the large is seven cents."

"Yassuh. Thank you, Suh." Etta backed for the door.

"Hey, Etta! Whut you doin' heah?" Dan came straight toward the front of the store.

The storekeeper turned and faced him, hands on his hips. "Get on back to work, Boy!" He turned back to Etta as she put her hand on the door handle.

"Thank you, Suh."

Dan ran forward and called out, "Wait, yuh ain't gots to ..."

21

The shopkeeper turned, catching Dan full in the face with the back of his left hand, sending him sprawling into the leg of a heavy table holding men's overalls.

Etta yelled, "No," took two full steps toward Dan before catching herself.

Dan, on his hands and knees, turned to her, blood running freely from a cut over one eye. Giles had turned fully on him now, though his voice was measured, "Didn't I tell you to get back to work? Now get that wagon unloaded before I take a strap to you!"

Tears streamed down Dan's cheeks as he tore his eyes from Etta's face, got up and slowly drug himself toward the back of the store, not looking back. Etta burst into tears herself and ran out the front. *Oh, God! Oh God! What have I done?*

The next day, Wednesday, after her deliveries, Etta crossed the street to avoid the front of Giles Dry Goods. She slumped as she walked slowly by, stealing glances across the street. *Shoulduh nevuh went in dere. What good gon come of it? What was I gon do, walk in de front door and strike up a conversation wid Dan? 'Howdy, Dan. Gets us two uh dem col' drinks you talked 'bout an' lets us sit together on de bench outside de store.'*

You crazy, dum nigguh, you! Whut you go in dere for? Wish I could stop thinkin' 'bout dat bloody face. How can dat man do dat to somebody nice as Dan? Hurt 'im like dat. Ain't right. He do dat to Dan jus' like he kickin' a dog. Crazy damn world we live in.

Ain't my fault. Etta thought of the reading she had done by lamplight in the *New York Times* the evening before. She lifted her shoulders and strode straighter down the street. *Some things got to change 'round heah.*

On Thursday, one of Etta's first deliveries was to the restaurant in the hotel downtown. As usual, there were several white men eating breakfast who stopped and looked at her as she came out of the kitchen into the dining room. Cap'n Jack, a stranger to Etta, came to the cash register to pay his tab as the owner was taking money from the till to pay Etta for her delivery.

Cap'n Jack spoke up, "John, you trust this nigger gal to handle that money?"

Without looking up, the proprietor handed over some change and smiled at Etta. "Yeah, Jack, I do."

Cap'n Jack looked at Etta closely. "I've seen you around town, gal. Who's your Missus?"

Etta looked him in the face. "I help my grandma in her business."

"Well, don't you talk pretty? You're the grandchild of that freewoman baker out on the edge of town, ain't you?" He was staring at her as if that was a serious accusation.

"Uhh… Yassuh." Etta put the money away, looked at him again and stepped back. She blinked, turned and headed for the door, but froze as the man continued, "Hey! I ain't done talking to you, gal. You think you can just walk off and not answer a white man?" His voice rose as others looked around. "Your grandma may be free, gal, but you ain't. You belong to the Wilsons, and I hear you're headed back to Bonita. I'd like to believe they're gon teach you some manners over there, but that ain't likely over in 'Nigger Heaven.' If you was mine, I'd put you under the lash and then sell you to somebody that'd stick you in the fields where you belong."

Etta, mouth open, stared at him. "Uhh, Yassuh." She could feel the blood pounding in her temples.

23

"Your grandma and your mama, too, done put ideas in your head. You think you good as white folks, don't you? Somebody is gon have to whip them ideas out of you one day. Maybe I'll be the one to do it." With that, Jack brushed by her and went out the door.

Etta stared after him in shock, her mouth still open as the store owner said quietly, "Don't you pay no attention to him."

Etta turned, headed out and down the street. She looked over her shoulder and approached each corner warily as she finished her deliveries. *Don't ever want to see dat man again. What he got 'ginst me? Wait a minute. Dat hotel man call him Jack. Dat's de man Grandma was talkin' 'bout.*

Chapter 4

Lonzo, Etta's grandfather, had a habit of coming by for Sunday breakfast with Medina. The last three years had been her chance to get to know her grandfather. He always had the latest news from around town. This Sunday, Etta wasn't listening. She had to take extra time on her hair and clothes. She finally served a plate and joined her grandparents at the table.

Lonzo looked up at her, nodded and smiled. "Yuh sho look pretty dis moanin.'"

Etta smiled at him. "Thank you, Grandpa."

Medina looked over at her and frowned. "You eat up now. We got tuh go."

Later, as she and Winne waited outside the Colored's entrance to the church balcony, Etta told Winnie what had happened to Dan at the dry goods store. Soon they were the only people still standing outside the church.

Etta looked around nervously. Winnie, frowning, turned to her friend. "Dey done started de music. Me an' you ain't gon have no place tuh sit. Dat boy ain't comin'."

Etta frowned and looked around slowly one more time before ducking her head and heading upstairs. "I'm skairt he ain't gon come 'cause he's embarrassed. Dem mean folks prolly not let 'im come. I don't know." Etta's voice trailed off as she reached the top of the stairs. Looking around she saw some empty seats on the top row. She strode up the narrow aisle steps to the last bench, letting Winnie in and saving a seat on the end for Dan. She liked this spot where she could watch the entrance without turning around. *What am I gon say to 'im if he do come? I'm sorry? It was my damn fault? Warn't my fault. It was his damn ol' massuh's fault. I wish I could talk to Dan 'bout what I been readin' in de paper, all de turmoil over slavery. Dat might make 'im feel better.*

The last person to enter the balcony was an older man. He looked around, then came to the top and stared at Etta, who had scooted toward him to cover the empty seat. He raised his eyebrows. Etta got up and made Winnie get up as well to let him in.

Dan never came. Etta crossed her arms and slumped in her place, making no effort to listen to the service. Winnie glanced over at her friend and sighed deeply.

That evening Etta began to collect the things that she would take with her back to Bonita. *I'm glad to be goin' back. I am ready to be done wid dis place.*

Medina walked in and stood in the doorway. Etta looked up briefly and went back to work.

26

"Etta, dere is sumpin else dat I ain't tol' yuh dat yuh need tuh know," her voice trailing off. Medina shifted her weight from one foot to the other as Etta furrowed her brow, turned, looked and waited.

Medina looked past Etta as she spoke. "Yoh mama and baby bruduh done been sent 'way frum de Main House."

"What?!" Etta's mouth dropped open, and her eyes got big. She stared at her grandmother. "Dey have what?!"

"Miss Frances done sent dem away frum de Main House."

"Oh, Grandma! What happened? What's Mama doin'? What will I be doin'? Do you know where I'll be stayin' and whut I be doin' over dere?" Clothes she was holding slipped from her hands to the floor, and she continued to stare at her grandmother.

Medina just shook her head and began to turn away slowly. "No, I ain't got no idea whut you be doin'." She shook her head again and added quietly, "You got famly over dere. Dey'll see 'bout yuh."

Her mouth still open and eyes still wide, Etta blurted out, "Dey just slaves! What dey gon do?" She burst into tears. She opened her mouth to speak again, but no words came out, but then, "When did dis happen?"

Medina bent over and leaned into the doorframe, as if she had been hit, her right arm across her stomach.

"Honey, yuh so smart. Always 'ave wurked 'ard, but yuh really 'ad hit easy. I don't know whut's gon happen, how t'ings gon wurk out obuh dere." Medina was shaking her head. "Dey sho don't always wurk out de way dey s'pose to." She bent her head. "We jus' gots tuh trus' in de Lawd. He'll take care uh yuh."

27

Etta put her hands on her hips. "Why didn't you tell me 'bout dis b'fo' now?"

Medina stood up a bit straighter and spoke with a stronger voice, "You ain't had no need to know b'fo' now." She turned away.

"Grandma, I ain't a chile no more! I be 15 dis summer. I be growed up, and you ain't tol' me de truth!"

"Yuh is still a chile! Me an' yoh Mama both been potectin' yuh frum de wurst uh hit since yuh wuz a baby. Ain't had tuh grow up."

Etta looked at her grandmother carefully. "What do you mean, 'worst of it'? You need to tell me what's goin' on. Tell me de wurst uh it. I know you. You done heard all 'bout it from Grandpa Lonzo, ain't you? So, you tell me just what happen. Did she get in a fight with Miss Frances? What dey fight 'bout? Somebody take sumpin and Mama get blamed?" Etta tilted her head, pursed her lips and waited, her hands still on her hips.

Medina looked at the floor and shook her head slightly. "I cain't 'splain it 'xactly. Your mama will tells you 'bout it w'en yuh gets obuh dere."

"Cain't 'splain it 'xactly?" Etta's eyes got big. "Why is you actin' so dumb all of a sudden? Is Mama working in de fields?"

"She's hepin' out in de fields, but her main job be cookin' fuh de foremens and de drivuhs."

Etta looked off, frowned and then stared at her grandmother again. "Well, tell me where I be stayin' an' what I be doin' over dere."

Medina shrugged. "'Sides hepin' wid de baby, I 'on't know."

"What else do you know?" Etta paused a moment, then asked again, "What did Mama do to get sent away from de Main House?"

28

Medina shuffled her feet and looked down, pausing before she answered, "You need to hear 'bout dat frum yoh mama w'en yuh gets obuh dere. Dat's all I gots to say. Hit too complicated to 'xplain. Hit be her bidness, and I ain't gettin' into hit."

Etta sat down on the bed and put her head in her hands, trying to grasp the impact of what she had been told. Medina turned slightly and glanced into the kitchen.

Etta's shoulders slumped, and she didn't look up. "So I ain't gon be livin' 'round de Main House, an' I ain't never gon be de cook fuh de Wilsons." There was a long silence. "Well, where is Mama over dere? I don't even know where to go."

"Rachel's down at Tabby Landing, Etta. Go down dere and somebody hep yuh fin' her."

Tears ran freely down Etta's cheeks. "Why you treat me like dis? Ain't I been good help to you?"

Medina's head dropped. "Lawd's my witness!" She shook her head. "Ain't nebuh done nuttin' but whut I t'ink wuz bes' fuh yuh. You 'ad hit too good, yuh and yoh mama. Neiduh one uh yuh 'as any idea whut yuh could be facin' obuh dere. Yoh mama should'uh done right. Wouldn'uh had dis mess."

Etta stared. "What yuh talkin' 'bout?"

Medina's head snapped up and she stared back. "Yuh need to be sho and pack yoh bible, be readin' hit 'stead uh dat uduh stuff dat put ideas in yoh head. Dat's all I got tuh say." Medina walked back into the kitchen mumbling to herself.

29

What is she talkin' 'bout? Etta's tears continued as she poked a few more things in her bag, then fell into the bed. She couldn't rein in her mind's wild gallop. She stared at the only finished ceiling in the house. *Why hadn't she told me 'bout Mama before now. Lawd have mercy, I sure hope Mama's got it worked out.* After an hour of tossing and turning, Etta drifted into a fitful sleep.

Chapter 5

Etta stopped suddenly, shook her head slightly and looked around. *Where am I?* Clutching her cotton bag, Etta looked down the dirt highway that formed the boundary between the freshly-ploughed-and-planted fields to her right and the old forests and protruding marsh to her left. Two hundred yards down the road on the right, a large farmhouse, barn, and outbuildings held out against an encroaching cotton field that extended to the horizon. A narrow lane with pecan trees along one edge reached out from the road to touch the huddled buildings.

Again Etta thought, *Where am I?* She glanced to her left, squinting, as the sun fought to free itself from the hardwood forest. *I don't remember nothin' 'bout how I got heah, but I must be close to de turnoff.* She frowned. *Got to get hol' of myself and think 'bout whut I'm doin'. All dese secrets is makin' me crazy.*

31

Grandma could'uh made dis a lot easier if she'd jus' stop treating me like a child. Etta turned and looked back the way she had come. *Can still see Brunswick, so I ain't missed de turn.* Setting off again, Etta's long, strong legs set a fast pace. *Watch now. Can't miss dat ferry.*

She was relieved when she saw the turnoff. Squinting, looking closely, the road to the ferry looked white against the grey lowland soil. She approached the turn. *Look at dat, dey done spread shells on de ground. Never seen dat before.* The shells crunched under her feet as she made the turn to the left and approached the forest of huge live oak and bay trees. Long moss beards hung from the tips of the limbs.

Oh my! Etta stopped and stared in disbelief, the back of her left fist over her mouth. She stepped back. The first few inches of each beard in every tree had suddenly bent in unison, curling sideways, all pointing to her right. She looked in that direction. *What dey all pointin' at? Looks like dey connected! Hit's like de woods can see me, an' de trees, dey twistn' dere beards at me like, "Who you? Stay out!"*

Etta moved forward slowly. *Is dis a warnin' 'bout comin' back to Bonita? An omen? Somebody puttin' a spell on me, an' I ain't even got on de island yet?* She frowned deeply and hesitated.

Come on now, you actin' like a looney bird. Stop it. Jus' puffs uh wind blowing 'em, and each one bend up de same. Now get goin'. Etta stepped into the dark, canopied forest, alert now, walking slowly, looking from side to side. With some relief, she saw a small opening through the forested tunnel into bright sunshine. It was there she knew she would find the wide-open marsh, the banks of the Dolphin River, the ferry to Bonita

Island and, there, the plantation where she had spent the first 11 years of her life.

Etta could see squirrels busy in the trees above her. The air was calm here, the moss hanging loosely. Etta's breathing slowed. She picked up her pace again. *Lots uh folks over on Bonita, if dey have de string of luck I been havin', dey be sure dat somebody's done put de hex on 'em. Hard to argue wid 'em, way things been goin' for me.* Etta shook her head.

You know, I didn't mind it when Grandma told me dat I was gon go back to Bonita. Wonder if she knew den dat I wouldn't be at de Main House?

Dat's always been my home. Stomach's been hurtin' since las' night. Don't know what to think. I reckon Mama'll know what to do. She prolly got a plan for us to get back up to de Main House, get dis mess straight.

To her right, just before reaching the river, Etta noticed the warehouse back in the trees. Several wagons were being unloaded at one large doorway. At another doorway, materials were being transferred by mules and wagons to the large paddlewheel steamboat tied at the dock. Etta continued into the sunshine, past the small office and waiting room and onto the dock. There she was engulfed in the rich, swirling aromas of the teeming marsh.

She stood for some time on the blustery dock, breathing deeply and looking out across the river to the green of the rippling marsh grass. *I'm glad Grandma gave me dis shawl.* She crossed her arms and shivered. *I thought it'd be warmer, but I guess it's still early in de day. It didn't seem dis cold when I left Grandma's.*

Etta wrapped the shawl around her but found it insufficient to the task. She clutched her bag of belongings and moved, head down, back toward the

33

buildings, knowing there would be some protection there from the swirling winds. She paced back and forth between the business office and the warehouse driveway, her thoughts again moving fast. *You reckon I could end up bein' a field hand? Never chopped cotton in my life. Out in de hot sun. Didn't think my life could be much worse. Mama might prove me wrong 'bout dat. Be livin' in a old leaky cabin. No books, no music, no newspapers, no conversation 'bout nuttin' I care 'bout. Everything I'm s'pose to think 'bout'll be at de end of a hoe handle.*

Tears began to roll down Etta's dark cheeks. She bent her head down and shaded her eyes from the looks of others. *Grandma could'uh told me whut wuz goin' on. Dis guessin' game makin' me sick at my stomach. At least I could'uh enjoyed mysef in Brunswick if she just let me have company besides jus' Winnie. I was gettin' my work done. Maybe wouldn't been dat mess wid Dan if'n he could'uh come to de house.* Etta kicked at a few small, dead limbs lying in front of her. *Prolly be enjoying my birfday out in de hot sun.*

She wiped her nose with one end of the shawl and looked around. The crew was carefully rolling heavy kegs up a ramp and onto the ship. No one seemed to be paying her any attention.

The Clara, a big side-wheeled steamboat named after the current Mr. Wilson's mother, lay against the dock, so big it was hard to tell, from where Etta stood, what was dock and what was open boat. She watched as a crew of slaves continued loading the ship with large sacks of guano as well as kegs of nails and stacks of finished lumber. There was also small kegs of flour, and coffee beans. Etta recognized wooden boxes that she knew held bottles of French wine.

34

Another group was preparing the ship for departure. As she watched, a large chute for loading coal down into the engine room was being removed from the deck.

I was good at my job at de Main House. Made sure everybody's glass stayed full. Edward de only one dat knowed how close I wuz listening to de goin's on. Etta smiled to herself. *Well 'cept for Mama or de cook dat would fuss at me when I run into de kitchen and spill sumpin cause I was in such a hurry to get back. All dat could be gone now, I reckon. Ain't seen Edward in a long time, but I thought we'd be friends again one day. No telling when I'll see 'im now. Not like he's gon ride down to see me!*

A future scene took shape in Etta's imagination. She was far out in the field with many other slaves, chopping cotton. As she looked up, Edward rode down the lane in his usual canter, sitting high in his saddle, surveying what would someday be all his.

Etta lunged toward him. *He's gettin' by.* She waved her hoe, then dropped it and ran forward, tripping over the handle and falling heavily on the ground. Down in the cotton on all fours, she could hear the already faint noise of the horse's hoofs recede as Edward continued down the lane.

Etta shook her head and refocused on the scene before her. Something twisted inside her. Her head drooped, and she again felt the dull ache in her stomach.

I got to get ahold of myself. It's gon be up to him. May not be much I can do on my end. Shouldn't be too hard, if he cares anything 'bout findin' me. If he don't, dat's another story. She looked away, blinking her eyes and biting her lip.

35

Etta glanced around looking for White passengers. They would board first and sit in the cabin while any slaves would board afterwards and sit on one of the benches along the outside of the cabin wall or sit among the cargo.

I ain't done nuttin' wrong, and heah I am goin' back in disgrace. It's been over three years since I've lived on de island. Don't know why Miss Frances hate me like she do. Ain't never done nuttin' to her 'cept try to do what she say. I noticed dat she different 'round me, like I made her nerves worse or sumpin.

Etta thought of the friends and relatives she still had on the island. Her father, James, had been over on the mainland for most of the past five years designing and building tabby warehouses on Thomas, Jr.'s new plantation. His mother, Hester, lived down at Tabby Landing. Abraham, Medina's father and Etta's great-grandfather, lived just south of there. Many aunts and cousins lived and worked at Tabby Landing.

Some of 'em are jealous of how Mama worked her way up to cook and den boss over all de domestics at de Main House. I bet you some uh dem think dis whole thing is funny. You know dey be laffin' 'bout it.

De slaves over dere are big on comin' up wid nicknames for folks. Some of 'em call me 'Bookuh' 'cause I usually had a book wid me. I wasn't never sure if dey meant it mean or just teasin'. Guess some folks are happy now dat we been brought down a peg or two.

Etta leaned back against the corner of the smaller building, her arms crossed over her chest. *What did Mama do to make Miss Frances dis mad? Whatever it was, it must have been bad. De truth is, it was usely me dat really got her goin'.*

She'll get obuh it an' have us back. Don't see how she gon run dat place widout Mama.

Glumly, Etta leaned more heavily against the corner of the unpainted building, staring down at the sweetgum balls at her feet. She smiled a tight smile and shook her head. *Miss Frances don't have to know how to work no spells to put de hex on me and Mama.*

She stepped out from beside the small office building, pulling her shawl around her. She moved up the dock and in behind three white people as they stood in front of the gangplank. The passengers waited for a signal that the captain was ready for the human cargo.

The two men in front of her were talking loudly. The shorter, heavy-set man spoke up. "I guess Thomas will be chomping at the bit to mount up and go hunting."

"No doubt about that." His companion turned and smiled at him.

"I think I'll just hang around the house, maybe go out to the beach."

The taller gentleman laughed. "You know Thomas is not going to let you get out of going."

"I'm really not feeling too well." The heavy-set man frowned as he helped the white woman standing next to him navigate the gangplank.

Etta shrugged her shoulders. *Guess everbody don't like huntin' like Mr. Wilson do.*

Others of African heritage were gathering to board behind her, but Etta didn't look around to see whom she might recognize. *I don't wan' tuh see nobody I know 'til I had a chance to talk to Mama 'bout what happened. I know Mama wouldn't steal nuttin'. I remember several times dey blamed some uh us for stealing sumpin dey found later, right where dey put it.*

37

Miss Frances ain't de only one wid a temper. It sure wouldn't be de first time Mama done let dat get her in trouble with buckra.

Couldn't been no problem wid Mr. Wilson. He don't hardly ever say nuttin' to de inside help. Her thoughts were interrupted as it was her time to board.

She watched her feet carefully as she stepped onto the gangplank and was startled when a tall, black man on the boat's crew hurried over and gave her his hand. She held her hand back in surprise, but then caught herself and offered it to the man. *Ought to be pleased, I reckon. He's older dan me. Show good lookin', but I ain't in de mood today.*

All she could manage was a quick glance up at him and a forced, brief smile. Etta made no effort at conversation but watched as the young man's crewmates teased him as he went back to work.

Onboard, Etta edged her way around a large stack of finished lumber on the deck and examined the bench on the east side of the cabin. *I think I can sit over heah in de sun, and maybe dem kegs dere up toward de front will block off some of de wind.* The other slaves had chosen seats on the near side. Etta thought about the Harper's magazine in her bag. *No, I don't dare take dat out. Don't need no trouble today like I've had in de past when people seen me readin'.*

She was vaguely aware of the buzz of activity onboard and below as the crew readied the boat to cast off. She jumped when there was a loud, low-pitched thump from the direction of the smoke stack, and a shudder ran through the boat as the paddlewheel was engaged. She glanced up as thick smoke blotted out some of the bright sun now rising well off the horizon.

Etta managed a more appropriate smile and nod as the same polite young man passed down her side of the boat.

"Moanin'," he said, touching the bill of his large cap.

She looked at him more closely. *He's a lot taller 'n Dan. He looks like he's several years older dan me. Almos' as dark as me. Handsome. Dis heah's a man, not a boy.* Etta smiled up at him. *"Morning, Suh."*

His smile broadened. "I'm Sam. Welcome onboad, or maybe I should say, *'Welcome home."* He took off his cap and gave it a wave along with a small bow.

Etta gave a quick lift of her head and her mouth tightened. She studied him closely, frowning. "I'm Etta, but sounds like you already know all 'bout me. You must be de head of de Bonita welcomin' committee." Etta displayed no emotion in her face.

He gave her an open, almost-laughing smile. "Don't mean no 'fense. I seen you on de boat b'fo' an' ax'd 'bout who you is. Wuz glad to heah dat a woman as beautiful as you is, wuz comin back to Bonita Island tuh libe."

"Well, I guess dat makes one of us den. So what else you done found out 'bout me?" Etta again tried to keep any expression off her face.

"Don't know nuttin but whut I sees wid my own eyes."

Etta tilted her head again and spoke slowly. "An' what is dat?"

"I sees a woman so tall and strong, she look like a willow tree bendin' in de wind. I see skin so dark and deep red, hit look like mulberries. Lips look lack dey come off a statue I seen one time in a school book."

Etta cut him off. "Nebuh knew dey had a poet on dis heah voyage." She caught herself. *Dat was mean. He jus' tryin' to be nice.*

"Ain't no poet, Ma'am." His smile faded.

39

Etta smiled at him again. "Sorry. Hard not to think dis is a bad day for me."

Sam smiled back and nodded. "Didn't mean no disrespect. I ain't a poet, but I is a boatman." He nodded again and bowed more deeply. "Anyways, welcome. De boatman gots to get back to wurk. I hope t'ings go good fuh yuh on Bonita. 'xcuse me." He touched his cap again, turned and walked down the boat.

Get ahold of yourself now. No need to be mean, 'specially to him.

They were soon loosed and heading downriver. Etta glanced nervously around. *Everbody know what's goin' on but me.*

She examined herself in the reflection of the cabin window and touched her lips and face. *I remember years ago Mama fussin' at me 'cause I got mulberry juice on my dress. 'Skin like mulberries'.* Etta held up her left arm and examined it closely. *I do love de coluh uh my skin. Funny how all de colored folks in Brunswick wants to be brown, while all de slaves on Bonita love dere black skin. Why is dat, I wonder?*

Etta's attention was taken by the gulls that were circling the ship and calling out, "Ha, Ha, Ha!" She put her hand in her pocket and felt the cured ham biscuit her grandmother had given her. *You reckon dem birds remember me frum b'fo' when I threw 'em some bread?* She frowned up at them. "Get on 'way from me now! I ain't got nuttin' for you." Etta stared across the river at the undulating marsh, her arms crossed over her chest.

The white people inside the small, glassed cabin laughed and talked among themselves. *Grandma tol' me dat I'm in for a change. Her white friends, like Miss Elouise, would talk to me and listen to what I had to say. It's funny. Bet dose people in de cabin dere would laugh at me if I offered*

40

my 'pinion on what dey talkin' 'bout. How can a person's life change so fast and so easy-like. Hard to believe dat I miss Brunswick and Grandma already.

Etta's breathing gradually assumed the rhythms of the boat and the paddlewheel. Her posture began to open to the growing warmth of the sun. She thought of Dan and imagined herself holding him, tending to his injured face. *I'm sorry, Dan. Maybe one day you'll have a dry goods store of your own. Be free. Be your own man. Maybe we'll see each other again. Sure do hope so.*

CHAPTER 6

Sometimes the ferry stopped at Lumber Landing, sometimes Tabby Landing, and sometimes both. Today the only stop was at Lumber Landing. There was the usual hubbub of activity as they arrived but no one there to greet her like there had been at Christmas when she had last come over to visit her mother. Then, one of the house servants had come with a buggy to pick her up. There was a buggy today, but Etta didn't recognize the driver, and he had immediately begun to load the luggage of the white visitors. He wasn't looking for her. *I prolly could hitch a ride, but I sure don't want tuh ask.*

A line of mules and wagons waited to be loaded, but Etta had no interest in waiting to ride in one of them. She strode out to the Main Road. As she turned right, she had to move quickly out of the way as the horse and buggy came out from the landing, in a trot. If she walked the entire six or seven miles to Tabby Landing, she knew it would take more than an hour to get to the Main House and then almost an hour on further to Tabby Landing. It would be a long, warm walk.

Etta looked around as she headed south down the 12-mile-long island. Etta was aware that Lumber Landing got its name because the northern end of Bonita was being logged and cleared of stumps. There was a large sawmill located across the road from the landing, that provided rough lumber for use on the island as well as some lumber for export.

Etta knew that the current Mr. Wilson had been expanding rice production on the cleared land. She had heard many discussions about how the river flowing in behind the north end of the island provided the large amount of fresh water needed to grow rice.

As she started down the road, Etta noticed new channels that had been cut across the road toward the river. She crossed a small bridge that looked to be new. Glancing to her left as she headed south, she could see a line of women and older children across the field, bent over. They were close enough to the road for Etta to see that they were sinking ankle deep in the wet, rich soil. She looked at the plants closest to her. *Dere de rice dey plantin'.*

The line of 12 or so was moving directly away from her, and she could see that each individual was planting a row as they moved across the field west to east. A woman on the end was keeping everyone in line.

Etta knew Miss Catherine, Mr. Wilson's first wife, had been against raising rice on the island. Everybody knew that rice production was associated with the deaths of large numbers of slaves. Etta remembered many discussions and arguments in the Wilson household over raising rice

43

and the reasons for the high death toll. *I remember dat Mr. Wilson kept records of how his slaves died. He could quote dem numbers from memory.*

Etta tried carrying her sack over her shoulder. *Dere was a lot of folks dat died from disease up heah, but dere was also a lot killed by fallin' trees or from de oxen dey had to work wid. I remember dey had a lot of snake bite up heah, too. Clearin' swamp land and digging channels in de mud was mighty danejus work, but disease was de big killer. Even though she was gone, some uh de family would quote Miss Catherine on dis subject, 'cause she was so set 'gainst it. She thought dere was something up heah in de swamp air dat made people sick. Crazy to think dat she died from yellow fever like so many of de slaves.*

Etta stopped and looked around. *Don't believe dis wuz a rice field de las' time I came obuh heah. Price fuh rice must be up.*

Etta began to set a pace. *Sure feel sorry for dose folks out dere. I remember how other slaves used to make fun uh 'em or talk bad 'bout 'em. If dere was a slave dat stole sumpin or wouldn't listen to de driver, dey would send 'im up heah to work. Some thought dat was like a death sentence.*

Some of dem girls look like dey younger dan me. What did dey do wrong? Do you reckon Miss Frances gon send me up heah to work? Etta felt a stab of terror and brought a hand up to her mouth. The bad feeling in her stomach ran its fingers up into her chest. She struggled for a deep breath. *I know PawPaw ain't gon let dat happen to me or Mama neither. Grandma say dey gon take care of me over heah. I sure hope dey can.*

44

As Etta began walking again, a breeze brought some sounds to her. She lifted her head. *Lawd have mercy, what have dem folks got to sing 'bout?*

Etta shook her head and continued her trek down the sandy road. It had become quite warm as it was mid-morning, and now the shawl she didn't think she could stuff in her bag had become a nuisance. One end dragged along behind her, collecting sandspurs, as she tried to keep up a good pace.

She had worn shoes, which were also a problem on the sandy road. She knew slaves on Bonita rarely wore shoes, but she was afraid her feet had gotten so tender that the sandspurs would be a problem. She trudged on, slick soles slipping in the sandy stretches of road.

Etta looked up as she felt a sudden, strong breeze. A large, dark shape flew across the road in front of her. "What's dat?" Etta stopped and threw a hand up over her face, then stared into the scrub woods and up in the sky to see if she had seen the shadow of a large bird. *Dat was too big for a bird. What in de world could dat uh been? Too fast for a cow or pig. Didn't make a sound.*

The field of shrubs and small trees sloped down from the road to her left. When Etta reached the point where she thought the shape had crossed, she checked the road for tracks but could find none. There was a small, curving lane to her left; it led toward a grove of large pine trees, roughly in the direction the shape had taken. Except for gators and snakes, Etta had never before been frightened by animals on Bonita, though she was wary of the oxen. *Dere is something down dere in dose trees, like maybe where dere was a buildin' of some kind.*

45

Etta stepped down the lane to see better. *De shrubs and trees are small heah. Believe I could see anything of any size out in dis heah field.* She continued down the lane several more strides--walking, then looking. Finally, only fifty yards or so away from the grove, Etta could see into the widely-spaced pines. *Dere's fresh turned dirt 'mong dem trees.* Frowning, she stared into the light shade. *Lawd have mercy! It's a cemetery, a slave cemetary, an' dat dirt I see is fresh graves. Lawd, I don't need dat now. Signs an' omens.* She turned and walked briskly away.

Now, even more unsettled and wary, Etta strode back up and continued south on the Main Road. After some distance, she paused in the shade of a magnolia tree and unwrapped the large, salt-cured ham biscuit. She nibbled on it and swallowed hard. *I should'uh got some water before I left de landin'. Let's see, I believe I'm pretty close to de Main House.* After a short walk she could see the grove of huge trees that surrounded the plantation house.

The Main House was a central two-story mansion set on a basement. High-ceilinged, one-story wings extended from each side. The south wing contained a large dining room and Mr. Wilson's office. The north wing housed the living room and master bedroom. The central, first-floor portion of the mansion contained the kitchen, a sewing room with Mrs. Wilson's piano and desk, and a small parlour or family room. There were five bedrooms upstairs.

Seven slave cabins housing domestic and other staff were scattered in the area behind the mansion. Between the mansion and the beach were a large chicken coop, horse stables, and the kennel.

Etta could see activity on the side and front lawns of the Main House as she approached. She recognized the men she had seen on the boat. They were part of a hunting party now mounting horses. There was Mr. Wilson and several other men.

Young slave groomsmen held the bridle of each horse as the men mounted. The young men seemed to be trying to control their laughter as they watched the efforts of an overweight guest struggling to get his foot in the stirrup and his body in the saddle. Etta stood behind a roadside bush, her hand over her mouth.

Dat po' man. Looks like dey picked a shorter horse for 'im. I reckon dat helps. Etta watched as the horse shied away in an effort to escape the coming burden. The man hopped around with one foot in the stirrup. With the help of a couple more groomsmen, the guest got his leg over the horse and both feet in the stirrups.

Dere's Mr. Wilson on dat big, black horse o' his. Easy to find him. Big man but not fat. Sits on dat horse all comfortable, relaxed, like he's sittin' at his desk.

Can't see from heah, but I know he got light skin and freckles like Edward. Can see dat he still got a bit of dat red hair in front and on de sides. Look at dat horse, rarin' to go, dippin' his head an' movin' 'round. He always talkin' 'bout dat horse. One of the boys handed up a western-styled hat. He put it on as he joined the other horsemen milling in the road.

The dogs were being brought around and loaded into boxes made with side slats so they could get air. *Look, dere's Nero, de chief dog handler. He's my friend.* After Nero got the dogs loaded, he climbed in the front and

47

took the reins of the two-horse wagon. He followed as the horsemen led the northbound procession.

Before they reached her, Etta slipped around behind the mansion, toward the well. There she saw her friend Katie cranking up a bucket of water. As Etta got close, Katie looked up and her mouth dropped open. She sat the water down on the edge of the thick tabby wall surrounding the well, ran to Etta and hugged her. Katie pushed Etta to arms length and looked around. She took a hand and pulled her to the other side of the well where there were some large sweet shrubs blocking the view from the house. "Whut you doin' heah, gal?" Katie asked, hugging her again, then looking around.

"Oh, Katie, I just got off de ferry. Grandma say I had to come back heah to work and help Mama, but she wouldn't tell me nuttin' 'bout why we got sent away from heah. What happen, Katie?"

Katie stepped back and was quiet for a moment, staring at the small live oak leaves on the ground. Finally, she looked up. "We ain't got time to talk 'bout dat now. Miss Frances, she don sent her 'way frum de house, an' she de one payin' de price fuh dat. Widout your mama heah to see obuh t'ings, hit's a mess, let me tell yuh. Mr. Wilson, he fit to be tied, an' Miss Frances, she's done screamed at ebuhbody least once tuhday. Meals ain't on time an' ain't never cooked right. Miss Frances done run yoh mama off jus' when dey trying to train a new cook.

"Turr'ble heah. Lucky yuh ain't wurkin' heah no moh, but yuh bettuh get on 'way from heah now. Hit sho wudn't do fuh Miss Frances tuh see you tuhday. She'd t'ink your mama done sent you up heah to spy, see how t'ings goin', and dey sho ain't goin' good."

48

Etta asked Katie for some water, drank deeply from the tin dipper and then dipped herself another and downed it. Handing the dipper back, she opened her mouth but was cut off.

"Lawd, you better get on now b'fo' Miss Frances sees you. We had 'nuf screaming fits 'round heah tuh las'. Yuh get on down tuh Tabby Landing. Yoh mama is down dere. She tell you whut happen."

Etta frowned but hugged her friend one more time and walked straight away from the back of the house into the edge of the thicker woods that lay between the house and stables. Etta skirted the edge of the beautiful live oak and bay-filled backyard until she intersected the road again, continuing south down the island.

Ain't dat sumpin. I had de run of dat place. Now I ain't even welcome dere. Etta laughed bitterly. *I knowed dey wud be in trouble widout Mama 'round. De fight 'tween Mama and Miss Frances must have been sumpin.* Etta smiled. *Poor Katie, havin' to live wid dat woman widout Mama dere to calm de waters. Might not be bad to chop cotton for a while. Won't be long before dey bring us back.*

Etta stood taller and walked briskly. *Wonduh why Miss Frances hate me an' Mama like she do? If she just leave us 'lone, everything go fine. She's a meddler, can't jus' go 'bout her bidness. Lawd, she could have it easy 'round heah but got to tell Mama how to do dis, how to do dat, 'specially in front of company. Guess Mama finally got fed up, give Miss Frances a piece of her mind. She'll wise up and have us back up to de Main House b'fo' long. Mr. Wilson'll talk some sense to her.*

49

CHAPTER 7

Etta slowed her pace and looked around. *Well, heah I am, my new home for de time bein'. Tabby Landing. I remember dat de name for dis place come from dem big warehouses over dere built out uh tabby. Know 'bout dat stuff 'cause Paw, he de expert 'round heah nowadays. Dey use dat 'cause dey can get de stuff to make it heah, and it is very strong. Got to protect dat precious cotton. Buckra can lose slaves, just can't afford to lose no cotton.*

On the east side of the road was the largest community of slaves on the island. About 150 slaves lived and worked on the North End, while 350 slaves lived at Tabby Landing. There were other small groupings of slaves at different locations, but Etta knew the Tabby Landing community was the main workforce for the cotton portion of the Plantation's business. She knew too that long-fiber, Sea Island cotton was by far the primary crop and money-

-maker for Bonita Island Plantation. It was a special crop only a few plantations in the United States could grow.

Etta turned left into the community, paused, and took a deep breath. She squared her shoulders but then frowned. *Where do I go to find Mama or find somebody to ask 'bout her? To de right obuh dere is de blacksmith shop. Prolly nuttin' but men in dere. I remember dat de barn and corral is over dere. Dis next set uh buildings heah on de right be de greenhouses.*

Tabby Landing was surrounded by large fields, though many of the cabins sat in groves of hardwoods. Some distance ahead Etta could see the zigzag of a low, split-rail fence that kept loose stock out of the community's main garden.

Etta could see scattered men and women working in the cotton fields around Tabby Landing, but all were some distance away.

Etta looked toward a large grouping of small cabins to her left. There was some activity, but it looked mostly like young children playing. *I remember playing down heah wid my cousins. Had a good time down heah, mostly.* Etta looked around again. *Everbody I could talk to is out in de fields. Guess I got to go out dere to ask 'bout Mama.*

As Etta turned to go to the closest group of field hands, a woman came out of one of the greenhouses and headed in her direction. Her head was down as she avoided some muddy spots. *Dat woman look familiar. She looks like Grandma, only shorter. I believe dat's Aunt Anna.*

Anna was watching her footing but then, as if she could feel Etta's gaze, looked up, tilted her head and squinted in Etta's direction. Her face lit up, and she hurried directly toward her.

Anna was a short, stout woman. Despite her small size and older age, she took Etta by the waist and lifted her from her feet. Etta bent her legs and let her aunt hold her. She found herself hugging her aunt back a bit too hard. *Don't break her neck.*

By slowing releasing her, Anna encouraged Etta to stand. "Honey, hit is so good tuh see yuh 'gin. I been lookin' fuh yuh up dat road. Yoh mama told me dat yuh be heah soon. All right, Baby, let me get a good look at yuh. I ain't seen yuh since yuh went to libe wid Medina."

Anna pushed her back at arm's length. "My goodness you done growed into a beautiful young woman. My, my, my. Yuh so tall an' pretty."

She shook her head slowly, then smiled. "Come on, Honey, an' I'll takes yuh tuh yuh mama. How is Medina? Lawd, I'd love to see her 'gin."

"She doin' good, Aunt Anna."

"Yoh mama oughtuh be headed back frum de fields 'bout now to put dinner on de table. She'll be mighty glad to see yuh. Le's go up dis way." Anna steered Etta straight into the community and then directed her to the left as they got to the garden.

Anna took Etta's hand. "Yoh mama serve dinner ebuh day but Sunday fuh de white foremens and de black drivuhs. She serve it up out unduh dat ol' pole barn we pass back dere." She pointed to the left. "Dey give 'er dat cabin right obuh dere an' put a iron stove in hit. Don't look lack she's back. She prolly up dis heah way." Anna led Etta north into the cotton fields.

People out in the fields were using hoes to cut out some of the cotton, creating the right space between the plants left standing. Etta was surprised at the reactions of the field hands. *How 'bout dat. Most everbody seem glad to see me.* Most smiled or nodded to her. Etta took a deep breath and began to smile back at people. She felt herself relax a bit. Memories took shape. A woman whose child she had played with smiled at her. Someone she had met at a church service years ago nodded and smiled.

As the people thinned, Etta could see a figure up ahead she knew was her mother. She dropped Anna's hand and began to walk faster.

"W'en yoh mama ain't cookin' an' servin', she bring watuh out to de hands."

Rachel spotted Etta and Anna while they were still a distance away. Across her back, she was carrying a notched pole with two buckets now empty of the drinking water she had brought to the workers. Burdened by the pole and buckets, she lurched forward in a shuffling run.

Etta heard her name; joy lit her face, and she ran to her mother.

Rachel dropped the pole and buckets, and they held each other in a long, strong embrace. Etta was shocked by the thinness and firmness of her mother's body. As she held her, all she could say at first was, "Oh, Mama. Oh, Mama." As they were holding each other, there was a sudden strong movement and a small cry between them. Etta jumped back, startled, then realized Rachel had the baby in a sling under her dress. Rachel pulled back the fabric and revealed Matthew's beautiful little face. Etta looked at the baby and stepped back again. Her eyes widened and her mouth dropped open, but no sound came out. The questions that leaped to her mind were answered by the pained apology on her mother's face. Rachel looked down. "I'm sorry, Honey." She extended the baby for Etta to hold.

Etta reeled as if struck, looking at her aunt and then back at her mother. Tears poured down her cheeks again as she could only mouth the words, "How could you?" For his part, little Matthew stared at her curiously, his

53

milk chocolate skin and red hair a strong contrast to the dark black skin and black hair of his mother. Rachel pulled him back to her.

Etta turned away. Blinded by the tears, she stepped into a shallow ditch and stumbled. Anna caught her as she went down on her knees. Etta heaved but brought up nothing of substance. Anna leaned over and patted her at the base of her neck. "Now, now, Honey."

Etta's shock quickly turned to fury. She struggled to her feet and headed back the way she had come. Anna followed, leaving Rachel and Matthew standing in the field.

Anna caught up and tried to take Etta's arm. She snatched it away. Anna backed off some, following, trying to talk to her. As they came back to the center of the Tabby Landing compound, Etta allowed Anna to put her arm around her waist and guide her toward Anna's ramshackled cabin. Etta leaned over the edge of the elevated porch, head down, still crying.

A young girl about nine, tending two other younger children, came running to the cabin and stared at Etta. Anna spoke to her quietly, "April, run up to de norf field dere and tell Rachel dat Etta gon stay wid us fuh de time bein'. Tell her dat I'll send fuh her w'en hit's time. Run do dat an' den come rite on back." She stared down at her. "Yuh heah now?"

"Yassum." April stared at Etta again, then turned and ran away.

Etta had her hands over her face. She turned and leaned her back against the porch as Anna walked over to the well, lowered the bucket and pulled up some cool water. She walked back and handed the dipper to Etta, whose fingers trembled as she drank. Anna took the dipper, put it down, leaned against the porch next to Etta and put her arm around her waist, pulling her closer.

Etta shook her head, mumbling to herself over and over, "How could she?" Then, "How could she ruin our life like dat? Carryin' on wid Mr. Wilson. No wonder we ain't welcome up dere. Ain't no way Miss Frances ever have us back up dere now."

Anna went into the cabin and in a few minutes brought a cup out to Etta. "Drink dis. Dis heah Life Ebuhlastin' Tea. Hit'll make yuh feel bettuh.

Etta took the tea, sipped it, and stood quietly for some time, shaking her head.

Finally, Anna spoke quietly. "Honey, hit's not her fault. She wuz trapped up dere wid no famly close. No frien's up dere. James gone. Mr. Thomas wouldn't let 'em libe togeduh w'en James wuz on Bonita. She didn't hab' no choice.

"Mr. Wilson, he be a very charming man w'en he puts his min' tuh it. Whut she gon do? Tell 'im 'No' 'cause he a married man?" Anna laughed out loud. "Where she gon go tuh get 'way frum 'im? Miss Frances ain't hardly ebuh dere no moh nohows. Pride de only reason she care. Fact is, dey all be bettuh off if'ns Miss Frances could'uh just smiled and bore de load." Anna took a deep breath, gave a long sigh, and shook her head slowly.

She started laughing softly. "Hmm, but I reckon she couldn't have dat red-headed bruduh uh yoh's runnin' 'round in front uh de company now, could she?" Quietly then, as if saying it to herself, Anna added, "Maybe yuh jus' 'as to be olduh to see dat yoh mama wuz in a trap an' dat she jus' human, Honey, lack all de res' uh us."

55

Etta began to cry again. *Don't nuttin' in my life make no sense no more.*

Anna didn't seem to notice and continued. "Oh, and one moh t'ing. Don't t'ink yoh mama de only one. Wilson, he got a couple uh gals obuh on Tom, Jr.'s place." Anna tossed her head back. "Not to mention a couple mo 'round heah." She started laughing again. "Hell, Honey, de two obuh at Tom, Jr.'s got in a fite coupla weeks ago, like dey got any say in who he gon get in de bed wid." She continued to laugh quietly to herself.

Etta's shoulders shook. She leaned away and stared back at her aunt. *Ain't nuttin' funny 'bout dis mess.*

CHAPTER 8

Two of Anna's great-grandaughters, Louisa and Harriet, lived with her in the wooden shack when Etta joined them. They were too young to work, so Etta told them stories and played games with them while her aunt worked in the greenhouses. The second day, Anna came home in the mid-afternoon and sat with Etta on the porch.

Etta called out to Louisa, "Come heah an' let me work on your hair."

Louisa, playing out in the yard, came to the porch and sat down on the floor in front of Etta, who began replaiting Louisa's hair.

Anna studied her young niece for a few moments. "I kin sho see de Ebo in yuh."

Etta looked at her aunt and raised her eyebrows. "See de what?"

"Ebo."

"What's dat?"

Anna nodded and waved to two women walking by. "Hit's a Afican tribe. Dey tend to be very dark, tall and strong, high cheek bones. Handsome peoples lack yuh is. Jus' sayin' dat I kin see yoh Ebo kin in yuh now dat yuh gettin' grown."

Etta frowned and cocked her head at Anna. "Dere's lots of tribes in Africa. Didn't know you could look at somebody and know what tribe dey from. Are you sure I'm Ebo?"

Anna smiled broadly at her niece. "Sho I'm sho. Yoh peoples is Ebo and Semnole on yoh papa's side. Ain't nobody ebuh told yuh dat?"

Etta looked up from Louisa. "I knowed dat my grandpa was part Indian, but ain't never heard nothin' 'bout no Ebo kin."

Anna nodded back. "Yuh need to know de story uh yoh peoples. Yuh know 'bout Abraham, Farah, an' our peoples on yoh muduh's side?"

Etta nodded.

Anna leaned back in her chair. "Let me tells yuh 'bout yoh Ebo kin." A passing gang of crows conversed loudly as Etta continued to work on Louisa's plaits.

"Yuh hear'd uh Ebo Creek, ain't yuh?"

"Yassum, I know 'bout dat creek. It's de one 'tween Bonita and Blackbeard, north of heah. Me and Edward spent lot of days playin' up dere 'round dat creek."

Anna stood up. "Dis heah a long story. Dere's a bit uh dat tea lef'. Let me get hit fuh us b'fo' I get started." Inside briefly, she brought back two tin cups and gave one to Etta. *I remember Anna tellin' stories to us when I was little. She got a lot of 'em.* Etta took a sip and put her tea down next to her chair. She went back to work on Louisa's hair.

58

Sitting back down, Anna took a deep breath, smiled at Etta and sipped her tea. "I'll tells yuh 'bout how dat creek got hit's name and whut dat's got tuh do wid yuh." Anna settled herself again and looked off.

She held her cup with one hand and rubbed her chin with the other. "Dere wuz a time w'en ships, 'specially dem whut didn't know de island too good, would pull into dat creek tuh unload whut dey be bringin' tuh Bonita. Warn't no road up dere back den, so de cargos would hab' to be carried by foots or by small boats to weh hit wuz needed on de island."

Years ago, back w'en Mr. Wilson's daddy wuz fus' gettin' started heah on Bonita, he was shopping fuh slabes up in Savannah. He met a Cap'n whut had jus' 'rived, an' Wilson, he bought a small shipload uh slabes frum 'im, sight unseen. Dis wuz w'en ol' Mr. Wilson wuz new at de slabe buying and tradin' bidness. He didn't know not tuh buy slabes whut all come frum de same tribe an' talk de same language."

Etta tilted her head. "Why was dat, Aunt Anna?"

"Dey didn't want dem folks able tuh talk 'mong demselves, make plans and brew up trubbles. Usely dey mix up dif'nt tribes b'fo' dey ebuh puts dem on de boat, but de Captain wuz new at de bidness, jus' lack ol' Mr. Wilson. Hit wuz a fact too dat some tribes wuz jus' too proud an' orn'ry tuh tame. Dat wuz a pro'lem wid de Ebo."

Etta smiled as Anna went on. "Ol' Mr. Wilson paid ha'f de monies fuh de slabes whut still be on de ship an' pointed Bonita out on de map. He tell dat Cap'n 'xactly weh dey needed de ship tuh come. He tell dat Cap'n too dat if'ns he would take 'is time, Wilson would meet 'im dere and have peoples ready to hep wid de unloadin'.

"Well, de Cap'n, he wuz havin' a awful time wid dis bunch uh slabes. Some uh de slabes be done broke de metal band whut hol' de chains dat control 'em.

"On slabe ships a chain run thu a metal anklet on de lef' leg uh one man, tuh de right uh de nex'. De womens and chilrens wuz not usely chained, but dey all wuz kep' in cages on boa'ds dividin' de bottom uh de ship frum de uppuh deck. Dere wuz barely 'nuf room to sit up in dem cages."

Etta shook her head. "Dat had to be terrible, Aunt Anna."

Anna nodded slowly. "I'm sho hit wuz. Dem slabes wurked hard tuh get free, an' one night a man got loose an' started freein' uduhs. Watchman seen 'im b'fo' he could get 'nough hep tuh obuhwhelm de crew. Might'uh done hit if'n dey hadn't been so weak frum de way dey been treated. De cap'n done swore dat w'en he got clear uh dis bunch, dat 'is ship ain't gon nebuh carry no moh slabes."

Anna leaned back and sipped her tea. "He wasted no time leabin' Savannah and, wid fabable winds, 'rrived at Bonita Island well b'fo' Ol' Mr. Wilson. De captain, he set in at de fus' place he saw whut wuz called Bonita on de maps, not payin' no 'ttention tuh whut Wilson tol' 'im. De ship wuz sittin' in 'bout 20 feets uh watuh at low tide, nosed up an' anchored in whut we'uns now calls Ebo Creek.

"All de male slabes on one side uh de ship wuz chained togeduh an' so wuz de male slabes on de uduh side uh de ship. As 'slabers' went, dis heah wuz a small ship wid only 'bout a hundred mens, womens, an' chilrens on boa'd. De whole bunch 'ad been riled up wid lots uh talk 'mongst demselfs

60

since dey pull up at Bonita. De Aficans belieb'd dat if dey got off de ship, dey would nebuh get back tuh Afica.

"A junior off'cer been sent off tuh find peoples on Bonita whut could take possession uh de slabes and hep march 'em to wehsumebuh dey need to be. De cap'n t'ought dat de plantation peoples could manage dese folks bettuh dan he been able to on de ship. If'ns he could get 'em off de boat, den dey could wait 'round wid no pro'lems fuh Wilson to show up an' pay de uduh ha'f uh de bill.

"De off'cer, he been gon a long time. De slabes wuz gettin' moh an' moh res'less, an' de cap'n, he wuz gettin' moh and moh nerbous. He wuz pas' ready fuh de Ebo to be somebody else's pro'lem."

Etta patted Louisa on the head. "Awright, Honey, dat's good." She felt her hair, then ran off toward a group of other children. Louisa bent her head over for inspection by a couple of older girls.

Etta picked up her tea and sat back in her chair. "But Aunt Anna, what has dis got tuh do wid me?"

Anna nodded. "We gettin' to dat part. Be patient." She leaned back again. "Well, de cap'n spoke to de fus' mate. He say, 'Le's go 'head an' be gettin' dese slabes onto de beach.'

"'Yassuh,' say de fus' mate, jus' as nerbous as de cap'n.

"Dey drops a gangplank down in de watuh on de Bonita side uh de ship, wid de end uh de plank in 'bout fo' or five feets uh watuh. De slabes on dat side wuz let out uh dere cages, broughts up frum below an' lined up on de deck. Dey look down at dat gangplank goin' in de watuh, an' dey 'fuse tuh go down hit 'less de chain be took off dere legs. De fus' mate an' de cap'n ain't sho whut tuh do."

Anna leaned toward Etta. "De cap'n tell de fus' mate, he say, 'Arm de crews wid swords and pistols, den go gets anuduh chain. Take dem mens loose at de top. Puts 'em back on as dey step on de beach. Gets dat lock back on w'en de las' man on dat chain gets out'uh de watuh. Shoot any man whut cause a pro'lem.'"

Anna opened her eyes wide. "Dey also give 'em a rope to hol' on to, mixing in all de womens and chilrens frum both sides so dese mens could hep de smalluh ones t'ru de watuh. Dey began gettin' ha'f de mens an' all de womens and chilrens off de ship w'en a chief or 'ligious man still onboa'd start to chant in dere native lang'age. His chant wuz a call to dere God uh de Sea tuh take all dere peoples back home rat den. Dere wuz a stir 'mongst de Aficans."

Anna looked at Etta, tilted her head and leaned in. "De cap'n warn't sho whut tuh do. He call on de 'mainin' crew tuh bring de uduh group uh mens up on de deck. W'en dey did, de mens start to join de chief in de chant."

"'Shut up!' de fus' mate yell at de mens. Dem whut wuz on de beach den start tuh join in wid de chant, too. W'en de Ebo chief wuz brought up, still chained to de uduh mens at de ankle, he keep on chanting fuh de Sea God tuh take 'is peoples home. By dis time, ha'f de mens an' all uh de womens and chilrens done lef' de ship. Dey wuz 'bout tuh fasten de lock back on de chain fo' de mens whut be on de beach."

Anna jabbed her finger toward Etta. "De cap'n pointed at de chief and yelled at de mate, 'Stop dat man rat dere! Shut 'im up!' De fus' mate, he raise up his short whip tuh strike de chief. De ol' chief, he back away frum 'im tuh de railin' uh de ship. Den all uh sudden, he t'rows hisself back'ards off de boat. Dem whut chained close tuh 'im jump off aftuh 'im into de deep side uh dat creek. Uduhs on de chain wuz yanked in wid 'im. De crew wuz desp'rate tuh stop 'em. In de melee, two crew members wuz grabbed by tribesmen and pulled obuhboa'd wid de Aficans into dat creek."

Etta sat back, mouth open and eyes wide.

"On de beach de uduh Aficans fus' started to run into de watuh wid dere tribesmen, an' mos' uh de crews try to get back up de gangplank to hep onboa'd. W'ens dey did dat, sev'al Aficans see dat de chain warn't fastened yet. Dey overwhelm de crew whut lef' on de beach an' tooks dere guns an' swords. A few uh de crew on de ship seen whut wuz happnin' an' fired dere pistols at de Aficans on de beach. Hin de confusion, all uh de Aficans whut ain't in the creek wuz able to turn, run into de woods an' be gone."

Anna let a breath out and sat back.

"De cap'n knowed dat Ol' Mr. Wilson would be furious. He done paid ha'f uh de monies, an' dere he wuz wid ha'f de men gone an' de res' uh his slabes runnin' free on de Norf End! De cap'n, he t'ought 'bout whut he could do."

Etta was up on the edge of her chair, listening closely.

"Shortly, de off'cer whut had been sent fuh hep called to de cap'n frum de beach. 'I got three mens, Captain! Do we need moh?' Wid 'im wuz sev'al Bonita drivuhs.

"De offcuh wuz tol' tuh come aboa'd. Den as de gangplank wuz raised, de cap'n spoke tuh de drivuhs stan'in' on de beach. 'Yuh peoples unuhstan' English?'

"De drivuhs smile at each uduh an' kinduh shift 'round, nervous-like. 'Yassuh,' one uh 'em say.

63

"Dere wuz a clankin' sound as de front anchuh wuz bein' raised. De cap'n, he say, 'Tell Mr. Wilson dat we's 'ad a few pro'lems an' dat we done lost some uh de slabes in dis heah creek. Duz you unuhstan' whut I is sayin'?'

"De drivuhs look at each uduh and shake dere heads, and dey don't say nuttin'.

"By dis time de crews done had de front anchuh up. De cap'n, he went on as de men starts usin' de rear anchuh tuh pull de ship back outs uh de creek. 'Tell 'im dat we hab' d'libuh'd well moh dan ha'f 'is slabes heah onto 'is prop'ty; dat for dose slabes, we gon 'ccept de ha'f payment whut he done gib' us."

Anna smiled and shook her head. "De drivahs look 'round an' say, 'Weh dey is?'

"De ship wuz now floatin' free in de open watuh.

"The cap'n call out loud and point to the woods. 'Dey obuh dere.'"

"'Bout dat time, de sails on de ship caught some wind, an' de ship turn an' start tuh move off whiles de drivuhs on de beach stare with dere moufs open at de footprints in de sand."

Etta was slowly shaking her head. "Dat's fascinatin', Aunt Anna. You gettin' to de part 'bout me?"

Anna laughed softly and nodded. "Awright, Honey. Dem Ebo whut run off didn't stay 'round heah long. Ol' Mr. Wilson t'ought dat a few days uh starvin' and livin' in de woods would hep tame dis bunch uh new slabes. 'Sides, he 'ad tuh 'round up a big 'nuf party tuh be ables tuh catch de Ebo in de thick swamps.

64

"In de week hit took 'im tuh organize a big 'nuf patrol, de Ebo done made weapons, killed game, fed demselfs, made some kinduh boats an' wuz gone."

Etta continued to stare at her aunt.

Anna put her hands on her knees and leaned forward, speaking more quietly. "Now we's be gettin' tuh de part 'bout Etta. De Ebo headed south an' hook up wid de Semnole Injins whut be down at Tallahassee. Florida. Dey lived wid de Semnole an' 'come part uh dere tribe. Many years latuh, dere wuz trubble 'tween de Semnole an' white settlers whut had moved onto Semnole land. War broke out.

"President Jackson, he sent a army to hep de settlers. De wars went on fuh a long time, but 'ventually de Semnole los' mos' uh dere lan' an' lots uh dere peoples. In 'bout 1825 yoh grandpa, Chocu, whose mama wuz a gal on dat slabe ship, come wid a group uh olduh Aficans back to Bonita Island tuh 'scape de 'Merican army."

"Mr. Thomas 'ad jus' taken obuh de op'ration uh de plantation, an' he sortuh took 'em in. Dey wuz treated good at fus' an' 'llowd to wurk fuh a place tuh stay an' fuh food. Hit warn't long b'fo' dey wuz treated lack ebuhbody else 'round heah. De mens soon tired uh takin' orders frum buckra.

Aftuh 'bout two years Chocu an' de mens whut come wid him, 'long wid a few Bonita slabes, took off one night back to Florida.

"Yoh grandma an' yoh daddy, who wuz jus' a baby, stayed heah wid her peoples. Mr. Wilson, he still angry tuhday 'bout dem running off, 'specially dem Bonita slabes." Anna leaned back and laughed. "He sent peoples tuh 'unt 'em down, but dey couldn't catch 'em an' come back empty-handed."

Etta smiled and nodded at Anna. "Mama had told me dat Paw was part Indian, but I sure never heard how all dat come 'bout. Paw's grandma lived wid de Seminoles, and her husban' was a Seminole Indian?"

Anna nodded deeply at her. "Ain't nobody ebuh tol' yuh dat story b'fo'?"

Etta shook her head, still smiling. "No, ma'am. I ain't never heard all of dat before. I been swimmin' in dat creek right obuh dem folks."

Anna gave a short laugh. "Hmm! Yoh Grandma Hester'll tell yuh dat yoh great, great-granddaddy be one uh de ones whut went obuh de side dere. She beliebs too dat dem peoples warn't in dat creek long. She'll tell yuh dat de Sea God done took dem peoples back tuh Afica. Dat's whut she say."

Etta furrowed her brow and studied her aunt's face.

Later that night, long after Etta could hear Anna snoring softly next to her, she lay with her hands behind her head. *Could dose people really been taken back to Africa? Sunday is Easter. Dat's when de precher say dat Jesus wuz taken back tuh heaven. Dat ain't all dat different. Could both dese things be true?*

I don't know what to think bout Sea Gods and stuff like dat, but dem men were sure brave to refuse to be slaves and jump off dat ship like dey done. Guess I always thought my people must be easy caught and easy to turn into slaves.

Etta slipped out of bed and lit a lantern, glad her aunt was a heavy sleeper. She found the small piece of mirror her aunt had and studied her face in the lamplight. *Ebo and Indian? Guess I know where dat mulberry*

66

tint come from now. Maybe dat ain't such a bad combination. She smiled to herself, slipped back into bed and soon was off to a deep sleep.

CHAPTER 9

Etta looked forward to sitting on the porch in the afternoons talking with Anna. *Grandma Medina would never sit and talk to me like Anna do. She too busy cookin', visitin' sick folks, and mindin' my business to talk to me.*

The next afternoon, Anna came right to the point. "Honey, folks know yuh is heah, and hit's time fuh yuh tuh get tuh wurk."

Etta looked up. "What work, Aunt Anna?"

"In de moanin' yuh kin go tuh wurk wid me in de greenhouses. Dat'll be good wurk fuh yuh. I talked to Lazarus, de drivuh, yistiddy, an' he say dat he could use yuh fuh a few weeks. Aftuh we's finish in de greenhouse, we'uns be outs hoein' de weeds an' den pickin' de cotton. Anna raised her eyebrows and tilted her head at Etta. "If'ns we don't gets yuh wurkin' somuhs, no tellin' weh dey apt to sen' yuh."

Etta shrugged. *Guess dat's better dan startin' out hoein'.*

The next morning, Anna got Etta up early. They fed the children breakfast, then Anna and Etta walked over to the complex of low buildings with glass-pane roofs. The first one they passed was quiet, but there was activity in the second building. A tall, thin, black-skinned and grey-haired man was standing in the doorway.

Anna, with Etta in tow, walked up to him. "Lazarus, dis heah is Etta. She de daughter uh Rachel, de cook."

"Yeah, I know who she is." Lazarus scowled at Etta and gave a short, quick lift of his head. "Come on, le's see if'ns yuh know 'ow tuh wurk."

He turned abruptly and stalked off with Etta suddenly trying to keep up. He led her to another building where several women were working. They looked up as Lazarus and Etta entered, but kept busy. Lazarus spoke directly to one of them. "Show dis gal whut tuh do."

Etta looked around. The women were pulling small plants, one at a time, out of thin flats of soil. When they had a handful, they would wrap each batch with twine and tie a loose knot. Each batch was then wrapped with wet burlap and placed in a burlap sack until it was about half full.

An attractive, older woman, her hair tied in a kerchief, looked at Etta for a moment. "Yuh be de runnuh. Charlene, you go wid 'er an' show 'er weh dey fixin' dat washout. Take all fo' uh dem sacks dere an' gets on back heah quick-like."

Etta watched as Charlene tied a knot in the top of each sack. She handed the first two to Etta and then tied off the last two, picked them up and headed out the door. Etta followed. They turned and took the lane south.

The cotton plants here were about a foot tall. The excess cotton had already been cut out, and soil was banked against the plants.

They walked for a mile or so past many working in the fields. Etta realized that the sacks were getting heavy, and soon she struggled to keep them up off the ground. *Dis ain't as easy as it looks. Never thought another girl be stronger dan me. She don't seem to be havin' no trouble.*

Etta didn't remember Charlene, but Charlene knew who Etta was. "You warn't livin' at de Main House wid yoh mama b'fo' yuh come down heah, wuz yuh?"

"Uh, no." *She kinduh nosey.*

"Weh wuz yuh den?"

"I was livin' in Brunswick wid my grandma when dey called me back heah."

Charlene spoke over her shoulder. "How come dey let yuh libe hin Brunswick?"

Etta shrugged and said nothing.

"We'uns 'as tuh wurk down heah. Ain't lack bein' in Brunswick or at de Main House neiduh."

Etta clenched her teeth and stopped momentarily. "Dey work up dere!" She took a breath to speak more loudly as Charlene kept going. *Don't reckon dere no need tryin' to 'xplain dat to her.*

Charlene slowed and turned to her. "Whut wuz yuh doin' hin Brunswick?"

Etta straighted up momentarily, struggling with the bags. "Helped my grandma. She a free woman and has her own bakery."

70

Charlene stopped and turned. "Sho 'nuf? Don't be dragging dem sacks now. Hain't good fuh de plants."

Etta renewed her efforts to keep the bags off the ground.

After another half mile, Charlene announced, "Dat's dem up dere." Etta could see a group of six or eight people up ahead. A couple were out in the field using their hoes while others were standing at the edge where there was a little shade. Several took long looks at her as they joined the group.

Charlene handed over her two sacks. "Heah yuh go."

Etta did the same, shook her arms and turned to walk away.

Charlene didn't seem to be in any hurry to leave. Pointing to some empty sacks on the ground at the end of the row, she spoke over her shoulder to Etta. "Pick up dem sacks obuh dere."

Etta jerked her head up, staring at Charlene whose back was toward her. She took a deep breath. *Who she thinks she bossin' 'round?* Etta breathed out and dropped her head. *But don't reckon dis is de time tuh get in a fuss wid her.* Etta walked over and picked up the sacks.

A man in the group untied a couple of the sacks they'd brought and began passing out bundles of plants to the other slaves. Charlene was busy making sure everybody knew who Etta was.

The man smiled at Etta. "Bookuh." He nodded to her. "Hit's Bookuh."

Etta lifted her head and examined his face. *What he mean by dat? Bein' mean or jus' tryin' to be friendly?* The smile seemed genuine, and he met her gaze. Etta nodded at him and smiled in agreement. *Yep, dat's me. Bookuh.*

71

Each field hand had a small, open burlap sack with a strap they used to carry the bundles. Those not doing the hoeing had a small, knife-like tool. Etta watched as they spread evenly apart and began to poke holes in the ground a little more than a foot apart. A plant was placed in each hole, and they would step next to the plant to close the soil around it. Another field hand followed with a bucket, pouring a small amount of water next to each plant. Those with hoes were using them to spread the soil evenly around in an area where heavy rain had washed out some plants and buried others.

The group gradually got to work, and Charlene turned and headed back. She was walking slowly, and Etta wanted to move faster. *Don't need to get in no trouble de first day. Take it easy now. Breathe deep. She know what she doin'.* Nobody made any comment when they returned.

Etta took over transporting the plants down to the lower fields. She learned to put a little less in the bags and to make faster trips. A day later Etta's arms and back ached when the bell was rung announcing lunch. She walked back to Anna's shack and lay on the porch while the children played in the yard. As Anna approached, she smiled at Etta. "Yuh awright, Honey?"

Etta sat up slowly and smiled weakly. "I'm fine, Aunt Anna. Jus' a little tired. Got any more uh dat tea?"

Anna walked up the rickety steps. "Sho. I'll bring yuh some."

She brought Etta a small cup of tea, went back inside and began serving up leftovers. In a little while she called Etta and the girls to dinner. They had some flat, thin cornbread with latticework edges, some collard greens, and rice with gravy. There was some streak-uh-lean pork that had been cooked with the greens. Etta got everyone a cup of water from the well.

72

She picked the meat off the bones of a fish left over from a previous meal and shared it with Harriet now sidled up under her right elbow.

As the days passed, Etta liked the feeling of strength that developed in her arms and shoulders. She liked getting out, walking back and forth to the fields, away from the gossiping women.

The cotton replanting slowed, and Etta began to work more with the syrup cane. Every afternoon a wagon of syrup cane stalks were parked outside the greenhouse. Using pitchforks, men had dug the cane out of shallow ditches where it had been laid and lightly covered with soil a couple of months earlier. The men covered the cane with burlap bags and wet them down to keep tender roots damp.

Etta's job was to cut the cane into smaller sections that would be used to replant the syrup-cane fields. She used a sharp knife to cut up the long stalks, being careful with the roots growing from the nodule on each cane segment. The tough cane and sharp knives took a toll on Etta's hands.

Work started early but ended around 3:00 in the afternoon. Late afternoons were for tending the small gardens around the cabins, caring for children, repairing nets, active fishing and small game hunting in the area around Tabby Landing. Etta had overhead discussions at the Main House about how the hours allowed time for the slaves to provide for a lot of their own care and feeding. *I remember Wilson hisself answering somebody 'bout allowin' 'is slaves tuh have guns. He say, "De squirrel and rabbits better for de slaves dan all dat fat pork meat dat we give 'em. Dey better workers when dey eatin' sumpin dey catch or kill. I'm not afraid of my people havin' guns."*

One afternoon after work, Etta strolled back to Anna's. She walked past the blacksmith's shop. On the right, a group of older children were playing a game. Etta stood on the periphery of the group and watched. The young people were playing with an axe handle and a ball. There was a thrower who threw the natural rubber ball toward a batter holding the axe handle. The batters tried to hit the ball and have time to run touch a piece of board 40 feet away and get back to the hitting area before the other children could catch the ball and hit them with it. Etta had played the game many times up at the Main House. *More players down heah might make it more fun.*

Etta took a place out with others trying to catch the ball. A boy a year or two younger smiled at her and moved over to give her room. Several children batted, and Etta chased down balls that no one caught.

June, a cousin of Etta's, about her age, was pitching. She caught a poorly-hit ball and easily hit the runner as he came toward her. June took the axe handle. Etta backed up. *Look how strong she look an' how she twirl dat handle 'round. I believe she good at dis game.*

Etta took a couple more steps back. On the first pitch, June hit a ball that looked like it was going over everybody's head, but Etta ran back, catching the ball in the air. She raced toward June as she touched the board with her foot, turned and ran back, unaware that the ball had been caught. Etta hit her squarely between the shoulder blades with the solid rubber ball. June stumbled and fell heavily on her chest, plowing up a foot of soil. She sputtered as she got to her hands and knees slowly, trying to spit the sand out of her mouth, her eyes pouring tears.

74

Etta ran toward her to see if she was all right, but June turned, lifted her head and charged her in a fury. She knocked Etta backwards, came down on top of her and began pounding at Etta with her fists. She got in one good blow to her temple before Etta could roll, get to her hands and knees and throw June off. Etta jumped to her feet, knees bent and fists ready.

June got up more slowly, tears still streaming down her face and snot running from her nose. "Yuh t'ink yuh so smart. T'ink yuh bettuh dan ebuhbody down heah. Dey needs tuh get rid uh yuh. Should'uh sent yuh tuh de Norf End in de fus' place. Yuh an' yoh mama ain't nuttin' but trubble."

Etta took a step toward June. "Didn't ask to get sent down heah, but I am heah, an' I belong heah just as much as you do. You gon fight me, or you gon talk? Come on. I ain't scared of you."

When June made no effort to charge Etta again, the other children began to mill around looking for the ball. June turned and walked away. Another girl helped her to get some water and wash her face.

A boy walked up and gave Etta the bat. Etta paused, handed it to one of the smaller children who hadn't had a chance to hit, and walked away.

Late that afternoon, Etta sat on the edge of the porch while Anna sat in a chair. The girls played with others out in the grassy area. Anna looked down. "How's de eye?"

Etta put her hand to her temple. It'll be awright."

Anna shook her head. "Yuh doin' good at de work, Honey."

Etta touched her eye again. "De wurk ain't de problem, now is it?"

Anna grunted a response.

Etta leaned back on her hands, swinging her legs slowly, watching the children playing out in front of the cabin. "People my age think I'm some kinduh crazy person. Ain't nobody to talk to, Aunt Anna. Get tired of listnin' to de women. Nothin' but gossip 'bout dis one layin' wid dat one. People I don't even know. Or some woman talkin' 'bout how de hag rode 'er all night long an' she ain't got no rest."

Anna shook her head. "Well, ain't nobody down heah dat's done de readin' lack yuh 'as. Yuh know, Ma and Pa taught dere chilren to read, but dere ain't nobody down heah dat keeps hit up. Ain't nuttin' down heah fuh folks tuh read.

"Hit won't hurt yuh none tuh jus' listen. W'en dey say sumpin dat ain't right, don't feel lack yuh got tuh be de one tuh set 'em straight. Dere's young folks dat's gon be yoh frien's. Jus' be patient. Hit gon take some time. Church be a good place tuh start."

Etta shook her head. "Can't believe Mama got us into dis mess, let dat man touch her. He don't care nothing 'bout neither one of 'em. His own child! I thought I knowed dat man."

Etta looked around at Anna. "Had me fooled. Always liked hearin' 'im talk. He a smart man; I give 'im dat. Used to admire 'im. I would find him lookin' at me sometimes, not in a bad way, just curious what I was doin'. He'd catch me readin' de newspapers an' jus' give me a funny smile.

"One time he and Thomas, Jr. were arguin' 'bout sumpin what had been in de paper, and he turned to me and say, 'Etta, what do you think?'"

I knowed I jumped like I been shot, but I jus' say, 'Nuttin', Suh.'"

"He and Thomas, Jr., dey jus' look at me an' laugh."

Anna sat up and looked around in front of the cabin. "Weh dem gals get off tuh? She got up, walked out in front of the cabin and looked around. "Etta, come on, let's go down tuh April's."

They turned to the left, walking slowly as Etta continued. "How could he have changed so? Would he be dif'nt if Mama was still dere at de Main House? How could he take dis out on her like he done? Not help her look after his own child."

Anna shook her head slowly. "Yuh bettuh off down heah 'way frum dem folks. Dat sit'ation done gone bad. Ain't none uh 'em fit tuh be 'round."

April and the girls were under the porch of her cabin. Bending over and looking under the porch, Etta realized that April was entertaining the girls by dropping ants into doodlebug pits. Anna bent over and looked under the porch as well. "You gals gets out frum unduh heah! Prolly snakes unduh heah."

Anna spoke to April as she came out from under the porch. "I'll see 'bouts 'em now, Honey. T'ank yuh. Harriet, come on, let's get on home. Louisa! The girls ran ahead toward their cabin.

Etta studied the ground in front of her. "Aunt Anna, I'm still tryin' to understand why hit happen, why she risk our situation for dat man. Feels like dere ain't nobody 'round heah lookin' out for me but me. I ain't talkin' bout you now, Aunt Anna. You been great."

They were walking slowly. Etta frowned and glanced over at Anna. "You know, I'm gettin' grown, and it's time fuh me tuh start figurin' things out for my ownself 'stead of listenin' to everbody else tell me what to do." Etta looked down and her frown deepened. "Sure can't depend on Mama to look out for me."

"You part right, dere, Etta, Honey. You 'bout grown, but dat don't mean dat yuh ought not be hepin' yoh mama. She needs yuh rat now.

"But too, yuh cain't fuhget dat yuh a slabe. Dem folks up at de Main House got dey own pro'lems, an' dey don't care nuttin' 'bout you 'cept whut yuh kin do fuh dem. We lucky both uh yuh ain't plantin' rice or hoein' cotton in Alabama somuhs.

"Now de part 'bout yoh Mama dat ain't quite right, she gon do de bes' she can fuh yuh. Whut happen warn't her fault. Yuh right, she warn't t'inkin' 'bout yuh w'en she dillydallyin' 'round wid Wilson, but dat's peoples fuh yuh. Dat's jus' de way folks is. Part uh growin' up is seein' yoh folks as peoples too, peoples dat get tangled up in dere own feelin's jus' lack yuh and me."

"Hmph!" Etta frowned and stared briefly at her aunt. "Well, she needs tuh think 'bout somebody 'sides her own self sometimes. Guess both of us need time to think."

Anna slowed her pace, looked off for a moment, then back at her great-niece. "Well, you kin stay wid us long as yuh lack, but you really need tuh be wid yoh mama. She needs yuh, an' yuh need her. Now, you go on an' figure out whut yuh got tuh figure out an' den get on back weh yuh belong. Yuh heah me now?"

Etta took several steps before replying, "Yassum."

Yeah, Mama need to think some more 'bout de mess she done got us in. I go sashaying back up dere, help her take care of dat baby, be like nuttin' ever happen. Wonduh who she be runnin' 'round wid nex'. How many more babies I have to take care of?

78

Chapter 10

The next afternoon after work, Anna came back to the cabin and started laying a fire in the fireplace. Before she lit the fire, she went and picked up a bag sitting on a shelf in the kitchen and shook it. She went to the door and spoke to Etta, who was sitting on the porch. "Etta, I is 'bout out'uh cornmeal. W'en's de las' time yuh seen yoh Grandma Hester?"

"Been a long time, Aunt Anna. I stayed wid Mama's famly mostly when I used to come down heah, but Paw would come obuh to PawPaw's or wehebuh I was and get me for visits wid him and Grandma.

Anna stepped out onto the porch. "I need tuh go get my staple goods. Yuh want tuh walk down tuh Hester's wid me? I'll light dat fiuh w'en we get back."

"Sure, Aunt Anna. I'd love to see Grandma."

"I need tuh get my food, but I'm gon come right on back an' see 'bout dem chilrens. Maybe yuh kin stay dere an' visit wid her fuh a spell dis aftuhnoon."

Anna stuck her head back in the door of the cabin. "You'ens don't be getting' into nuttin' now. I'll be right back."

Scattering a small flock of chickens hunting in the grass, they walked deeper into the community through an open area toward the large, five-acre garden that dominated the center of Tabby Landing. To their left were clusters of cabins set back in scattered groves of sweetgums, pines, and hardwoods.

Anna laughed and looked over. "You know, lots uh folks is skairt uh yoh Grandma Hester. She 'bout de number one root doctuh 'round heah. Folks always little nerbous 'round de root doctuh."

Anna looked at Etta and raised her eyebrows. "Hit's a fact too dat her job givin' out de produce an' de staple goods 'round heah make her somebody yuh wants tuh stay on de good side uh." Anna nodded deeply.

Etta smiled back at Anna. "When I'd visit down at PawPaw's, de other chilren would call her a hag, say she come in de night and ride people when dey try to sleep."

Anna laughed quietly and nodded.

"I'd tell 'em, 'No, she ain't!'" Etta looked around at her aunt. "She was always good to me."

Hester's cabin was made out of tabby and was a little larger than most of the others even though she lived there by herself. Anna and Etta stepped up on the porch and knocked on the door. A burlap bag lay to the right of the doorway. Hester opened the door and smiled broadly. "Come in. Come in."

Anna put her hand on Etta's shoulder. "How yuh doin', Hester. I brought somebody by who wanted to see yuh."

Hester looked Etta up and down. "Look uh heah! Look uh heah!" She opened her arms wide as Etta entered the cabin. "My goodness, I hear'd dat yuh wuz down heah. I've missed yuh. Sho glad tuh see yuh, Baby."

They hugged. "Yuh done growed so tall. Look so much lack yoh daddy." She smiled broadly. "Know he gon be glad tuh see yuh." Hester stepped back. "If'n he ebuh get back obuh heah, dat is. Come on in, Anna."

Etta hugged her grandmother again and stepped back. "Good to see you, Grandma. Thought I might visit some dis aftuhnoon, if dat's awright?"

"Sho, Honey. I wuz goin' on a little walk. Yuh can come wid me if yuh want tuh."

Etta smiled. "I would like dat, Grandma."

Anna looked around. "Yuh got some stuff fuh me, Hester?"

"Yeah, Anna," pointing to a corner of the cabin. "Take one uh dem sacks dere. Hit's got yoh rice an' cornmeal. We'll add some uh dis uduh stuff to dat sack."

Anna looked at the few sacks left. "'Bout de las one tuh gets my food dis month."

Hester looked around at her. "Don't make a ol' woman hab tuh carry dat stuff down to yuh now." Laughing, she helped Anna pick out bundles of early vegetables including collards, turnips, potatoes, and onions. She also gave Anna some dried red peas, some cured pork, and a half-gallon of cane syrup sealed in a metal can with a lid and wire handle.

Etta looked over at Anna. "You can't carry all dat. Leave part for me."

Anna smiled at her, took most of the food and left some items next to the door. Hester helped with the door as Anna spoke over her shoulder. "I'll see yuh aftuh while, Honey."

"Bye, Aunt Anna."

Hester shut the door, turned, and pulled out a chair for Etta from the small table. She stood, hands on her hips, smiling down at her grandaughter. "How you lack hit down heah in Tabby Landing, Etta? Lot dif'nt, I reckon. Dey wurkin yuh hard?"

"It's a big change from what I was doin' in Brunswick, Grandma, but it ain't too bad. Just need to make some friends down heah.

"Dat'll come, Honey. Dat'll come."

Etta looked closely at her grandmother. Even at her age, Hester Brown was an imposing figure. *Tall as me. Broad shoulders. Ain't no fat. Strong, I reckon.*

Plaits stuck out in various directions from under a thin cotton rag Hester had tied on her head. *Sure ain't a pretty woman.* Hester's left eye drifted away from her right.

I always liked being wid her. I liked it dat she talk to me like I was growed up, even when I was little.

She sat down and looked up at her grandmother. *She'd tell you what she thought. Sure warn't one to 'beat 'round de bush. I have always liked comin' tuh see Grandma Hester.* "How you doin', Grandma?"

Still standing, her grandmother put one hand on the table. "I hab my pro'lems, but dey don't 'mount to much. Doin' good. I wuz t'inkin' 'bout taking a walk an' seeing whut spring plants I kin fin'. Dat soun' awright tuh yuh?"

Etta smiled up at her. "Sure, Grandma. Maybe you could teach me some more 'bout plants."

Hester pointed to the door. "Get me dat croaker sack off de po'ch out dere." She took the sack and put several small jars in with others already there. She moved around the room, picking up a paring knife and a small, flat digging tool.

Etta leaned back in the chair. "Grandma, folks call you a root doctuh." I knows a little 'bout dat, but what is root? Is dat like roots from a bush?"

Hester nodded as she looked around for something. "Sometimes hit be roots or dif'nt parts uh plants dat yuh use. Hit all kinduh run togeduh, but dere is healin', and den dere is root doctuhin', conjurin'. Yuh see, Honey, dere are t'ings, spirits, yuh may not kin see, whut kin hep yuh or, fuh dat mattuh, whut kin hurt yuh, too. Root be de way whut yuh kin get de spirits on yoh side an' try tuh keep 'em dere."

Etta stared at her grandmother. "Yeah, I've heard folks talk 'bout de spirits."

Hester had picked up a pair of heavy shoes and looked down at Etta's bare feet. "Kin yuh weuh dese?" She shook her head. "Dere is sandspurs an' prickly pear out dere weh we goin'. Need some stout shoes."

Etta put the shoes on and tied the leather laces. She followed her grandmother out the door, down the steps and to the right, back toward Anna's and the road. Before they got that far, Hester turned right, into the woods.

"Aunt Anna was telling me some 'bout Paw's daddy an' how he come to be heah. I sure would like it if you'd tell me more 'bout 'im."

"Sho, Honey. W'en we gets back, I'll fix us some suppuh, an' I'll tell you whut I know or whut I kin 'membuh."

Etta continued behind Hester as they wound their way along a faint trail through the trees. "So, Grandma, you were sayin' dat dere are two types of root doctorin'?"

Hester kept moving as she talked. "Yeah. Well, dere's usin' roots, leabes, an' berries tuh cure sumpin whut ails yuh, and den dere's conjurin'. Hester stopped and looked back at Etta. "De conjurin' be usin' wha'ebuh wurks tuh gets on de good side uh de spirits. Get dem to potect yuh frum bad spirits or peoples whut wants tuh hurt yuh."

Etta's eyes got big, and she spoke quietly. "Are spirits de same as ghosts, Grandma?"

Hester bent a pine limb out of the way and passed it back to Etta. "No, not 'xactly. De spirits be free. Dey kin go an' do as dey please. Dey mostly 'ttached tuh places or peoples dey lub'. Ghosts is lack spirits whut ain't free. Dey still draggin' 'round dere bodies. Lot uh folks kin see ghosts. Dey be walkin' 'round wid no head, all bloody lookin'. Dey ain't as powful, danejus as spirits."

Etta stopped and shuddered. "Eww. But you sayin' dat ghosts can't hurt yuh?"

Hester laughed quietly. "Well, dey kin, I reckon, but dey's don't care much fuh peoples. Dey dun got stuck wid dere bodies, an' dey worried 'bout getting free. Dat's 'bout all dey care 'bout."

The trees began to thin out as they continued north. Etta moved up beside her grandmother as a field opened up in front of them. It looked like it had not been planted for the past several years. Sweetgums and some pines

84

had sprung up, but the landscape was dominated by a variety of shrubs and small plants.

Hester scanned the field. Etta frowned. "Are all spirits mean, Grandma?"

Hester smiled at her. "Lawd, no, Honey. W'en a nice person die, dey be a good spirit, an' w'en a mean person die, den dey prolly be a mean spirit. Danejus. Dey a lot moh good 'uns dan dere is bad 'uns, but dem few bad 'uns kin sho cause some mischief."

Hester turned and skirted the open field, examining the ground for plants along the tree line.

Etta looked around, too. *I don't know what to pick.* "Can you get me some Life Everlastin', Grandma? I want to make some of dat tea."

"Oh, dere plenty uh hit out heah. See dis plant heah wid de small white leabes rite on de stalk?"

"Yassum. Dat's what Edward call rabbit tobacco. We tried to smoke it one time."

Hester laughed. "Dat's hit, but I don't pick hit 'til hit got flowers. Dere won't be no flowers fuh a while yet. I'll gibe yuh some dat I dried last fall.

"Look dere. You see dat plant wid de big, fuzzy leabes?"

Etta reached for a short plant with large leaves. "Right heah, Grandma?"

"Yeah. Feel uh hit. Feel lack a rabbit's eah, don' hit. Dat's mullen. Pull up de whole plant. See if'ns you kin fin' some moh. Good fuh de febuh. Shake de dirt off an' jus' drops dem in de sack."

Etta looked for more mullen. "Grandma, why do ghosts still have dey bodies dat dey drag 'round?"

Hester pulled up a mullen plant, shook it, stood and tossed it to Etta. "Dat happen if'n dey warn't 'pared fuh burial lack dey should'uh been, dere people don' take care uh de body lack dey should'uh, or if'n dey wuz murdered or killed in some kinduh bad way."

Etta tapped a plant against her boot to clean the roots. "I saw sumpin up at dat graveyard past de Main House. It was a dark shape, flew cross de road in front uh me fast-like. Wuz dat a ghost?"

Hester was bent over pulling up a plant. She looked at Etta. "Dat's prolly a new spirit, somebody whut jus' died. Dey hang 'round de graveyard lack dat. New spirits easier to see dan ol' spirits. Ain't l'arn tuh blend intuh de woods, swirl in de breeze lack ol' spirits."

Hester stood up, put her hands on her hips, shook her head and smiled at Etta. "Yuh ain't changed a bit. Still ax'in' one question right aftuh de las' one."

She bent back over another plant. "I go up tuh dat grabeyard sometime. People t'ink I'm up dere gettin' buckets uh grabeyard dirt, but I jus' sit out dere, listen an' talk tuh de spirits, gibe my 'spects. Dey lack company sometimes."

Etta smiled to herself and was quiet. She allowed her mind to swirl like the spirits as she tried to consider the meaning of all her grandmother was saying. *Sure hard to fit all dis together wid what de preacher say over in Brunswick. Maybe it'll make sense to me one day.*

Hester was pointing with the metal tool. "Etta, see dat plant obuh dere, dat little tree whut got dem lite green leabes? Look kinduh lack a white oak leabe, but dey pointier. Yeah. Take dis heah and dig up any uh dem yuh see out heah dat's not too big." She held up the tool about four feet off the ground to indicate a good size, then handed it to Etta.

Hester took a jar out of the sack and opened it. She walked over to Etta, took the small tree, pulled the paring knife out of her pocket, and cut the root off. She chopped the root into the open jar, using her calloused thumb to press the root against the sharp edge of the knife. "Make a good tea aftuh hit dry some."

Etta had found another of the small trees. "I've smelled dat root before. What's it called?"

Hester answered without looking up. "Dat's called sassfras. Sipping sassfras tea good fuh de stomach."

Etta stood up and took a broader look around. "What is it like tuh conjure, Grandma?"

Hester spoke as she worked. "Somebody who conjure be lookin' fuh peoples tuh slip up, leab a hair brush out weh yuh kin get dere hair or be leabin dere bare footprints 'round weh yuh kin get de dust out'uh 'em."

She stood, a plant in one hand. Glancing around, she spoke quietly. "Yuh take de hair or de dust, tie hit up wid some grabeyard dirt whut come frum a fresh grabe at midnight, an' you got yohself de beginnin's uv uh pow'ful spell."

Etta stood, frowned, and stared at her grandmother.

Hester put one hand up on her waist. "As fuh me an' conjurin', I is tryin' tuh get folks tuh lets me be 'bout dat stuff and jus' come tuh me w'en dey sick, w'en dey's got a rash, been hurt. I is tellin' folks, 'Don' come tuh me fuh no conjurin'. I is tiud uh ebuhbody 'round heah t'inkin' I done put a spell on 'em ebuh time dey gets de runny nose. Mos' I do now be a turnback ebuh once hin uh while."

Hester pointed into the edge of the woods. "Etta, dere's a patch uh vines obuh dere I want tuh take a look at." She walked over to a small spring that was almost covered by a dense tangle of vines five feet high.

Etta called from the field. "What's dat, Grandma?"

Hester picked up a vine and looked at it closely. "Dis heah's greenbrier. I ain't gon fool wid de leabes or vines tuhday; I need gloves fuh dat, but I is glad tuh know dat dis is heah."

Etta walked over and looked at the vines.

Hester went down on one knee. "Le's dig up some uh de roots, cut dem off an' jus' drop dem in de sack. Kerful uh de vines; dey'll scratch yuh."

Etta joined her grandmother on her knees pulling up roots. "What's dis used for, Grandma?"

"Hit hep womens get bettuh aftuh dey hab a baby. I gibe hit tuh de midwife tuh use. Chocu say if yuh hungry, dat you kin eat de root lack a little tater. Hit don't taste like much. I ain't nebuh cared fuh hit."

Etta continued to work as she asked, "What was you sayin', Grandma, 'bout a turnboot or sumpin?"

Hester turned and stared at Etta. "Whut? Oh, a turnback. Well, if'ns yuh knows whut yuh doin', yuh kin cure somebody whut been conjured by turnin' de spell back on de one whut done hit. I sho cured lot uh folks lack dat." She handed Etta the knife.

Etta's mouth was open, but she took the knife and cut several roots off the vines.

88

Shortly, Hester stood and brushed off her apron. "Dat's 'nuf uh dem."
She looked closely toward the field. "Look right dere." She pointed. "See
de plant wid de white flowers? Dem's stingin' nettles, Honey. You know
'bout dem?"

"Yassum. I know dey sure do burn and itch if you rub 'ginst 'em."

"Take dat tool an' dig up all you see. Careful. Hold dem by de root,
take de knife, cut de roots off an' puts dem in dis heah jar."

Etta went to work. "Whut dey good foh, Grandma?"

Hester laughed. "Let me see dat root." She took it, twirled it in her
fingers, and looked at it closely. "Got tuh hab dis stuff. De ol' mens down
heah be knockin' on my doh, askin' 'bout stingin' nettle root. If any uh 'em
fin' a penny, dey gon come see me fuh sho."

Hester held it up and twirled it at Etta. "Dis stuff rat heah turn dere
little ol' hangin' root intuh a big ol' stout branch." She bent over laughing.
"Sumpin dere wives kin hang de wash on, Baby."

They both laughed. "Aw, Grandma!"

Hester put her hands on her hips and looked around slowly. "Yuh wuz
talkin' 'bout makin' frien's. I knows de boys be swarmin' 'round yuh like
bees 'round honey."

Etta was bent over working. "No, Grandma. Ain't been no swarmin'
'round me."

"If'ns I know anyt'ing, I knows dat gon change." Hester walked
around pulling a couple of more plants as Etta worked on the stinging nettles.
"Get de rest uh dem nettles dere, an' we kin head on back. We got plenty uh
plants tuh wurk wid fuh de time bein'."

Chapter 11

Etta and her grandmother approached the cabin. She took the sack over to
two tall cedar posts that had been put in the ground four feet apart. They
supported five board shelves. A piece of tin had been nailed onto the tops of
the posts.

Hester removed all of the whole plants and larger roots that had been
collected, then spread them out on the shelves. Etta had sat down on the
steps and was taking off the boots. As she looked up toward her
grandmother, she realized there were two squirrels on the corner porch post,
hanging from a string tied to a back leg. Etta pointed. "Look, Grandma."

"Yeah, I seen'em. We'll 'ave 'em fuh suppuh. Bring'em obuh heah
tuh me an' den draw up some watuh." Hester took the knife out of her
pocket, walked over and sharpened it on a grinding stone that was sitting on
the stump of a small tree. In a few quick movements, she had skinned and

gutted the squirrels. Etta brought water in a small bucket. Pouring slowly from the bucket, Hester washed the blood and hair off each carcass, rinsed her hands, tossed the water, and dropped the squirrels in the bucket. "Take dese."

The jars clanked around as Hester picked up the croaker sack and led them inside. She removed the jars and set them on shelves along with a number of jars already there. She looked around. "Honey, see if dere's 'nuf coals in de fiuhplace tuh gets a fiuh goin'." She pointed. "See my kindlin' obuh dere? Dere some small oak on de poach."

As Etta added split slivers of heart pine to the coals, the rich, rising vapor filled her nose. One blow on the coals restarted the fire. Etta added hardwood and soon had a hot fire that would leave coals for cooking.

Her grandmother smiled at her. "I'll take care uh hit now, Honey, but bring me some more uh dat oak and stack hit obuh heah." She pointed to the right side of the hearth.

Hester worked on a worn board counter, peeling and chopping vegetables and herbs.

"What else can I do, Grandma?"

Hester nodded toward a deep cast-iron pot with a lid and a curved, hinged handle over the top. "Get me some watuh an' put 'bout dis much in heah." Hester leaned over and put a finger on the outside of the pot and went back to chopping.

In a few minutes Etta brought in a bucket and poured water in the pot.

"Yuh kin sit hit rite heah." Hester wiped a spot clean of peelings.

She added the vegetables and herbs, then cut each squirrel into four small hams. She added them and the skinned squirrel heads to the stew.

91

Hester took the pot by the hoop handle and slipped it over the metal hook extending from the right top of the fireplace. She swung the pot of stew back in, over the pile of coals.

She turned to Etta, who had sat in a chair on one side of the table. "So yuh want to heah 'bout yoh Grandpa Chocu?" An old rocker held together with wire sat out in front of the fireplace. It creaked its complaint as Hester sat down.

"Chocu?" Etta wrinkled her brow. "Wuz dat his name? I don't remember ever hearin' his name before."

"Dat wuz 'is name. Chocu. His pa wuz a Semnole Injin. His mama wuz part uf a bunch dat 'scaped at Ebo Creek."

Etta nodded. "Aunt Anna told me 'bout dat."

"Well, dem Ebo went south and hooked up wid de Semnoles. De Injins took dem in, and dey lived togeduh an' got along. I'll tell yuh 'bout all dat aftuh we eat."

Hester began mixing up ingredients for cornbread. She pointed to her right. "Honey, get dat oven dere nex' tuh de fiuhplace and set hit on de hearth."

Etta got up and found a footed, cast-iron oven with a flat, heavy lid and sat it out in front of the stew pot.

Hester raked a small pile of coals out from under the stew and sat the oven on top of them. She rubbed the inside of the oven with a piece of fat meat. She came back and added the cornbread batter, using her long forefinger to cleanly wipe out the mixing bowl. She added the lid, reached for a small shovel, and scooped hot coals onto the top of the oven. She put the bowl in the washtub, wiped her hands with a rag, sat down in her rocker and leaned back.

Etta could see the steam begin to escape the lidded pot hanging in the fireplace. She leaned back too, allowing the odors of the cooking food to take her back to more carefree times. She closed her eyes and let the memories of her grandmother's cabin drift over her. After a while, she asked, "Grandma, do you think I can be happy down heah?"

"Baby, I knows yuh 'ad a 'ard time lately. Yuh an' yoh mama 'ad it good in lots uh ways, but dat sitchation at de Main House done turned bad. Mr. Thomas? "He ain't got no wife no moh, an' dat ain't good. W'en she dere, which ain't a bunch, ebuhbody wish she warn't. Yuh an' yoh mama bettuh off down heah.

"Yoh daddy still mad 'bout whut happen, but he don't blame yoh mama. He say Mr. Thomas kep 'im 'way frum her. Sho warn't no su'prise dat dey got her tangled up in dere mess. Be easy tuh feel sorry fuh Mr. Thomas, take 'is side, w'en she so mean and hateful, but he 'bout as bad 'n 'is own way. He connivin'. He smooth an' he smart, but he dun got weh he don't care nuttin' 'bout nobody 'cept 'isself and 'is white chilren."

Hester took a deep breath and stopped rocking. "Buckra takes care uh buckra. Dat's de whole crux uh hit. Ebuhbody else gottuh make do wid whut ebuh's lef' obuh.

"James knowed dey wurk her too hard, kep' her cut off frum 'im an' de uduh famly dat she could'uh spent time wid. I hate hit's wurked out like dis, but yuh and Rachel bettuh off 'way frum dem peoples. Yoh mama leabin' dun hurt dem worser dan hit's hurt anybody else."

93

Hester got up and stirred the pot with a long wooden spoon and arranged the coals under it with the small hoe. She turned and looked at Etta. "I hope dat Miss Frances jus' leabe well 'nuf 'lone an' let yuh be. Hit seem tuh be wurkin' out so fah."

She sat back down in the rocker. "But whut 'bout yuh, Honey? How yuh doin'? I got a chaince tuh talk tuh Anna uh few days back. She say dat all dis been hard on yuh, but yuh doin' good obuh hat de greenhouses." Her chair registered each movment as Hester rocked slowly, studying her granddaughter.

Etta smiled back at her and nodded slowly. "I'm doin' awright, Grandma. I like de work pretty good, 'specially bein' able to get out and walk. I'm tryin' to make some friends, and Aunt Anna, she been wonderful to me."

Hester nodded at Etta. "Bein' wid Anna is good. She de storytelluh 'round heah. Keeps up wid t'ings dat happen. Makes sho de chilren knows 'bout de pas'." She frowned. "But de main t'ing right now is dat yuh need tuh be back wid yoh mama." She raised her eyebrows and leaned back. "Dat's all I gon say 'bout dat fuh de time bein'."

"Yassum, Grandma. I'll be back wid her b'fo' long."

There was silence except for the creaking chair. "Hab yuh been tuh talk tuh Abraham?"

"No, Grandma, I ain't seen PawPaw."

Hester cocked her head at Etta. "He de only one whut can really do sumpin 'round heah. Yuh need tuh go down an' talk to 'im, gibe yoh 'spects."

Etta nodded. "Yassum."

Her grandmother looked off and spoke softly, "Yoh mama wuz sho smart tuh get yuh out uh heah b'fo' Miss Frances done sumpin crazy 'bout yuh an' Edwud."

Etta lifted her head and frowned. "What you talkin' 'bout, Grandma?"

Hester looked at her. " Yuh knowed dat Miss Frances hate yuh 'cause Edwud, he care 'bout yuh so much."

Etta jerked up straight in her chair, her mouth partly open. "What was dat, Grandma?"

Hester leaned up. "I wuz sayin' dat, b'fo' yuh went off to Brunswick, Miss Frances all de time be raisin' a fuss wid yoh mama obuh yuh an' Edwud spen'in' so much time togeduh. She couldn't sell yuh off, sen' yuh tuh de Norf End, eben sen' yuh down heah tuh stay long, 'cause Edwud, he'd throw a fit. Yuh know dat boy gets 'is way."

Etta frowned and nodded.

"Well, yoh Mama come up wid de idea uh yuh goin' to hep Medina. Warn't nuttin' dat Edwud could say 'bout dat. Miss Frances could stop worrin' 'bout yuh an' Edwud bein' so close, and yoh mama could stop worryin' 'bout Miss Frances doin' sumpin crazy, lack sellin' yuh off."

Etta blinked, her mouth open again. Her shoulders slumped, and she shook her head. "Dey didn't tell me nuttin' 'bout dat. Mama say it was Grandma's idea."

Hester resumed rocking. "Well, maybe hit wuz, but we wuz desp'rate tuh gets yuh in some safe place b'fo' Miss Frances hab one uh her blowups."

Etta sat up once more. "So de problem was dat Edward, he care a bunch 'bout me?"

Hester nodded and leaned toward her granddaughter. "Yep. Dat wuz de crux uh hit. Warn't no white gals 'round heah. She t'ink he wuz too wild. T'ought you wuz part uh de pro'lem. Boy needed tuh be tamed. 'Membuh dem parties she had wid dem young peoples frum Brunswick? De dances?

Etta nodded. "Yeah. She made 'im dress up, take dancin' lessons." Etta put her hand over her mouth and laughed. "He hated dem dances."

Hester leaned back. "She sho didn't lack peoples seein' yuh two playin' togeduh, and she t'ink hit wuz yoh fault he didn't care nuttin' bout spen'in' time wid dem town gals."

Yeah, it embarressed her when dere was anybody other dan family 'round. Didn't even like for Mr. Luke to see Me and Edward together. When she had company at de Main House, I knew we had to get up de beach to have any peace. Etta smiled broadly at her grandmother.

Hester laughed as she spoke. "Dat woman can sho fin' plenty tuh worry 'bout. Aftuh yuh lef', she agg'avate Mr. Wilson 'til he finally 'llowed her to get Edwud in boa'din' school obuh in Brunswick." She shook her head, still chuckling. "Reckon dey done civilized 'im obuh dere."

Etta took in a sharp breath. *Wonduh how he's changed, if he ever think 'bout me anymore.*

Hester wiped the tears from her eyes. "We'uns gon get de nubie out right aftuh dinnuh an' ax' de spirits 'bout yoh fuchuh. Fin' out whut's comin' yoh way." Hester smiled. "Don't take no root tuh know dat dere's boyfrien's awready linin' up. Aftuh dat, I'll tell yuh 'bout yoh Grandpa Chocu."

Etta went out to the well, cranked up some fresh water and dipped them out two large cups. Hester took out two bowls, serving large helpings

96

of squirrel stew and setting them on the table. She went to the hearth, brushed the coals off the top of the Dutch oven with a rag and slid it forward. After removing the lid using the cloth, she cut large slices of thick cornbread and placed them on the edge of each bowl.

Etta leaned over the table and blew on a spoonful of stew. *I ain't 'ad no squirrel in a long time.* "Hmm, dis is good, Grandma."

Hester served her own bowl, fishing out one of the squirrel heads from the pot.

Etta laughed quietly. *Dem squirrels prolly tuh pay fuh some stingin' nettle root or fuh uh turnback.*

Etta ate until she was uncomfortably full. She sat back in her chair. "What's a nubie, Grandma?"

Hester got up, walked over next to the door and took something hanging from a nail. She laid it on the table in front of Etta. "Dey all dif'nt, but dis heah's mine."

Etta picked up the nubie and examined it closely. It was a two-foot string tied to a small piece of quartz crystal. Hester took their bowls and put them in the washtub. She sat back down in her rocking chair. Etta gave the nubie back, and Hester laid it across her lap while she rubbed her hands together. "Now tell me, Honey, whut question do yuh want de nubie tuh ansuh?"

"What do you mean, Grandma?"

"De nubie kin ansuh yes an' no questions 'bout de present time or de fuchuh. What's hit dat yuh be wond'rin' 'bout?"

Etta looked off and was quiet for several moments. "Will I ever live in Brunswick again?"

97

Hester rubbed her hands together and took the end of the string in her right hand, suspending the crystal over her left palm. She gave Etta a look that seemed to say, "Be quiet." Then she asked out loud, "Will Etta ebuh libe in Brunswick 'gin?"

Etta stared intently at the crystal. Nothing happened. Then the crystal began to swing back and forth above Hester's palm. "No, Etta. De nubie say you won't be libin' in Brunswick no moh."

Etta frowned and stared down for a moment. "Will I be happy living heah on Bonita?"

Again Hester rubbed her hands together and held the crystal over her palm, but then laid it back down. "Yuh need tuh unuhstan' now, dat w'en yuh lookin' tuh de fuchuh, dat whut you do 'tween now and den kin change whut happen. Yuh unuhstan'?"

Etta nodded.

"Awright den." Hester rubbed her hands together, picked up the nubie and asked, "Will Etta be happy libin' heah on Bonita?" Again the string moved back and forth. "Well, Honey, hit say yuh won't be happy heah, but 'membuh yuh kin change t'ings yoself by doin' t'ings dif'nt. Got anuduh one?"

Etta brought her forefinger to her lips, and her frown deepened. In a moment she asked, "Will I ever live anyplace else?"

She sat quietly, watching intently as Hester went through the process. Again, nothing at first. Then the nubie began to move in large circles around Hester's palm.

Hester laughed quietly. "De nubie say fuh sho yuh gon libe somuhs uduh dan Bonita.

98

Etta smiled broadly.

"Dat make yuh happy, but not me. Anuduh question?"

"Will I ever see Dan again?"

Hester went through the motions and asked, "Will Etta ebuh see Dan 'gin?"

As Etta looked down on the nubie, it began to circle.

Etta smiled, looked off and paused. "Let's leave it at dat right now, Grandma. Got to think 'bout all it had to say." Etta watched Hester put the nubie in her pocket.

Hester leaned forward. "How 'bout some sassfras tea, Honey?"

"Sure, Grandma." Etta put her hand on her stomach. "I think I need some."

"Take dis 'ere kettle an' fill hit 'bout ha'f full uh watuh."

Etta took the kettle, walked out to the well and lowered the bucket. The light was fading as she returned to the cabin.

"Hook dat bail obuh de arm dere and stir up de fiuh, Honey. Yuh might need tuh add some small pieces uh dat oak wood." Etta tended the fire and pushed the kettle over the flames. She came back and sat down at the table.

Her grandmother was shaving off thin pieces of a root into a small crockery pitcher. "Hit don' take much sassfras tuh make a good tea. She sat back in her rocker. "Yuh ax' me earliuh 'bout yoh grandpa. Whut yuh want tuh know 'bout 'im?"

Etta frowned and stared into space for a moment, then looked at her grandmother. "What's his name again? Chocu? How did you meet him, Grandma?"

99

Hester took out a small, round, tin container from her pocket, opened the tight lid, took a large pinch of the dark brown powder and tucked it into her lower lip. She looked off and rocked. "Lawdy, dat wuz a long time 'go."

Etta shifted around in her chair and leaned back.

Hester packed the snuff down with her tongue. "I 'membuh w'en I fus' seen 'im. Hit wuz wintuh w'en he an' two uduh mens jus' showed up. Chocu wuz lot lightuh skinned dan mos' folks 'round heah. Talluh dan me. De uduh men wuz older Aficans. Dey an' Chocu's muduh 'ad been part uh de Ebo bunch whut 'scaped from de fus' Mr. Wilson." Hester pointed. "Han' me dat can on de table dere, Honey."

Etta leaned up, picked up the empty can and gave it to her grandmother.

She spit into it. "T'ank yuh. Hit wuz cold weaduh, an' Chocu wuz wearin' uh long coat an' uh turbin. Dat turbin wuz de fus' t'ing dat caught my eye. I nebuh seen a man wear uh turbin b'fo'. Hit wuz a long, wool scarf whut he would wrap an' tie on 'is head. I 'membuh too dat 'is coat 'ad ruffles 'round de shoulduhs an' was dec'rated on de ches' wid beads. Peoples 'round heah didn't wear nuttin' like dat."

There was steam from the kettle over the fire. "Etta, take dat kettle an' fill dat pitchuh 'bout ha'f full."

"Yassum." Etta got up.

Hester pointed. "Take dat rag an' use hit. De 'andle might be hot."

She went on as Etta managed the kettle. "My daddy, he run de sawmill, an' we'uns libed sortuh isolated up towa'd de Norf End. I wuz uh liddle olduh dan yuh is now w'en yoh grandpa showed up. Lawdy, he wuz a feast fuh my eyes."

100

Etta sat up straighter in her chair, looking intently at her grandmother as she spoke. "Chocu an' de uduhs say dat dey 'ad been out huntin' an' comes back tuh fin' dat dere town 'ad been burned tuh de groun' by 'merican soljurs. Some uh dere frien's an' famly been killed, an' dey t'ought uduhs been shipped off tuh de West. De mens didn't hab no place tuh go. Hit warn't safe dere, so dey come back norf lookin' fuh a place tuh libe an' wurk 'til t'ings settle down.

"Ah don' t'ink Wilson knowed whut tuh do wid 'em. Been so long since de olduh men 'scaped, dat he didn't feel lack he could whip 'em or go tuh de law. 'Sides, he ain't nebuh lack habin' de law out heah nohow. He t'ink dat he could slowly bring 'em unduh control. He all de time talkin' 'bout how happy 'is slaves be. He prolly t'ink dem felluhs be glad tuh give up dere freedum, start saying, 'Yassuh' an' 'Nawsuh' lack ebuhbody else 'round heah. Prolly t'ink hit be a lesson to uduhs 'bout runnin' 'way.

"Anyhows, he lets dem stay up at a cabin norf uh Lumbuh Landin' weh dey s'posed to be sawing down trees an' runnin' teams uh oxen tuh haul de logs tuh Daddy at de sawmill." Hester got up, put a spoonful of honey in each of two cups and filled them with tea. She stirred them, brought the cups over and gave one to Etta.

Hester walked out the door and spit off of the porch. She came back inside and sat back down in her rocker. "Dem mens would wurk some, but dat Chocu, he wuz born tuh hunt. Wilson, he didn't lack peoples huntin' up dere, 'cause he wanted dat game fuh 'is ownse'f an' 'is frien's."

Hester leaned back and sipped her tea. "W'en dey would bring in a tree, I'd sneak a peek at de man in de turbin. He noticed me too, an' hit warn't long b'fo' we be slippin' 'round, spenin' time togeduh. My mama an'

101

daddy didn't lack me bein' roun' 'im, tried tuh keep me in de cabin w'en he wuz dere, but I would slip out at night an' meet 'im aftuh dey went to sleep."

Etta's eyes got big, and she put her hand to her mouth.

Hester looked over at her granddaughter. "My daddy, yoh great-grandaddy, wuz bad tuh drink. Up weh we wuz, we'uns didn't see too much uh buckra. In de Fall, my paw, he gets de felluhs up dere to fin' 'im all de bullis grape dey kin fin' out in de woods. He make jugs an' jugs uh wine an' hide 'em down in de well. He would get rip-roarin' drunk mos' Sat'd'y nights. He warn't no bad man mos' uh de time, but he be 'bout de meanest man yuh ebuh seen w'en he be drinkin'. I wuz sick tuh deaf uh hit."

Hester spit in her can and sat it next to her chair. "Chocu tol' me dat he wanted me tuh come libe wid 'im in whut he call a 'chikee'. Didn't take me no time tuh make up my mind. I lef' an' took up in de woods wid 'im. Hit wuz de bes' time uh my life. We wuz happy out dere fuh a long spell. Lawdy, Lawdy, dem wuz good times." She looked at Etta, smiled, and shook her head.

"Daddy, he start complainin' to buckra dat he warn't gettin' no trees, tellin' 'im 'bout de huntin, an' me takin' up wid Chocu, not wurkin' neiduh. Dat wuz de buhginnin' uh our trubbles."

Etta let the sassafras aroma fill her nose as she sipped slowly.

"Chocu wuz dif'nt frum anybody I ebuh met. He wuz very kind tuh me. He knowed ebuh plant an' animal in de woods. My mama, she taught me root, but Chocu, he taught me de plants an' hows tuh use 'em tuh heal."

Hester sipped her tea. "Chocu, he spoke Injin. At fus' I 'ad a 'ard time figurin' whut he wuz talkin' 'bout. He wuz very wurried 'bout 'is mama an' whut happen'd tuh her. One or two times dey gets a little news. Word wuz

102

dat Chocu's mama's body wuz not found, an' he t'ink dat she been caught an' sent out West somuhs. He wanted tuh go look fuh her out dere."

Etta frowned deeply. "Yeah. I read 'bout President Jackson. He sent lots uh Indians out to de West. Settlers wanted dere land, and he round dem Indians up and sent 'em off. Dey on what dey call reservations out dere, all dem what dey didn't kill. It's a long ways out dere, Grandma."

Hester nodded at Etta. "Well, Chocu, he wuz res'less, an' I knowed he wouldn't be stayin 'round heah too long. 'Course dat mainly 'cause he didn't take no orders frum nobody, 'specially buckra. Fuh de two yeahs I libe wid 'im, I knowed whut hit wuz lack tuh be uh free woman. Dey warn't gon get no chain on dat man."

She looked off. "He would stan' dere while de obuhseeuh talk. He frown, bob 'is head up an' down lack he would be glad tuh do whutsumebuh dey ax'in' if'n he could jus' unuhstan' whut dey talkin 'bout. Later, I'd try tuh 'splain whut buckra say he 'ad to do." Hester laughed. "Figured out quick he didn't care no moh 'bout hearin' whut buckra say dan whut de bird's be sayin' in de trees. Yuh know dat sort of t'ing gon bring trubble 'round heah 'ventually, an' hit did."

"Yuh want any moh tea, Honey."

Etta smiled and shook her head.

Hester continued, "Sho 'nuf, Wilson, he sen' de obuhseeuh up dere tuh find Chocu an' tuh tell 'im dat de dogs don' foun' blood on de groun' weh hit look like a hog 'ad been kilt an' dressed. He wuz tol' 'gin dat he 'ad no right tuh de game on de Norf End an' Blackbeard weh Chocu lub' tuh hunt. Hit wuz kinduh hard tuh act inn'cent, 'cause w'en Buckra fin' us, we'uns 'ad a hog quartuh on uh spit obuh de fiuh."

103

Etta and Hester both laughed. Hester paused, then raised her eyebrows and continued. "De obuhseeuh, he rant an' rave while Chocu kinduh shuffle 'is feets an' try tuh look sorry. Buckra say dey would bring moh food up dere if'ns he would stop de huntin'. Den he went into our chikee an' start takin' anyt'ing whut look lack sumpin' tuh hunt wid. He took Chocu's bow an' arrows an' busted dem obuh 'is knee. He missed Chocu's dart gun but took a spear an' spear thowuh, 'long wid de hog quartuh."

Hester looked down and shook her head slowly. "I knowed Chocu soon be leabing w'en by de next day he don' made anuduh bow an' arrows an' kilt a turkey. Den wid de arrow still stickin' in 'im, he t'rowed dat turkey on de back uh buckra's buggy dat wuz parked down at de sawmill. Hit wuz lack he sorry an' he payin' fuh dat hog."

Hester gave a brief laugh, picked up the can and spit into it. "He tol' me 'bout stan'in' in de woods an' watchin' de obuhseeuh fin' dat turkey." They were both laughing now. "I 'membuh hit well, 'cause I nebuh seen 'im laff out loud b'fo'. W'en he told me 'bout watching dat obuhseeuh fin' dat turkey, he wuz laffin' so hard, I t'ink dat he gon fall in de fiuh." They both wiped tears from their eyes.

"'Course he jus' slappin' Buckra in de face wid dat bidness. De sad part wuz he tell me dat he gon be goin' an' dat he cain't take me an' liddle James wid 'im. In less dan a week, de men whut come frum de Semnole town wuz all gone, 'long wid some uh de slabes whut wurked wid Papa at de sawmill."

Hester grinned at Etta. "Wilson, he wuz 'side 'isself, he so mad. He los' dose mens whut come heah an' two good slabes tuh boot. He went

104

'isself wid de huntin' party, but dey come back empty-handed." She clapped her hands together and laughed out loud.

"What did you do, Grandma?"

Hester frowned and looked down. "Chocu wuz gone, an' I wuz sad fuh a long time, but I 'ad James." Hester looked up at Etta and smiled. "An' now I 'as Etta 'til she moves tuh Araby 'r sumuhs." Hester smiled broadly at her granddaughter.

Etta smiled back and sat her cup on the table. *She 'bout de most fun of anybody I ever met.*

Hester emptied the contents of her lip into the can. "Yuh know hit's funny, but I nebuh took up wid anuduh man aftuh dat. Dey lets me move down heah, an' dat wuz awright by me. Me an' James done jus' fine in Tabby Landing. Wid me knowin' plants, dey 'ventually took me out'uh de fiel' an' puts me obuh de garden. I knowed dat Chocu would nebuh be back. Dey'd'uh put 'im in chains tuh wurk, an' dat would'uh kilt 'im fuh sho."

Hester stared off. "Ebuh night fuh a long time, I'd lie in bed an' wonduh if he wuz still 'libe. Heah noises at my window, I jump up an' t'ink dat he 'ad come fuh us." She shook her head slowly. "But hit warn't nebuh 'im. Wish we'uns could'uh been togeduh 'gin in dis life, least one moh time. Wish he could'uh met 'is pretty gran'chile."

Hester gave Etta a sober stare, then looked down and shook her head. "Been hearin' some rumblin's frum de spirit wurl. I belieb Chocu's done passed obuh."

Etta sat quietly in her chair for some time. "Thank you for tellin' me 'bout Grandpa. I sure wish I had knowed 'im. Guess I need to get on back over tuh Anna's."

"Wait jus' uh minute." Hester got up, pulled some items out from under her bed and began looking in a large handmade basket. "Heah hit is." She held up something small between her fingers. She paused again, then went to another part of the cabin and began going through another smaller basket. "Dere, dat'll wurk." She came back over and held out her hand for Etta to see.

"Yoh grandpa wore dis all de time, an' he give it tuh me w'en he lef'. Hit's time fuh yuh tuh hab hit. Said hit wuz good luck, would connect us." In her palm was a shiny, flat, ebony item that was about two-and-a-half inches long and about an inch-and-a-half wide.

Etta's eyes got big. "It's a shark's tooth, Grandma!"

She held it up. "Lawdy, didn't know whut hit wuz."

"Edward found one of dose on de beach, but it was much smaller dan dis one. A doctor visiting Mr. Wilson saw it on de mantle at de Main House and was tellin' dem 'bout it. He say dat dese were fossils and dat dey was so old dat dey done turned to stone." Etta stared at her grandmother, who frowned and tilted her head.

A hole had been drilled into the top of the tooth. Hester strung a thin piece of dried sinew through the hole. "Turn 'round, Honey." She tied the sinew around Etta's neck.

"What 'bout Papa?" Etta sat down and rubbed the polished fossil between her fingers. She looked up. "Wouldn't he want to have dis?"

"James be glad I give hit tuh yuh." Hester sat back down, took her tin out and reloaded her lip. "Now, yuh bettuh get on back obuh tuh Anna's."

Etta stood up, bent over and hugged her grandmother. "Thank you, Grandma. I loved bein' wid you today." Picking up the food items Anna had left, Etta headed out the door and down the steps into the descending evening. *What did Grandma say? She say dat Miss Frances worried 'bout how much Edward care 'bout me. Dat's de reason Miss Frances let me go to Brunswick. How 'bout dat. 'Worried 'bout how much Edward cared 'bout me.' I love de sound of dat. Maybe he still do.*

An' all dat 'bout Grandpa Chocu. Didn't have no idea 'bout who he was, what he was like.

The moon was rising full. A vibrant ensemble of insects and amphibians captured Etta's attention, delivering it back to her senses and to the present. She felt her feet stirring the warm, sandy soil. Her face caught the light touch of a cool breeze that offered the Spring's first taste of honeysuckle. She took a full breath and slowed her pace, noticing the trees' grey moon shadows. *Dis heah is a special place. Maybe I can belong heah wid my people. It ain't so bad.*

I'll see Edward sooner or later. Hope it ain't later. Might have to help dat along a little bit. Maybe Grandma could make me a potion. Maybe I ought to just find out when he's gon be over heah, get somebody to take 'im a note. We'll see. Reckon he'll be out 'uh school b 'fo' long.

Etta took the stone from her chest and touched it to her lips, thinking of a handsome man wearing a turbin. Wind stirred the trees. *My people.* She strolled back through Tabby Landing. *Maybe de nubie's wrong. Maybe I can be happy heah.*

CHAPTER 12

As soon as the workers left the fields on Saturdays, most slave families built fires in their yards to heat water for washing clothes and bathing. Etta cranked up water, poured it into a 20-gallon syrup kettle and tended the fire she had built under it. Anna came and dipped out the water she needed for washing clothes in a washtub on the porch. "I 'preciate yoh hep, Etta."

Etta kept adding water. "Glad to, Aunt Anna. I have clothes to wash, too."

Etta and Anna washed clothes and hung them on a line. They put supper on the table, washed the children in the tub on the porch and put them to bed. Etta emptied the large washtub off the porch into the yard, turned it on edge and rolled it inside. She pulled the table over to make room. More water was brought in, and Anna and Etta had their baths.

Etta pulled a clean cotton gown over her head. "Guess Grace 'piscopal gon send de vicar over for de service tomorrow?"

Anna was sweeping ashes off the hearth back into the fireplace. "I reckon so, Etta. He been comin' obuh heah doin' de Easter service fuh a long time."

Etta laughed as she got in bed. "Be another good day tuh stay 'way from de Main House."

Anna looked around. "Why's dat?"

"De vicar always brings a bunch wid 'im, and dey usually stay around for several days eatin' an' drinkin' big. For some reason dat group make Miss Frances more nervous dan usual. Dey a little nosy, I think. She prolly think dey gossip 'bout her back in Brunswick. Dey'll sure ax' 'bout Mama an' miss her guidin' hand in de kitchen. Etta laughed. "Poor Katie."

Anna smiled back as she came to bed. "Yeah, I bet yuh right 'bout dat."

The next morning Anna dressed quickly as the children finished their breakfast. "You bettuh come on now, Etta, an' get dressed."

"I don't think I'm gon go,' Aunt Anna. You need some help wid de girls?"

"Whut? Folks are gon miss yuh. Come on now, get dressed. Bet dere'll be some boys dere."

Etta shook her head. "I heard enough out'uh de vicar up at de Main House tuh las' me from now on."

Anna cocked her head. "Yuh know we be havin' dinnuh on de groun' tuhday."

109

Etta had propped herself up in bed and was looking at an old Savannah newspaper that Anna had come up with. "I'll be dressed when you come back for de food."

Anna looked at her great niece, put her hands on her hips and frowned deeply, but gave a nod. "Awright den, I'll be back in a little while."

Etta had always heard the vicar's Easter sermon up at the Main House. *Dat man could talk de most and say de least of any preacher I ever heard.*

Etta put her hands over her head and extended her legs in a long stretch. *Wonder if Grandma Hester and PawPaw will be at de service. Wonder too how dey get all dis stuff straight in dere head. It's funny, PawPaw and his wife were Muslim, but dere family all Christian. He still follows de Muslim ways, far as I know. Grandma Medina told me one time dat she was taught Muslim prayers when she was little and, lawdy, nowadays she 'bout de biggest Christian dey is.*

And Grandma Hester, Etta smiled to herself and shook her head, *dat's a whole other ball of wax dere.*

Etta read for a while longer but soon got up, washed her face and slipped on her clothes. She lay back across the bed and picked up her well-worn magazine, flipping pages.

Later, Anna came in. "You ready?"

"Yassum."

"Heah, take dis tablecloth. Heah, carry dis pot."

As they walked back toward the barn, Etta spoke up. "Aunt Anna, how come PawPaw an' his wife were Muslims, and now all of dere children and grandchildren are Christians?"

Anna looked down for a moment. "Well, dey started out tryin' tuh teach de Muslim 'ligion tuh us. Papa eben make up a little book whut told us whut we s'pose tuh do, but de missionaries wouldn't 'llow no Muslim service out in de open. Mama and Papa tol' us tuh keep quiet 'bout it.

"De actual truth is dat some uh whut dey do at church now comes frum whut Papa wuz teachin'. Yuh notice heuh dat de men and de womens don't sit togeduh. Notice too dat dey set de benches up so ebuhbody face de east and pray tuh de east."

They reached the Main Road and turned right. "Well, what 'bout Grandma Hester's conjurin' and all dat she say 'bout ghosts and spirits and stuff like dat? Don't believe dat stuff is in de Bible."

People were gathering next to the barn as they approached. Anna stopped and looked at Etta. "We ain't 'ad no new slabes frum Afica in a long time, Etta, but I belieb folks knowed 'bout conjurin' an' spirits an' such foh dey gots heah. Way back den w'en new slabes wuz comin' heah frum Afica, de Wilsons had a regluh school fuh teachin' 'em a little English, how tuh take orders, do farm wurk and gets along heah. A part uh dat little school wuz a missionary group whut taught slabes 'bout Jesus." Anna smiled. "Dat Afican stuff still heah, but us slabes took tuh de Beatitudes like ducks tuh watuh."

Etta was lost in thought as they walked up to the barn that sat across the Main Road, next to the tabby warehouses.

Food was being uncovered and placed on tables made of rough boards nailed between trees. Church services had been held in the barn. Anna put the new potatoes, turnip greens and cured meat she had brought, onto one of the rough tables.

111

Etta watched as Anna spread the tablecloth on the ground but hesitated when she realized that Anna had positioned them next to Rachel. The men were pulling out a few benches from the barn, and there were some chairs for the more elderly. Most people served themselves, then sat on one of the cloths to eat.

Rachel reached over and touched Etta on the knee. "Miss you, Honey."

Etta gave her mother a small frown, then a forced smile and looked down at her food. She turned slightly away from her mother and ate in silence. As she was finishing, a cousin came over and whispered that Grandpa Abraham wanted to talk to her.

Etta looked around and saw him sitting in a chair under a tree some distance away. She put her plate down and went straight to him. His mouth was full as she walked up. He pointed to the empty chair next to him. He soon leaned over and spoke quietly. "Etta, I'd lack fuh yuh to come see me early next week aftuh wurk."

Her eyes downcast, she responded. "Dey been workin' us late, PawPaw, tryin' to finish de plantin.'"

He nodded. "Hmm. Reckon dey is. Lazarus'll let yuh go midday on Tuesday. Come on down aftuh yuh eat."

"Yassuh, PawPaw." Etta felt close to tears. "Have I done somethin' wrong?"

He looked directly at her, smiled, and shook his head strongly. "No, Honey. I jus' want tuh talk tuh yuh 'bout yuh an' yoh mama's sitchation. Dere's some t'ings yuh need tuh know."

112

Etta blinked several times and looked up. "Awright, PawPaw." She took a deep breath and let it out slowly. She stood, smiled at another of Medina's sisters and offered her the chair.

Children chased each other while the adults sat or stood in the shade, ate, and visited. With Matthew in her lap, Rachel slipped over next to Etta. "When you coming home, Honey?" Matthew twisted and looked at Etta.

She sat Indian-style with her dress pulled over her knees, staring at her plate in her lap. "Don't know, Mama."

Matthew tried to crawl toward Etta, but Rachel held him back. "Got a pretty nice place, Honey. You kin have de loft all by yohself. I put a book up dere, an' yuh got yoh own window tuh read by. I put some curtains up, too. Dey nice. Light blue."

"Dat sounds good Mama, but I want to keep it like it is for de time bein'. Got a lot to think 'bout. Need some time to figure things out my own self."

Rachel closed her eyes briefly. "All right den. You know where we is when you ready. Matthew and I wants you home." He strained toward Etta. She lifted one corner of her mouth and shook her head at him, looked down, shook her head again and spoke quietly, "I'll be home b'fo' long. It's been good bein' wid Anna. Learn a lot from her."

Rachel leaned back, pulling Matthew with her. "All right. Don't make it too long, Baby. Miss you." She turned away as tears fell.

Later, deep in thought, Etta strolled around the barn and the warehouse that sat behind it. The ferry was tied up at the dock. It was empty and quiet. She leaned against the corner of the tabby warehouse and looked out across the river to the marsh. *Damn, why does it have to be like dis? Should be up*

113

at de Main House. Don't nuttin' ever happen down heah. Never thought Mama do what she done. Brought us both down.

There was movement to her left. She glanced in that direction. There was a railing at the end of the dock that was used to tie up teams of mules. *Dere's a couple down dere leanin' 'ginst dat rail. Ooo, dey kissin'. Look, dat's Sam. I should'uh known dat he got a girlfriend. Can't see her good but don't believe I know her. Prolly ain't de only one.*

Etta stepped back around the warehouse and toward the gathering in front of the barn. She scanned the large open area between the road and the barn. Scattered groups of people filled it. Children chased each other out in the road. Adults stood or sat on their cloths, some still eating, everyone talking and laughing. *Where's Mama and Aunt Anna? Dere's PawPaw's big group.* She continued to look around. *Where's my group? Where do I go?* She walked over to the far edge of Anna's empty cloth and sat with her head down. *Maybe I jus' ought to go on back over to de cabin.*

Etta wrapped her arms around her legs and again sat watching different groups. *People seem to be havin' a good time. Dere's Mama. Anna, too.*

Etta felt her mood lift. She watched the children run and play.

"Howdy, ma'am."

Etta flinched and looked around and up. She put her hand up to shield her eyes. "Hello, Sam. You scared me." She frowned at him as he stood above her.

He dipped his head. "I'm sorry. I belieb I hab tuh 'pologize tuh yuh ebuh time I see yuh."

Etta offered her hand and stood. She nodded. "How yuh doin'?"

114

Smiling still, he tipped his hat. "Doin' fine, Miss Etta. Like tuh go fuh a walk?"

Etta looked around for the other girl. *Why not. He ain't married.* She smiled to herself. *Dat I know of, anyways.*

"Sure, Sam. But what happen to yoh friend?"

Sam's smile broadened again as he offered an elbow "She, uh, 'ad tuh get on home."

Etta smiled to herself and shook her head.

CHAPTER 13

Sam had pushed off. It was a warm, lazy afternoon as Etta lay in a cotton hammock tied to small trees in the side yard of Anna's cabin. She was thinking of her mother. *Why am I bein' so mean to Mama? Is it dat I don't want to help her wid her mistake? Truth is, always trusted Mama tuh know what tuh do. Now? Feel like I'm driftin' in de wind. Truth is, too, dat I miss de Main House. Dat's de crux of it. I want to be back up dere. Ain't so bad down heah, but I sure miss de goin's on up dere.* She snorted bitterly. *Least some of 'em.*

Anna called to Etta from in front of the steps. "Etta, me an' de gals gon be gone fuh a spell. Dere's some leftovers. Sho would lack fuh yuh tuh go tuh services and de Shout wid me tonight."

She sat up a bit. "Awright, Aunt Anna." *I ain't been to a Shout since I was little.*

The girls ran ahead and Anna called out, "I'll be back in plenty uh time tuh gets ready an' go. I'm gon leabe de gals down at Paw's tuhnight."

"Awright, Aunt Anna."

Etta wished she had something new to read as she lay back in the hammock. Her mind drifted to what she knew about the Shout and the church service that came before. She knew the nightime services and Shout would be very different from the day service. *I remember talk 'round de table at de Main House 'bout dese services. Frances Wilson believed dat ever' gatherin' of black folks was gon lead to a uprisin'. Mr. Thomas would jus' shrug her off.*

De service I remember was outside. After de preachin', dere was women dancin' 'round de fire an' doin' de Shout. Some folks call it de Ring Shout. Men standin' 'round clappin' outside de ring of women. Everbody singin'. Don't remember no white people dere at all. It's funny, dem nighttime services an' de Shout is 'bout de only doin's on de island what was run by slaves an' not by Buckra.

Anna returned several hours later, and they dressed and walked over across the road. Benches were being taken from the back of the barn and set up in a space between the barn and the warehouse behind it. They faced east toward the back of the barn. Two pallets were placed at the front of the benches, and a large fire was laid between the pallets but not lit.

"Honey, I wuz t'inkin' 'bout some uh de questions yuh ax' me. Us Geechee is a bunch uh mixed up tribes, but we is all Afican jus' de same. De dancin', lack de conjurin', come wid us w'en our peoples wuz brought heah."

As they walked up, Anna struck up a conversation, and Etta took a seat on the women's side. She watched as a man brought the last piece of wood

117

to the stack. A small metal washtub was brought and turned upside down behind the benches. Another man leaned a hoe handle against the warehouse, next to the tub.

A slow, steady trickle of people came and took seats. *Everbody sure seems to be in a good mood.* Most spent some time greeting and hugging those that had preceded them. Etta looked down, not meeting anyone's gaze, trying to avoid these open displays of affection. She was glad that Anna had gone several steps away and was talking to a relative.

Etta looked over the older crowd. *I know de young people heah think de Ring Shout is ol' timey.* She looked up at the pallets. *Dey'll start wid regular services first, I do believe. Maybe some young people will come shortly.*

A middle-aged African man carrying a book and wearing a worn but well-fitting suit stepped up on the pallet platform in front of the men's side and waited. The congregation took its place and became still and quiet.

Etta put her hands in her lap and watched closely.

Another but younger man stepped up on the pallet to the preacher's right. One spoke. "Let us pray." The men bowed their heads.

Etta watched for a moment and then closed her eyes.

The preacher spoke in a strong voice. "Jesus, we's come as yoh 'umble servants to ax' fuh yoh forgiveness fuh our sins."

The congregation responded. "Have mercy, Lawd."

The preacher raised his voice. "Give us strength, oh Lord, tuh forgive dem whut sin 'ginst us, dem dat strike us and curse us, oh Lord."

The congregation came back strongly. "Give us strength!"

The preacher used his hands as if lifting. "Lift your people up, oh

118

Lord. Lift us up so we can see de promised land."

The congregation responded. "Lift us, Lawd. Lift us up."

He spread his arms above his head. "An' we's will fly to yuh, Lord. Yoh 'umble servants will spread our new wings and fly to our home wid yuh, Jesus. Have mercy on our souls. Amen." He bowed his head for another moment. Then both men raised their heads.

"Amen, Amen," many called out.

The younger man on the platform raised his arms to the congregation. "Join me in song." He lead the hymn off with a strong tenor voice. "Oh, po' moanuh, won't yuh jus' belieb!"

The congreation knew the song. "Livin' 'umble, livin' 'umble."

The song leader, "Oh, po' moanuh, won't yuh jus' belieb."

Again the congregation, "Livin' 'umble, livin' umble."

"Oh, po' moanuh, won't yuh jus' belieb. Christ is waitin' to receib."

"Livin' 'umble, livin' 'umble."

The song leader began to move and sing louder. "King Jesus camp in de middle uh de air."

"Livin' 'umble, livin' 'umble."

"King Jesus camp in de middle uh de air."

"Livin' 'umble, livin' 'umble."

"King Jesus camp in de middle uh de air. None but de righteous gon be dere. Halleluya!"

"Halleluya!"

They sang several lively songs. The song leader turned, bowed to the preacher and stepped down from the platform. He sat on the front of the men's section.

119

The preacher cleared his throat and opened the book in his hand. "From the Holy Scripture, Psalms, Chapter Seven, Verses nine an' ten: An' de patriarchs, moved wid envy, sold Joseph into Egypt. But God was wid 'im an' delivered 'im out of all 'is afflictions and gave him favour and wisdom in de sight of Pharaoh, King of Egypt, and He made him gubnuh over Egypt and all his house.'"

Etta sat up straight. *I wonder how many folks over heah can read like dat?*

The preacher closed the book with a snap and raised his right hand in the air. "What did de song say? What did de Word say? Dey say de righteous gon rise up, take dey wings an' fly home to Jesus."

The congregation responded. "Fly home to Jesus."

"Dey say de meek gon inherit de erff."

"Inherit de erff!"

The preacher increased the volume and the speed of his preaching, and soon he and the congregation had a rhythm going. Etta added her voice and looked around. *Everbody sure seems to be enjoyin' de service.* The congregation began to clap and shout out along with the preacher's rhythm. Men and women moved to the rhythm as the preacher got warmed up.

Ain't like dis in Brunswick. Ain't no dozin' off in dis church. Etta looked up at the sky as she smiled to herself. *Pretty big church.*

The preacher continued for some time, maintaining the intensity of the service. Clapping and shouting out her response, Etta was surprised when, at a fever pitch of emotion, the preacher suddenly stopped, knelt down and prayed silently.

Many in the congregation shouted out, "Halleluya!" and "Yes, Lawd!"

120

Soon from the back of the group, Etta heard a 'thump, thump, thump' as one of the men began to hit the hoe handle onto the metal washtub, establishing a base rhythm. With this, the preacher dragged the pallets away, leaned them against the barn, came back and lit the fire.

Most of the women stood, one bench at a time, forming a line and moving in a slow shuffle in front of the fire, then around the fire, counter clockwise. The men stood up and spread out on the outside of the moving circle. Etta kept her seat.

I remember dis better now. Dere was singin', too. Lots of singin'. Etta watched closely. The women were bent slightly at the waist, with elbows bent, hands open and held down.

Look at de way dey move. Dey doin' a little shuffle step, slidin' dere feets. Don't think dey gettin' 'em off de ground. Now dey twistin' dere hips an' pausin' right in de middle. Look at 'em. I believe de men like dat part. Look at how dey encouragin' de women, clappin' an' gettin' loud.

Dey steppin' in time to de thumpin'. The women began to clap in counterpoint to the base rhythm.

One of the women raised her voice. "Membuhs!"

The other women responded. "Plumb de line."

Again she sang. "Membuhs!"

The women answered. "Plumb de line."

The lead singer danced around the fire with the others. "Oh, membuhs!"

"Plumb de line."

"Want tuh go tuh heaben, got to plumb de line."

The chorus sings. "You got to sing right."

The men add, "Plumb de line."

"Yuh got to sing right," the women sing.

The men … "Plumb de line."

The women come back. "Yuh got to sing right."

"Plumb de line."

The soloist … "Want tuh go tuh heaben, got to plumb de line."

The women sing, "Oh, Sistuh."

The men add, "Plumb de line."

Etta is absorbed in the performance as Anna comes by, takes her hand and pulls her into the circle behind her. She positions Etta's hands on the outside of her hips, just below her waist. "Do lack me now."

Anna almost twisted out of her grip several times as Etta tried to match Anna's slide steps and twists. Soon Etta had gotten the movement. She held her back a bit straighter, released Anna and began to clap along with the other women. After another round, Etta focused on the singing.

As the men observing the women took over the clapping of the complex rhythms, the dancers added another element by raising their arms over their heads and twisting more fully side to side. All the women made similar movements with their open hands. The song rises in volume, and the men respond with more vigor.

The women circle as the fire throws shadows of their movements on the walls of the barn and warehouse. The oversized shadows of the women's hands and the smoke from the fire create images not unlike a flock of birds flying through a wispy fog.

Etta watches as two beads of sweat run down the back of Anna's neck. *Dis ain't easy.* She gave her attention back to the dance and soon became more comfortable. She glanced at the men as she rounded the circle. *Dere's a couple of young fellows over dere. Where did dey come from? Dey both smilin' at me.* Etta smiled back. *Dat's good to see.* She focused back on the dance.

Etta slowed her concious thoughts and allowed her body and mind to join the women's circle, free to dance and sing. *Dese sweaty ol' folks are sumpin'.*

Etta had lost track of the time and was exhausted as the dance ended. She collapsed onto a bench, elbows on her knees, sweaty head in her hands. She noticed movement in front of her and looked up. Two of the dancers had walked over. "Becky an' me heah wuz jus' talkin' 'bout how we lub' yoh dancin'."

Etta's mouth dropped open. She shook her head and smiled back broadly. "Y'all very sweet to say dat. I sure like doin' it. I want to learn more."

Other dancers came over to Etta, and Anna introduced them, often telling how they were related. Everyone hugged Etta and welcomed her. One of the older dancers was last. "Etta, my name is Beulah, an' I wanted tuh ax' yuh tuh come dance wid us all de time."

Etta smiled up at the greying lady. "I would like dat very much. Thank you, Miss Beulah."

Etta and Anna slowly walked around the back of the barn and back toward the cabin. *Dey wants me to come sing an' dance wid 'em. How 'bout dat?"*

Etta found her legs wobbly, but for the first time in a while, she found her mind still. She smiled into the darkness and spoke softly. "Thank you

Aunt Anna."

"Yuh welcome, Honey. Glad yuh enjoyed hit."

CHAPTER 14

The next week was their busiest for the women at the greenhouses.
Replantings had to be completed in time for the plants to mature and
produce. Tuesday morning Anna and Etta walked over together. "Lazarus
say fuh yuh to go on down tuh Paw's aftuh dinnuh today."

Etta nodded. "Awright, Aunt Anna." She beat Anna back to the cabin
after the noon bell. She had served her plate and was on the porch eating
when Anna approached. "Aunt Anna, ain't Grandpa Abraham's place down
de Main Road on de right?"

The girls ran noisily up onto the porch. "You ain't neiduh," Harriet
yelled at her sister.

Anna frowned at the girls. "Wipe yoh feets now!"

She turned back toward Etta. "Yeah. Hit's 'bout a ha'f mile. Fus'
cabin you see on de right."

Etta walked out to the Main Road and turned south. She looked around as she walked. *Road look dif'nt down heah. Dey never cut de trees next to de road. Gives a nice shade.*

As she walked, her thoughts drifted to her mother's family and their history on Bonita Island. She remembered that her great grandmother Farah and her great grandfather Abraham had belonged to an African tribe that was Muslim and valued education highly.

Farah and Abraham had been captured and sold to British slave traders by a neighboring tribe. As teenagers, they were bought by British planters who brought them to the Caicos Islands to work in the cotton fields. There, a planter and close friend of Thomas Wilson's father offered to sell them to the older Mr. Wilson who had been down on a visit.

Wilson bought Abraham, Farah, and all the children they had, in 1802, and brought them to Bonita Island Plantation. He had been told that Abraham knew how to grow the high-quality cotton that could only be grown in moist, tropical climates such as in the Caribbean. Respect for his abilities had allowed Abraham to insist that his whole family come with him. They had brought seeds for the new cotton, and Wilson had high hopes that, with Abraham's help, he could get this better grade of cotton to grow on Bonita Island Plantation.

Farah had taught all of her and Abraham's children to read and write. *Mama told me 'bout how Grandma Medina kept dat goin' wid her, even teachin' Mama 'bout numbers.* Etta laughed to herself. She knew it was against the law in Georgia for Whites to teach Coloreds to read. *Reckon dere was nuttin' dey could do 'bout Grandma teachin' Mama, an' Mama teachin'*

126

me. Wonder if PawPaw bein' able to read was another reason dat Ol' Mr. Wilson made Abraham driver over all de other slaves.

Etta tried to remember a clear image of her great grandmother but failed. Farah had died when Etta was three. As she got older, Etta had spent some time down at Abraham's. *I remember dere always bein' a bunch of cousins down heah. Always somethin' goin' on. Wonder what PawPaw want tuh talk to me 'bout? He might fuss at me for not stayin' wid Mama and helpin' her.*

Her pace slowed for several steps. *Ain't nuttin' I can do to change what he gon say. Might as well get on down dere.*

Her great-grandfather's cabin was a "shotgun" house. The original one-room slave cabin had two more rooms built straight out the back, separated by only doorways. She climbed the steps to the porch. The front door was partly open. She stuck her head in.

A woman about her mother's age was rinsing dishes in a small washtub sitting on a table against the wall. She turned. "Etta? Hey dere, Honey. Come on in."

Etta smiled and stepped in.

She smiled back, dried her hands and gave Etta a hug. "'Membuh me? I'm Ruth, yoh mama's first cousin. Goodness gracious, you done growed up since I seen yuh las'! You lookin' fuh Abraham?"

"Yassum." *Dis house still smell de same, like fat-lightered wood.*

Ruth nodded to her left. "He in de nex' room dere. Go on back."

There was a living room with an old broken-down sofa and an easy chair where Abraham was sitting. The threadbare chair looked like it may have been in the Main House in some far earlier decade. Abraham's head

127

drooped, and a tiny piece of wood stuck out the side of his mouth. Etta cleared her throat.

Abraham lifted his head, blinked a couple of times and smiled broadly. "Etta! Good tuh see yuh, Gal." He looked down. A cane was on the floor next to his chair. "Hand me dis stick heah, Honey, an' come hep me up. We'uns 'll go out on de po'ch weh dere might be a breeze." He leaned heavily on her as they shuffled through the kitchen and, with some difficulty, through the doorway outside. Abraham nodded toward a large wooden chair with arms, sitting on the covered porch. They made it over, and he lowered himself slowly as Etta held his elbow and arm with both hands.

"T'ank yuh, Honey. I warn't so stove up de las' time yuh seen me, an' yuh warn't near so big as yuh is now." He smiled broadly at her.

Etta sat in a chair to Abraham's left and returned his smile.

"How yuh doin'? How de wurk goin'?

"I'm doin' awright, PawPaw."

He smiled at her for a moment longer and went on. "How's Medina doin'?"

Etta frowned. "She was fine when I left, PawPaw. Ain't heard from her since I been down heah."

Abraham tilted his head, leaned forward and looked at Etta. "How's yoh Mama doin'?"

Etta shifted slightly in her chair, looked down and spoke without looking up. "She's awright, I reckon."

Abraham reached out and patted Etta's arm. "Hit's a big change frum de Main House tuh bein' down heah at Tabby Landin'. Sorry dat yuh lost yoh place up dere. Hit prolly mean a lot tuh yuh."

128

He sat back in the chair. "Been doin' whut I could tuh keeps yoh mama an' yuh safe down heah. Ain't lack hit used tuh be. Cain't do a whole lot no moh. Thomas, he stop by heah ebuh once a while, but he don' want tuh talk 'bout nuttin' but de 'good ol' days.' He don' want my 'pinion on de goin's on nowadays, 'specially not 'bout de mess dey done made up at de Main House."

He stared off at the trees. "Some uh de drivuhs still listen tuh me some. Jus' want yuh an' yoh mama tuh know I'm doin' whut I kin. I wuz sho glad we could get yuh in de greenhouse fuh a spell an' not throw yuh right out in de fiel.'"

Etta stared at her great-grandfather, her mouth half open. *I nebuh thought dat PawPaw knowed whut was goin' on wid me.*" She gave him her full attention.

"De bidness wid yoh Mama done turn t'ings upside down fuh 'em up dere. Ebuhbody knows dat yoh mama wuz de one whut really run t'ings. Miss Frances awready jealous uh her. I belieb de goin's on right under her nose done ruined hit foh her and Thomas." He laughed quietly and shook his head. "She blame all de pro'lems in de wurl on yuh and yoh mama."

Me?

Still shaking his head, he looked at Etta. "She been makin' hit mighty hard on yoh mama, but so fah she ain't stuck her nose into whut we been doin' fuh yuh."

Etta's frown deepened. *Ain't thought 'bout how Miss Frances gon hold a grudge 'gainst me. Lord, what we gon do?*

Abraham tilted his head. "We'un's seems tuh be awright fuh de time bein'. Jus' be sho not tuh rock de boat right now. I's hopin' dey gon ease up

129

on yoh mama. I do belieb t'ings settlin' down. Jus' cain't be sho wid dat woman whut's gon happen nex'." He took in and let out a deep breath.

Etta sat up straighter, frowning. "Thank yuh fuh helpin' us."

The door swung back to the inside, and Ruth brought out two cups of cool water.

Etta took one and nodded at Ruth. "Thank you."

Ruth handed a cup to Abraham. "Oughtuh get on back tuh wurk. Yuh need anyt'ing 'b'fo' I go?"

Abraham took a long drink and wiped his mouth on his sleeve. He looked up and smiled at Ruth. "No, Honey, dat's fine. Jus' move dat slop jar obuh heah so I kin reach hit. I'll be awright out heah 'til yuh gets back."

Abraham turned to Etta. "Warn't surprised dat she called yuh back frum Medina's. Miss Frances wuz goin' on at fus' 'bout sendin' yuh boff tuh de Norf End. We'uns holdin' her off fuh de time bein', but we sho don't need no moh upset 'round heah, or she could get her way." He gave two short nods.

Etta, eyes wide, took a quick breath and stared back at her great-grandfather.

He smiled at her. "I t'ink hit's gon be awright. Made hit dis long."

They were quiet for a moment, and then Abraham went on. "I wuz worried too dat yuh been wid Medina so long dat yuh done fuhgot whut hits lack tuh be a slabe down heah. Abraham leaned toward her. Gotuh be careful. Don't give nobody no cause fuh complainin' tuh de Main House."

Etta sat up straight and nodded. "Yassuh."

"T'ings wurk a little dif'nt down heah, yuh know dat. Don't be lookin' no white folks in de face. De less talk 'round white folks, de bettuh." He

130

looked directly at her. "I 'membuh dat yuh wuz a talkuh, but 'Yassuh' an' 'Nawsuh' 'bout all yuh needs tuh say tuh white folks an' drivuhs.

"Miss Frances, she a dif'nt bird fuh sho, but don't fuhget she got her eyes and ears down heah. Don't want tuh lose dat smart little 'Bookuh'." He smiled at her."

Etta frowned and nodded slowly. "Yassuh, PawPaw."

He shook his head at her. "I know dat young folks gon try a new'un out, an' yuh needs to stan' up fuh yohse'f, but no moh fightin' down heah." He nodded. "Yuh heah?"

Etta nodded and bit her lip. "Yassuh."

Abraham looked serious and leaned over toward her. "'Membuh, keep yuh eyes down w'en you roun' de bosses. Stay 'way frum 'em much as yuh kin an' jus' keeps yoh t'oughts tuh yoh ownse'f.

"W'en dese folks got dis much powuh obuh yoh life, Honey, dere ain't no shame in doin' whut yuh got tuh do tuh keep yohse'f an' yoh mama safe. Yuh heah me now?"

Etta nodded at him.

He tilted his head down at her. "If yuh do talk, tell 'em how smarts dey is and how yuh 'preciate all dey do fuh yuh. Cain't do widout 'em. You hear'd dat kinduh talk b'fo'."

"Yassuh, PawPaw." Etta frowned and stared at the floor. *Dat ain't gon be easy. Easier dan workin' in de rice fields, I reckon. Remember dem girls out in de muck.* She took a deep breath, looked up and, with a serious expression, spoke slowly. "I believe I know what tuh do."

Abraham gave her a small smile and nod. "Don't fuhget."

"Yassuh."

131

He looked off again. "Hit ain't jus' yuh and yoh mama dat I's worried 'bout. Wid all de talk and doin's in de Country 'bout slabery, white folks 'round heah done got nerbous. Our folks get dere hopes up 'bout bein' free, an' de Whites get moh an' moh scairt. Hits uh unsettled time, an' I's worried 'bout whut gon happen. Dey a lot uh talk 'bout war. De mess in de Country and de mess up at de Main House all togeduh ain't good. Make hit 'specially danejus fuh ebuhbody right now."

Etta nodded slowly. "Yassuh." *Hmm. I been wantin' things tuh change. Guess dey could change fuh de worse.*

He smiled at her, finished his water and sat the cup on the floor next to his chair. Etta's mind churned, but she was quiet. She waited for him to go on.

"Now one moh t'ing. Yuh bein' at de Main House an' now down heah give yuh a look at de wurkin's uh t'ings dat mos' folks don't see. Yoh readin', too, heps yuh." He nodded.

"Anna say dat fuh a young person, yuh knows lots 'bout whut goes on out in de wurl, dat yuh read de newspapuhs w'en yuh kin get 'em."

Etta nodded a bit eagerly. "Dat's so."

"I'd lack tuh ax' fuh yoh hep, Etta. I kin get de papuhs. I'd lack hit if'ns yuh would come down heah an' read 'em tuh me. My eyes done got bad, an' I'd be mos' grateful. If I's gon be any hep tuh folks, I need tuh know whut's goin' on in de wurl."

Etta nodded. "Sure, PawPaw. You know I'd love to help."

He put his hand on Etta's arm again. "W'en yuh bigger, yuh gon be lot uh hep tuh yoh peoples. I kin see dat awready."

132

Etta shook her head. "Oh, PawPaw, I just want tuh get along down heah."

He smiled at her. "Yuh gon be awright. Jus' 'membuh whut I told yuh, an' maybe t'ings gon settle down 'round heah."

Etta nodded. "Awright, PawPaw."

There was a moment or two of silence. Abraham shifted in his chair and leaned back. "Dere wuz a time I could'uh done moh. Ol' Mr. Wilson an' me built dis place, got tuh be good frien's, but me an' Wilson bein' frien's warn't gon change t'ings fuh our peoples. Slabes still be slabes. Peoples still bought and sol'.

"His boy Thomas wuz lack one uh my own. I hep raise 'im. Good boy, fine young man. Mr. Wilson an' 'is fus' wife, Miss Catherine, wuz good for each uduh an' fuh dis place. Almos' make peoples fuhget dey wuz slabes, but times an' peoples change."

Etta leaned back, too, as Abraham looked over her head. "Miss Frances an' Thomas jus' a bad mix. She don't know how tuh get 'long wid folks. An' Thomas?" Abraham snorted. "He done got greedy. Not doin' whut he oughtuh fuh folks. Pushin' fuh moh rice 'cause de price is up. He tryin' tuh gits all he kin while de gittin' is good. Hurt's ebuhbody."

"Yassuh, PawPaw."

Abraham frowned and shook his head. "W'en dey brought me heah, I wuz proud tuh be put obuh de uduh slabes. Didn't see de peoples heah as bein' my peoples. Buckra made me feel impo'ant. I's sad tuh say dat I raised de whip to de uduh slabes a few times."

He gave Etta a tight smile. "Hit took me a long time an' lots uh chilrens an' granchilrens 'round heah fuh me tuh unuhstan' dat all de Aficans

133

on dis heah island wuz my peoples, an' folks is impo'ant heah not jus' 'cause uh whut we kin do fuh Buckra." He leaned forward. "It's impo'ant whut we kin do fuh each uduh."

Etta's eyes were big as she stared at her great-grandfather.

He looked directly at her. "Yuh talk to yoh mama now an' tell her whut I done tol' yuh."

Etta nodded. "Yassuh, PawPaw. I'll tell her."

He tilted his head down and raised his eyebrows. "She needs yuh wid her rite now. Yuh need to fuhgive her. Yuh needs tuh be togeduh an' doin' fuh one anuduh."

Etta lowered her eyes and spoke softly. "Yes, PawPaw."

He leaned back. "Now Etta, kin yuh come down heah Sunday aftuhnoon? I'll hab us a papuh by den."

"Yassuh."

"I be lookin' fuh yuh."

She smiled. "Awright, PawPaw." Etta waited for Abraham to continue, expecting more, but after a bit of silence she stood up and took her and her great-grandfather's cups back inside.

When she came back out the door, Abraham looked up at her. "I'll see yuh Sunday."

Etta put her arm around Abraham and hugged him. "Thank you for what you doin' for us."

He patted her on her shoulder. "Sho, Etta. Hit's gon be awright. Jus' be keerful. 'Membuh whut I say."

Etta walked back up the road toward Tabby Landing. *Damnation. Ain't done nuttin' to dat woman but try to help. We jus' easy to blame for all*

134

de problems dey got between dey ownselves. We do all de work and still get all de blame. Guess I'm lucky dat I don't have no more dealin's wid Buckra dan I do.

Her pace had slowed. *Maybe Mr. Wilson doin' more dan I thought tuh help us. Reckon what PawPaw sayin' is dat we can't cause no more problems. He could let dat woman have her way.*

She need to quit blamin' everbody else and look in de mirror.

I knowed he wuz gon say somthin' 'bout Mama. Etta, still walking slowly, turned into Tabby Landing toward Anna's. She went past the cabin, through the fields, east, deep in thought and not aware herself where she was going.

135

CHAPTER 15

Etta felt herself drawn toward the beach, her mind again a jumble of conflicting thoughts. The familiar knot was back in her stomach. *No matter how hard I try, I can't 'magine Mama and Mr. Wilson lying down together.* She laughed a bitter laugh. *Now de most powful woman on de island, woman who owns me, hates Mama and me, too. What was Mama thinkin' tuh get us into dis mess?*

The knot in Etta's stomach rose toward her chest, affecting her ability to get a full breath as she crossed over the dunes. She drifted up the beach, away from the Landing. She walked into the surf and splashed a handful of water on her face. Walking slowly back up on the beach, she took a deep breath and looked around. *Still de same out heah.* She stared out at the ocean.

Pelicans were diving for fish in deeper water. To her left was a large, mixed group of birds milling on the beach. A few of the smaller birds frantically searched the last little gasp of each wave, looking for a treat under the white foam. *So lovely heah. May be de one place in my life dat ain't upside down.*

As Etta strode north, she noticed the strength of the wind on her back. Soon it was picking up sand and stinging her legs, urging her on. She began to jog north, her mind settling on her many memories of running and playing on this beach.

She became more aware of her body, feeling the wind pressing on her back and finding her rhythm in a steady, strong pace. The shark's tooth tapped a rhythm on her chest. *Been a long time since I could run on dis beach.*

Etta increased her stride and continued for some time, enjoying the strength she felt in her legs. She filled her lungs with sea air. *I'm movin' now. Feel like I could do dis forever.*

Places she recognized slipped past. After she had jogged for some time, she glanced to her left. *Dere's de path to de Main House.* She held her pace for some time, noticing the birds, pushing some groups to fly ahead of her while others circled and landed behind. She ran on.

Extending her stride and increasing the speed of her legs to the edge of comfort, Etta moved much faster. *How odd, de wind change direction. It's in my face.* She smiled. *No. I'm outrunnin' de wind. Flyin'. Flyin' wid de birds.*

Etta felt herself whipping up the beach, her simple cotton dress plastered against her lithe frame, only the balls and toes of her bare feet touching the packed sand. *Nothing heah now but de wind in my face, sand poundin' my feet, and de air rushin' in an' out'uh my ches'. Mind's clear as de sky.* She flew low and fast up the beach.

Etta began to ease her pace until again she felt the wind on her back. She slowed to a jog and then a walk. Her heart pounded. Bending over, she breathed deeply. As she stood fully, she looked around. *Hmm, where am I? Ain't no trees. Dis heah's where de dunes go all de way 'cross de island. I is almos' to de North End. Didn't think I'd come dat far.* She turned around. *De wind stopped blowin' all a sudden.*

Etta moved away from the water and toward the dunes. She vaguely remembered this small section of beach. *De island ain't very wide right heah.* A path in front of her wound back through the dunes. *Don't remember dese dunes bein' so tall.* She followed the path. *Dey even larger back heah next to de river.*

A profusion of vines with trumpet-shaped flowers grew in the hollows between the dunes, while sea oats stood watch on their wide, sandy shoulders. Etta tried to climb the last and largest dune. Going to her hands and knees, she got high enough to see over the top to the mainland. *Right dere is where de river runs in.* Looking down, Etta realized that this last dune was actually undercut by the river that started its curve south just beneath her. She caught her breath. Making the top, still on all fours, she rose carefully to her full height. "OOOOHHhhh..."

The whole island broadened dramatically before her, expanding as the river curved broadly to her right. Far downstream she could see several ships anchored at what she thought must be Lumber Landing. *Dem ships look like toys.*

138

Etta took in a deep breath. *It's like what dey call a 'mural'.* She surveyed the island and river carefully from left to right.

Suddenly a shadow flew in front of her and across the base of the dune toward the river. Etta jumped but resisted the impulse to look up. Instead, she closed her eyes and spoke to herself. *Quiet. Listen.* She stilled her thoughts and understood. She touched the warm stone on her chest. "Hello, PawPaw."

"Hello, Child. I wanted yuh tuh see whut's rightly yohs."

She kept her eyes closed. *Mine? Mine, PawPaw? Dat don't feel right.*

"I nebuh say dat hit wuz yohs 'cause yuh earned hit. Hits yohs 'cause yuh ancestors done bought an' paid fuh hit. As much as hit do anybody, dis heah place belongs tuh yuh an' tuh yoh peoples. Lots moh Afican an' Injin spirits heah dan white folks. Don't nebuh fuhget dat."

Etta nodded slightly. *Thank you.* Taking another slow breath, she stood at her full height and opened her eyes. The wind swirled around her, and her world that was Bonita Island lay before her. *Dis heah is my home. One day we'll claim dis place fuh hits rightful heirs, de heirs uh our ancestors whut died heah, give dere lives tuh dis place.*

Slowly dropping her arms, Etta looked west towards Brunswick. *I can almos' see Grandma busy in her kitchen. Hope Winnie's doin' good. Hope Dan safe an' sound. Maybe I'll see 'em again one day.*

She turned and looked north towards Ebo Creek. *My creek. I see de ship an' my peoples fightin' tuh be free. We still fightin'. I may be in a bad place right now, but I ain't alone.*

139

Turning again, she looked east. *Got tuh be patient. Tomorrow de sun will rise on a clean day when all will be new, an' more may be possible. Ain't climbin' on no cross, but dat don't mean I got to 'ccept de way t'ings is.*

Etta took a deep breath. *Can't control dem, but I can control me. Gon get along heah 'til things change. Our time is comin', an' I'll be ready when it do.* The sea oats nodded in agreement.

Etta turned around slowly once more and slipped down from the dune, into the world at hand. She strolled back to the beach and turned north again. The world was vibrant and alive, her senses keen. She smelled the ocean, felt the air on her skin and the sun on her cheeks. She marveled that the birds no longer ran nor flew from her but just made room for this tallest of kin.

Chapter 16

The beach curved sharply to the left. Etta had reached Ebo Creek that separated Bonita from the smaller and wild Blackbeard Island. Blackbeard was now uninhabited, though the story was told that the pirate Blackbeard had made it his home for a time.

The middle of Blackbeard was a mixture of sand hummocks and swamp. Edward had learned the island from fishing and hunting there with his father. Etta and Edward had explored Blackbeard in his boat. She remembered a structure he said had been built by an Indian. Now she knew that Indian's name. *Chocu, my grandpa.*

She walked around the end of the big island to see if Edward's boat was still stashed in the edge of the woods where the beach ran out. She was surprised to find it still there turned upside down with a paddle, push pole, and cane fishing pole lying on top, just as it had been three years earlier.

Etta turned to the left again, skirting the edge of the live oaks and bay that grew here. She looked among the trees. Tied to a pine and a bay on the edge of the woods was Edward's ship hammock where they had often napped.

Testing it carefully, Etta slipped onto it. She laughed to herself when she realized that her feet stuck off into the ropes. A gentle breeze rocked the hammock and kept the insects at bay. The setting led her to memories of her childhood.

Etta's earliest memories were of being with her mother and Edward at the Main House. Rachel had been bought from Miss Julia Gates to serve as caretaker for the new son of Thomas and Frances Wilson.

She remembered her mother's stories of her own first few years at the Main House. *'Bout de time Mama got over heah, Mr. Wilson was plannin' another tabby warehouse down at Tabby Landing. My Paw James knew 'bout buildin' wid tabby. He was spendin' lots of time up at de Main House makin' plans wid Mr. Thomas. Mama caught his eye dere. Dey start spendin' time together, an' 'ventually he and Mama wanted to get married. Dey beg, but Mr. Thomas never would allow 'em to live together. Dey did manage to see each other some, and I come along two years after Mama came to Bonita Island.*

Jus' natu'al dat I be wid her when she cared for Edward. First thing I remember is sitting in Mama's lap while she read us a story.

Lizbeth, Mama's friend and daughter of Missus Gates, would get schoolbooks for her to use wid us. Mama taught Me and Edward how to read and do numbers. Edward liked to paint and draw, and Miss Frances was good 'bout havin' plenty of paints, pencils, and paper. She'd bring all kind

142

of books and drawing supplies when she come back from visitin' her family up North. She sure didn't like it if she caught me using dat stuff, but I'd take pencils and paper back to de cabin and practice my writin'. She never come out dere.

Mama was our teacher for a long time. Dey were plannin' to hire a live-in tutor, since dere warn't no way dat Edward could get to school ever' day. Mr. Wilson was so pleased wid Edward's progress, he put dat off for years.

When Miss Frances was at home, Mama would try to keep me out'uh sight. Miss Frances didn't care none for me from de get-go. De older I got, de more she frown at me. Didn't like seein' me readin' or doin' schoolwork. Don't know why dat unsettle her so.

I remember dat time she got so mad at me when one of her visitors caught me readin'. Mama like tellin' dat story. It was a nice fall day, Mama say. De men were huntin', and de ladies were playin' croquet out in de front yard.

Dis lady got tired of de game and walked 'round to de back of de Main House. I must'uh been six or seven years old. I never knew she was dere, but she come 'round to de veranda, and I was out dere readin' to my dollies. Mama say dat woman stan' dere, watch and listen while I went on, page after page, readin' to 'em 'bout Rollo doin' dis and Rollo doin' dat.

Mama would laugh out loud when she told 'bout de woman, eyes big, hurryin' back 'round de Main House. She say de woman call out loud, "Frances! Frances! Are y'all teachin' de Coloreds out heah to read?" Reckon dat embarressed Miss Frances, 'cause after dat I cain't be in de room wid Edward when Mama was teachin', at least when Miss Frances was 'round.

Warn't jus' de readin' dat stirred up dat woman. She sure didn't like Me and Edward spending so much time together. In de afternoons we both were pretty much on our own. At first we played in de yard, climbin' trees, chasin' chickens or th'owin' a ball.

We learned dat we had to get 'way from de house if we was to have any peace. We'd go to de beach to get 'way from pryin' eyes. I remember one of Miss Frances' big blowups. Mama filled in de details, but it was one afternoon dat Me and Edward was playin' out on de beach.

Miss Frances was gon order some clothes fuh Edward from a mail order catalog, and she needed to measure 'im. She called for 'im 'round de house and den went out in de backyard lookin' for 'im. It was one of de dog handlers, I believe, dat tell her he seen Edward headed out to de beach.

She didn't like bein' outside dat much no how. I can 'magine her headin' out to de beach, gettin' sand all in her shoes, thinkin' she should'uh sent dat boy after Edward. She struggle up de big dunes out dere and looked down on de beach. Me and Edward, we down dere in a tidal pool; both got little reeds we sharpen for spears. Edward, he ain't got nuttin' on but a short-sleeve shirt. Me, I done took off my step-ins and tied my dress up over one shoulder. We bent over, heads together, arm-in-arm, peerin' an' pokin' at a jellyfish or sumpin down in de water, our bottoms stickin' up in de air back toward Miss Frances.

Lord have mercy! Dat woman flew down on us like a hawk on biddies, flailin' her arms an'yellin' at us to get out of de water. I think I was sent

144

down to Tabby Landing for most of a month dat time. Mama told me dat she warn't sure if I'd ever be 'llowed back up at de Main House.

As we got older, we'd run, usually race, further and further up de beach to get away. I remember dat Edward had been taught how to swim, but dat most of my folks was scared to death of de water. When we got a little older, we began to play in de waves. Mama done spoke to us both 'bout being in de water. But you know Edward, he run out in dere, and I'd be right behind 'im. I remember dat if I got knocked down by a wave, or step in a hole, he was always watchin' out for me, makin' sure dat I was awright. Course it warn't long b'fo' I could swim jus' as good as he could.

I can see him now. He warn't real tall, but built sturdy. I was faster, but he was stronger. In de summer he get brown all over, but his face, it be full of freckles. He had de thickest, reddest hair of anybody I ever seen.

Dat boy ought to be called Christopher Columbus, 'cause he sure did love to explore. We get 'is boat out and go 'round behind de island or over to Blackbeard an' look for treasure. He was a good big brother to me. Reckon he was 13 or 14 de las' time I seen 'im. Let's see, he had a birfday back in March. He already 17. Finish school dis year, I reckon.

Sure feels good to be out heah again. Breeze feels so nice. I forgot what it was like out heah.

Etta dozed in the hammock. Sometime later she was bothered by what she thought was a large insect that kept landing on her face. Half asleep, she swatted at the bug. When it landed on her nose, her eyes flew open, and her hand came up and caught the sea oat. Etta looked at what she was holding, trying to wade out of her sleep enough to make sense of it. She looked down the stem to see the young hand that was holding the other end. With understanding, Etta looked up directly into Edward's grinning face.

He was hugging her before she could get out of the hammock. His arms around her waist, he pulled her up on her feet. The strong hug continued as she gave in to his rough affection. They broke the embrace, and she kissed him on the cheek.

Etta stood back and stared at him for a moment. An inch or two taller than her now, she noted his auburn hair had kept its thick waves. His skin was lighter, and she noticed only a few freckles as he flashed her his familiar smile. *His mama and daddy spoilt him rotten, but he was a good friend to me.* She hugged him again. *How much has he changed, I wonduh?*

He took both of her hands in his and looked into her eyes. "Etta, I've missed you."

Etta smiled at him, and her heart melted. "I missed you, too, Edward." *At last, heah we are together.*

Still holding one hand, he smiled and steadied the hammock for her to sit back down. "So what are you doing here?"

Etta was turning to sit but stopped and stared up at him, eyes wide, not really sure what he meant. "I live back on de island, Edward. I been down at Tabby Landing for most of a month." *He had no idea.* She looked away from him and pulled back, though not taking her hand from his. "I hoped I'd see you. Thought 'bout you lots."

Edward sat down on the edge of the hammock, turning slightly, looking down and speaking softly. "Sorry. I didn't know. I've been out of touch with things around here."

146

The curve of the hammock threw them against each other. Etta leaned away. *How much does he know, I wonder?* She still held his left hand. *Hand so soft. Hmmm. Mine must feel like leather.* She pulled her hand back. "I work in de greenhouse down dere fixin' cane for plantin', carryin' bundles of cotton plants out to de fields, cleanin' up, and stuff like dat."

He looked at her and frowned. "That sounds like hard work. I wish you were back at the Main House."

The silence grew as Etta frowned and searched for something to say.

He blurted out, "I guess I been trying to stay away from down there. Rather be at school." He looked around. "Or out here."

She spoke quickly. "Let's don't talk 'bout dat right now."

His head dipped, but he looked back up and tried a lighter smile. "We had a lot of fun out here, didn't we, Etta?"

She looked around and nodded. "Yes, we did."

He pushed the hammock back and forth with his feet. "We didn't have a care in the world. Happy time."

"Well, I'm sure you are happy at dat school you go to in Brunswick. I walked by it one time visitin' some sick folks wid Grandma. I could picture you in dem big ol' brick buildin's." *Dere wid all of your rich friends.*

Edward shrugged and swung his left hand in an arc in front of them. "Well, this is our world, Etta. No worrying 'bout school books out here."

Hmm, I'd love some books to worry 'bout. Etta looked closely at him. "No, ain't no school books out heah."

He stood up, took her hand again and pulled her to an opening in the trees. "You remember our house? Come here. Let me show you. I have kept most of our things here in the hollow log." He reached up in a huge

147

hollow tree that was lying across the middle of the opening and pulled out a pot containing their big spoon and knife. He had the plates they had made from driftwood.

Etta looked around where they had played away many afternoons setting up tables and putting up pretend walls. She looked again at the clearing, memories flooding back. She was stunned to realize how free they had been and how that freedom was now just an unsettling memory. She 'roused herself and pulled Edward away toward the creek.

As they came into the low dunes just above the water, Edward hesitated. "Wait here." He went back into the edge of the undergrowth and cut off five or six large palmetto fronds with his pocketknife. He brought them to the narrow beach and began to spread them out carefully, 10 or 12 feet from the water.

She smiled, recognizing that he was doing this for her the same way he had done in their childhood past. She watched every move and expression. *Guess he tellin' me dat he always showed me respect. Dat's de truth. Maybe he ain't changed much after all.*

Edward was busy in his work of arranging the palmetto fronds just right. After he finished he turned and, with a stern expression, bowed and offered his hand.

She took it, putting her other hand over her mouth, laughing as she assumed her place on their throne.

He picked up a broken stem from the palmettos and began to draw in the sand. *Dat's one area I could never match 'im. He got a natu'al gift for drawin'.* Etta shook her head. "I belieb' dat sand's too dry."

Edward nodded and moved closer to the water. There he drew a map of the streets and buildings where he lived and went to school. As he drew, he talked about his teachers, friends, and what life was like in Brunswick. "Been staying there on weekends." His voice broke a bit. "Haven't had much interest in coming home."

He smiled up at her, and his speech quickened. "There's a farmer behind the school that lets us ride on his farm." He moved more quickly as he drew the school's small barn and stables. "Dad gave me a gelding out of Sultan. Call him Caliph, and I keep him in the stables there at school. Ain't a horse there that can catch him."

Etta worked to maintain her smile. "Sounds wonderful." She rubbed one palm with the fingers of the other hand. *He sure live in a dif'nt wurl dan me.*

Soon the last gasp of high tide rushed up and erased much of Edward's drawing. She put her hands to her face. "Oh, no-o-o-o!"

Edward looked at her with his lips poked out. "There goes my life."

"Come on," he yelled suddenly. Tossing his "brush" and taking her hand as she stood up, he startled her by turning around, pulling his shirt over his head, dropping his pants and underwear. Within a moment he was naked and diving into the creek. "Can't catch me!" He swam strongly out toward the middle.

Etta's mouth dropped open, and she stood frozen in place. Edward waved enthusiastically. "Come on."

She stepped forward and lifted her cotton dress slowly over her head, hesitating, then tossing it down on the palmettos. Looking around, Edward waved at her again. She hooked her thumbs in her step-ins but then

149

hesitated, keeping them on. Turning, she strode the remaining steps to the water. Looking up, she realized that Edward had gotten still, treading water as he stared back at her.

Did he still think of me as a child? She hesitated. *Hmm, I ain't got nuttin' to be ashamed of.* She stood up tall, strode to the edge of the water, waded out and dove in toward Edward.

The tide was exactly at peak with no obvious currents. He turned to her left and swam up the creek toward the mainland and the river. He wasn't trying too hard to get away, and Etta quickly caught him, taking him by the shoulders and pushing him under forcefully. He went way under, grabbing her foot as he slipped past. She gave a little squeal and yanked it free just before her head was pulled under.

She swam back down the creek with Edward in pursuit. He swam up next to her and threw one arm over her back as if to dunk her. As she twisted to get away, his hand slipped down over her bottom. As she rolled onto her back, she realized he was staring at her breasts. They both stopped swimming for a moment. She pushed hard off of him with one foot and swam directly back to the palmettos. *Dis could head off in de wrong direction.*

She slipped from the water and turned back toward Edward. *We ain't children no more, and dis ain't playin'.* The water dripped from her nipples and beaded on her black body, sparkling in the bright sunshine like liquid diamonds. Edward stared, his mouth open. *Why shouldn't I be out heah with a boy? 'Bout time something good happened in my life.*

Etta shook the water from her hair, then stood, hands on her hips, accepting his attention. She turned, muscles in her legs and back glistening

150

as she walked slowly to the palmettos. She moved her dress and lay down on her stomach. She closed her eyes and welcomed the warming sun. *Dat sure feels good. Maybe out heah I can feel free again. What's wrong wid dat?*

Several moments later Edward called her from waist-deep water. "Etta, you coming back in?"

She turned and sat up, one hand shading her eyes and the other covering her breasts. "You go ahead. Feels fine right heah to me."

He paused, turned toward the creek, then turned back and waded out of the water toward her. She frowned. *Hmm, look at 'im. Dat's different. I don't know if dis is good.* She stood up quickly.

He walked up, put his arms around her and pulled her toward him. She kept her hands and arms between them as he attempted to hug her. She kissed him on the cheek, pushed him back and turned to sit back down. He held one arm, pulled her back to him and tried to kiss her on the lips, missing slightly.

She looked him in the face, put her arms around him and kissed him back on the lips. Edward pulled her closer, pressed her to him and kissed her again. *Dis is nice.* She put her head on his shoulder and nuzzled his neck, feeling the warmth rise between them.

His hand slipped down her back. *Hmm. So dis is what it's like to be wid a boy.*

There was a stirring behind her. She raised her head. *Listen to dat wind!*

Edward pulled back, frowning. "What's wrong?"

"It's nothing." She kissed him more strongly on the lips. He put his arms back around her.

151

A hawk called from the trees behind them. Her eyes blinked open, and she looked past Edward to the creek where her ancestors had leaped to their freedom. She looked back at him and kissed him gently, without passion. She smiled and shook her head at him and turned away, her great aunt's voice quietly echoing in her head, "She jus' human, Honey, jus' lack de res' uh us."

Edward stared, his mouth open as Etta calmly picked up her dress and dropped it over her head. "Wait. What's wrong?" He tried to take her arm and pull her to him.

She jerked her arm out of his grasp, turned, shook her head and looked him in the face. "We ain't gon do dat." She walked away.

Edward struggled back into his underwear and pants, calling out, "Hold on! Wait!"

Etta stopped but didn't look back. "I care 'bout you Edward, but dere's been 'nough of dat bidness 'round heah awready."

He put a hand on her shoulder and tried to turn her so he could look in her face. "What's between us doesn't have anything to do with our parents."

Etta laughed and stared at him again. "Sure it do! Have you met OUR little brother yet?"

Edward reeled away as if struck in the face, but turned back and spread his arms. "Look around. We're free. There's nobody in this world but the two of us. We can do whatever we please out here. Nobody at the Main House even knows we're out here." He lifted his arms. "We're free as birds!"

Free as birds. Etta put one hand on her hip, stared at the sand and shook her head. "Dat's 'bout as make-believe as our house. What would

152

happen if a fisherman went back and told your mama dat we was runnin' 'round naked out heah? You might be free as a bird, but I ain't. She might be yoh mama, but she owns me."

Edward frowned but walked over and took Etta's arm again. "What difference does it make? We are both almost grown. Come on, let's sit back down on the palmettos. Nobody going to see us out here."

Etta pulled back, folded her arms over her chest and studied the horizon, looking in all directions. "No. Guess you gon have to bring one uh dem Brunswick girls out heah to go skinny dippin' wid you."

He laughed out loud. "That won't ever happen."

She frowned and looked at him. "So it be wrong for dem girls to come out heah and get naked wid you, but it ain't wrong fuh me to do it? Dat what you think?"

Edward frowned deeply and shook his head strongly. "I didn't say that. I don't know. Those girls are crazy. Not like you."

There was a long silence as Etta looked out on the creek. "Yeah, Edward, you're right." She looked down at her scarred palms. "Dey ain't like me. I'm goin' back to Tabby Landing."

He stepped forward and reached for her. "Wait!"

She headed down the beach. He followed her, trying to get back into speaking range. "I'm going to come down and see you!"

Tears streamed down her face. She stopped and whirled around, hands on her hips. "Don't you see? You can't come see me! Lord have mercy! Yoh mama already wants me out in the mud on de North End with de snakes and the gators. You gon be gone off to school somuhs. I'll be heah, and she'll make me pay. You come see me? Me an' Mama 'll end up in Mississippi, or worse."

Edward looked down, his voice softer. "No, now, she wouldn't do that."

Etta stared back, speaking slowly and carefully. "De hell she won't! Dat woman wants Mama and me both 'way from heah. She thinks she ain't got no husband 'cause of Mama. She sho ain't gon want you hangin' 'round me now. Look, don't mention my name. Don't you say a word 'bout me or Mama at de Main House. You understand?"

He nodded and looked down. She walked away. Tears had turned to anger.

He called out to her. "I'll ride down the beach late tomorrow afternoon. Meet me out there!"

Etta shook her head but didn't look back. *I should'uh knowed dat I can't be friends wid Edward widout causin' more problems for me and Mama. Hellfire and damnation! All my dreams turn to sand. What did I do wrong?*

She picked up her pace. *PawPaw told me not to do anything stupid, and dere I wuz runnin' 'round half naked on de beach wid de Massuh's son. Lord, I hope Miss Frances don't get wind uh dis.* It was a long walk home.

The sun was almost touching the horizon as Etta approached Tabby Landing. She chose a path that would take her back by her mother's cabin. Soon she could see her mother moving around under the pole barn. Etta was close before her mother looked up. Rachel stood, stared, and hurried out to meet her.

154

Etta came directly, hugged her mother and held her, speaking over her mother's shoulder. "I'm sorry, Mama. I love you. I'm heah to help, not to make it worser."

Rachel kept an arm around Etta as they walked back to the barn and sat down on one of the rough benches. Matthew was in a basket on the table. "You ain't got nuttin' to feel sorry 'bout, Honey." Rachel dropped her head. "I'm de one dat's sorry. I should'uh stopped it if I could'uh."

She looked up at Etta and grimaced. "Miss Frances knowed dat Mr. Thomas done took a likin' tuh me, and she hated me fuh it. I warn't gon last much longer dere nohow. She warn't sure de baby was his'n 'til Matthew was born. Warn't no denying dat red hair and freckles. Midwife went right to her." She gave a crooked smile and shook her head. "I was gone de nex' day."

"You don't have to 'splain nuttin' to me, Mama."

Rachel looked up at Etta. "I been busy tryin' tuh 'splain it tuh my ownse'f." She gave a short laugh. "I t'ink I 'ad kinduh a crazy dream. Yuh spend so much time wid folks, yuh forgets dat dey don't see things like yuh does. Yuh start tuh think dat yuh a reg'luh person dere, like dem, dat it ain't really massuh and slabe."

Rachel looked down and shook her head. "T'rough dis whole mess, I t'ought dat Thomas would claim Matthew."

She gave a short, bitter laugh. "I knowed better, but I t'ought 'e would claim me too. I cared fuh dat man. T'ought he might'uh cared fuh me, too. If he do, he sho care 'bout sumpin else a whole lot more."

They sat quietly for a moment. Matthew fussed and kicked his cover. Etta got up and walked around to his basket. As she approached, he began

155

kicking and waving his arms. Etta poked him in his bare tummy. Matthew froze and stared back at her for a moment before he grinned and began kicking in excitement again.

Etta smiled back and tickled him. He laughed, and they laughed together. She picked him up, spun him in a circle and walked with him back to their mother who was smiling broadly at them. Holding him under his arms, Etta lifted him over her head. "Matthew, I'm Etta, your sister." Matthew gurgled his response as Etta dodged his drool. "You mind if I move in wid you?" She looked at her mother.

"Mama, I need to tell you what PawPaw have to say."

Chapter 17

Etta, Rachel, and Matthew settled into a routine where Etta would hurry back from the greenhouses every afternoon to care for Matthew and help her mother prepare for the noon meal she would serve the next day to the overseer, foremen, and drivers.

On Sundays, Etta would walk down to PawPaw's after her noon meal with her mother. Most Sundays, Etta would come back by her Grandmother Hester's on her way home. They would go on an outing or work with plants at the cabin. Often she would stay for supper.

Sam had come by to see Etta on several occasions, but their busy schedules had not allowed for them to spend much time together. Their relationship settled into a friendly, mutual respect.

One Monday morning in late June, Etta walked into a tense scene in one of the greenhouses. The women were gathered in a group, heads together, everyone listening intently to the speakers. Etta walked up to the edge of the group and spoke to Charlene. "What y'all talkin' 'bout?"

Charlene turned around. "You ain't heard 'bout whut happen?"

Etta closed her eyes for a moment and resisted saying something smart. "No, Charlene, I don't know what happened. Why don't you tell me?"

Charlene pulled her away from the group and leaned in close. "Three mens wurkin' up at Lumber Landin' tried tuh 'scape last night. Dey got word dat dey wuz gon hab tuh go up and start movin' stumps an' diggin' a new channel fuh de rice fields. Dey hid on a ship headed up norf, but de crew squeal on 'em b'fo' dey ebuh got unduhway."

Etta frowned deeply. "What's gon happen to 'em?"

Charlene's eyes were wide. "Dey bringin' 'em down heah and gon put 'em in a room obuh in one uh de warehouses while dey decide whut tuh do wid 'em."

Etta stared back. "Who are de mens dat got caught? Would I know 'em?"

"You know June, dat gal dat yuh got in dat fight wid?"

Etta rolled her eyes. "Yeah, sure."

"One uh dem is June's oldest bruduh, Malcolm. Dey calls 'em Buster. De uduh two is bruduhs, Joseph an' Nathaniel. Dey a few years olduh dan we is. Dey folks lib an' wurk at de sawmill. Dey might be some kin tuh yuh." She shook her head. "Don't know 'em good." Charlene turned back to the other women.

Etta stood back but listened carefully to the conversation. One of the older women spoke up. "Dey crazy to do dat. Dey gon bring trubble down on ebuhbody."

158

Anna stared at her for a moment, then spat on the dirt floor, then stared again. "Huh! Growin' rice is whut brings de trubble. Diggin' up dem stumps whut brings de trubble. Wurkin' in dat mud is whut brings de trubble." Anna's voice rose as she spoke. "Dealin' wid dem snakes whut brings de trubble. Wadn't dat long ago we wuz 'avin' a funerul fuh yoh cuzzun whut got pinned in a ditch up dere an' drownt. Dem boys knowed whut dey wuz facin'."

The woman looked away from Anna, sneering. "Yuh jus' wait an' see. Gon be a mess fuh ebuhbody. Dem boys won't be de only folks gettin' whipped. Should'uh done whut dey wuz tol'."

Anna shook her head at the woman. "Mr. Luke ain't gon whip nobody. W'en de las' time dey whipped somebody 'round heah?"

The woman turned back, laughing at Anna. "Dat's whut de white folks gon t'ink is de pro'lem. Mr. Luke bettuh look out, too. Mistuh Wilson? He ain't a happy man, an' dis mess gon 'barress 'im b'fo' 'is frien's. Dey all scairt dat if peoples down heah figure out some way whut tuh get norf, dat white folks might hab tuh get out and pick de cotton dey ownse'fs."

Anna tilted her head. "Well, dey caught 'em, didn't dey?"

"Yeah, but you know Mistuh Wilson been tellin' his frien's dat 'is slabes lub' hit heah and wouldn't try tuh run away fuh nuttin'. Been de 'xample in dis part uh de wurl fuh treatin' slabes decent. He say he don't have tuh whip us.

"Yuh know my boy is his carriage drivuh. He wid 'im ebuhweh he go. He say dat de uduh plan'ers worried, sayin' hit's time tuh get tough an' dat Wilson be settin' a bad 'xample."

159

Anna leaned back. The other women were quiet. Etta stood with her hands on her hips, watching. Anna lifted her head and shook it slowly. "Yuh might be right. We'll know b'fo' long."

The women drifted apart. Etta went back to work. She brought in part of the load of cane parked outside and piled it against one wall. *Dis heah is some of dat red ribbon cane Mr. Wilson used to talk 'bout so much.*

She went to the well, filled a large watering can and, in several trips, wet the pile down. She cut each stalk into rooted segments and put all of the segments she could carry into a croaker sack. She wet down each sack after she had loaded it back on the wagon, knowing the segments would be planted in the next day or so.

Wonduh what dey gon do to dem men? Can't see Mr. Luke whippin' nobody. Dat woman was sayin' dat dis mess could cause trouble for 'im. Wonduh what she mean by dat? From de talk I used to hear up at de Main House, Wilson was very proud of his crops most years. Thought we did better dan most. Is he so scared of us runnin' off, dat he fire Mr. Luke when de farmin' goin' so good? Is sumpin like dis what PawPaw was worried 'bout?

Wednesday morning the drivers and foremen caught the workers going to the fields and told them to gather in front of the barn at noon. Rivulets of workers fed a growing pool after the noon bell was rung.

Etta stepped out of a greenhouse. She noticed Thomas Wilson in the back of a buggy along with someone in the shadows sitting next to him. The black carriage driver stood by the steps of the buggy. Wilson was watching the large group of slaves gather.

160

Etta noticed Anna on the edge of the crowd and joined her. Etta nodded toward the buggy. "Dat's Mr. Wilson. I ain't seen 'im since de day I got heah."

Anna stood with her arms crossed, frowning, her lips pressed tight. She nodded at various friends and family but said nothing. Leaning over to Etta, she whispered, "I don' lack de feel uh dis."

Etta watched as Mr. Wilson put his arm on the driver's shoulder and stepped slowly down from the buggy. He walked out in front of the barn and stepped up two steps to a small platform that been set up that morning. The other man, his back to her, stepped down from the buggy. *Dat ain't Mr. Luke.*

Up front heah we got one white foreman and five black drivers. The drivers stood to the right of Mr. Wilson. To the left was the foreman. He had left space between himself and Thomas Wilson.

She looked closely, frowned, and leaned over to Anna, whispering, "Where's Mr. Luke? Overseer ain't heah."

Anna looked around and shook her head.

Etta looked over the crowd. *Got to be several hundred slav es out heah. Dey sure are quiet. Everbody is so serious-lookin'. Nervous, worried.*

Thomas Wilson cleared his throat. The mixed crowd of men and women pressed forward, most still holding the hoes they brought with 'em from the fields.

Etta and Anna moved up close to the front as Etta shifted over to be able to see. Mr. Wilson spoke loudly. "Nothing hurts a parent more than being disappointed in their children." He pointed up the Main Road. "I

161

came down that road today with a heavy heart. I have been told that my people want to run away from all that they get from living here, in our home."

Several voices from the crowd called out, "Nawsuh!" One voice added, "We lack hit heah wid yuh, Massuh. Yuh and Massuh Luke is good tuh us."

Wilson looked down. Etta could see his jaw muscles moving. *I ain't never seen 'im like dis.*

Wilson clenched his lips for a moment and then went on. "I'm told that my people want to leave, risk their lives with strangers out in the ocean to get away from this life, this home we have built here together."

Etta put her hand up to her mouth as she watched Thomas Wilson's face turn bright red. He began shouting and waving his arms. "FOR WHAT? If you people could get up north, the Yankees going to put you to work in their cotton mills and pay you just enough to KEEP YOU ALIVE! You think anybody up there cares anything about you the way I DO? Anybody up there going to pass out bags of flour, rice, and cornmeal? They going to pass out CURED MEAT?" Wilson's voice began to break.

Etta stood with her mouth open. The crowd produced a few weak "Nawsuhs."

Wilson took a deep breath and went on with some composure. "A parent can't just love their children. They have to teach them right from wrong. As many have warned me, it seems I have failed you in that regard."

One strong "Nawsuh" rang out from the crowd.

"I know now that those who do wrong have to be an example of what can happen when you don't listen to your Massuh, the one white man in this world that cares about you and knows what's best for you."

He paused and took a couple of breaths. "Now, I understand that it's not always going to be fair. Some do have to sacrifice more and work harder than others." Wilson made a circular movement with one arm. "But it is for the good of us all!"

There was some movement and murmuring in the crowd. Etta heard Anna mutter under her breath. "'Specially for you."

Wilson cleared his throat. "Many have told me that I was not doing right by you, that I was not teaching you right from wrong, because I was too kind. Too forgiving of my people when they did wrong."

The crowd called out, "No! We lub' yuh, Massuh."

"I told 'em, 'No. My people would never leave me! They tell me they love me. Love what I do for 'em.'"

Cries came loudly from different places. "Dat's right! Yassuh! Sho 'nuf!"

Thomas Wilson hung his head and shook it slowly, then looked up and jabbed his finger toward the crowd. "Looks like THEY were right! I've been listening to lies around here. Starting tomorrow morning, Mr. Luke will be relieved of his duties here and will be working on the mainland for Thomas, Jr., on his plantation."

There was not a sound from the slaves. The man, who looked vaguely familiar to Etta, approached from the buggy. *Reckon dat means we in for trouble. What's dat man got in his hand? A rope?*

163

Etta looked again at the man's face. A bolt of lightening went through her; her knees buckled, and she lost her breath. She bent over deeply from the waist. "Oh, Dear Lord, have mercy! No! No!"

Anna stared around at her. "You awright? Whut's wrong?"

Etta looked up, put her hand over her face and shook her head.

Cap'n Jack climbed up on the platform next to Mr. Wilson. Wilson put his hand on Jack's shoulder. "This man is Cap'n Jack Morris, your new overseer. He is here to make sure that everyone on Bonita Island Plantation understands what is expected of 'em. "You talk to'em, Jack."

"Yes, sir." Cap'n Jack stepped forward. There was a plaintive, "We lub' yuh, Massuh," while people in the crowd looked at each other and shook their heads. Etta looked at Anna who was staring at the new overseer. The crowd moved back, and people began to talk among themselves.

"LISTEN UP!" Jack forcefully cracked the whip in his hand.

Etta jumped as if she had been shot. The crowd gasped and moved back another step.

Jack stood with his feet wide apart, brandishing the whip. "THAT'S THE PROBLEM! When white people are talkin', you people gon shut up!" The crowd became quiet. "You people have had it easy for way too long. I've seen it time after time. A kind, Christian man like Mr. Wilson here loves his slaves and is kind to them, and then they turn around and stab him in the back."

Wilson's head jerked around, and he gave Cap'n Jack a startled look.

Jack didn't notice. "In my many years working with the Negro, I have learned that there ain't but one thing that you all understand." He cracked the whip again. "From now on, the slaves on Bonita Island Plantation are

164

going to follow the rules and show respect for their betters, or they gon feel the lash right then and right there. You people understand that?"

There were murmurs and movement in the crowd.

"Every one of you, young and old, better mind your manners from now on, 'cause things are about to change."

Darkness closed in around Etta, and she put her head down.

From the crowd came numerous "Yassuh's".

She stared at the ground, feeling tears welling up in her eyes. *Guess I'll be de first one he whips.*

Wilson stepped forward and spoke again. "Now, for the three boys that embarassed us all, brought this down on you, they're the first ones that need a lesson. Bring 'em out here, Fellows."

Each of the young men, in arm and leg chains, were led out by a foreman using a heavy rope tied to the chains at the wrist. The slaves were lined up in front of the crowd to Mr. Wilson's left.

He turned and addressed them directly. "You boys have brought shame on me, on your families, and on Bonita Island Plantation. The first job of a slave is to do as he's told by his betters. You boys don't seem to understand that. We're going to see right now that you do."

The young man in the middle fell on his knees and raised his clasped hands under his chin. "We're sorry, Massuh. We don't mean no disrespect."

Wilson stood staring down at him but didn't respond. He nodded to the driver to his immediate left. Malcolm, the young slave closest to Thomas Wilson, was led to the corner beam. A large metal hook had been bolted to the rafters about eight feet off the ground. The driver tossed the rope over the hook, cinched it up and tied it, almost pulling Malcolm off his feet, face against a large beam. He began to cry and beg, trying to look around at Mr. Wilson.

"Ple-e-ease, Mr. Wilson, don't let 'em do dis! I lub' yuh, Mr. Wilson. I lub'd yuh since I wuz a baby." Malcolm, eyes big, looked at the foreman who had picked up a large paddle.

His voice got louder and higher pitched. "Dey made me do it, Massuh. I didn't want tuh go. Please! Please!" The young man wet himself. The foreman pointed to the growing stain on his pants and laughed. The other foremen and drivers laughed with him.

Holding the paddle with both hands, the foreman began striking the young man in the buttocks and the back of his legs.

Malcolm screamed in pain. A woman in the crowd screamed out and collapsed on the ground as others tried to hold her up. Etta doubled over in pain herself. She looked at Anna, who had her head in her hands. Etta began to work her way toward the back of the crowd, each movement in that direction hastened by the preceding scream.

Etta looked closely at those around her. An older man squeezed his hoe handle, flinching with every blow. Next to him, Etta recognized one of the dancers at the Ring Shout; her lips were moving soundlessly. *Dat woman dere is angry, but most folks look scared.*

Etta continued to move through the crowd away from the barn. She paused and looked back. As he was hit, Malcolm would jump from one foot to the other. The foreman was laughing. "That's it, Boy! That's it! Dance!" Then he would hit him again. He put the paddle down and picked up the short, thick-leather whip with multiple strands.

166

Etta turned and continued moving away, the screams following her. *I don't see nobody keepin' folks heah.* She walked over to the closest grove of trees, then straight away from the gathering toward her mother's cabin, keeping the trees between her and the barn. Going in the cabin and climbing up to her bed in the loft did not silence the screams. There was a pause, and they began again. Etta threw up in a bucket she got from under the bed.

She put her hands over her ears and buried her head in the shuck mattress. It seemed to go on forever. The screams echoed in her ears after they had finally stopped. She was suddenly chilled and couldn't get warm. She pulled up her cover, crying and shivering. She heard her mother on the porch and began to rub her face on the bedclothes.

"Etta! Yuh home, Honey? I been lookin' fuh yuh."

"Uh, yes, Mama, I'm heah."

"Yuh all right?"

"Yassum, I reckon." Etta slipped out of bed and wiped at her face. "Dat was awful. Made me sick."

"Come down heah and get in my bed."

Etta climbed down from the loft, and her mother studied her carefully. Rachel held out her arms. "People can sho do mean things tuh one anuduh."

Etta returned her mother's embrace, holding on for several moments. She finally sat on the edge of the bed.

Rachel walked to the stove, bent over and was blowing on coals in the firebox.

Etta lifted her head. "Mama, I know dat man."

Rachel didn't look up. "What man?"

"Our new overseer, Cap'n Jack. I'll prolly be de first one he whips."

167

"What?" Rachel stood up straight, wiped her hands on an apron hanging over a chair and stared at Etta. "How yuh had any dealin's wid dat man?"

"I was deliverin' pies down to de hotel restaurant dere in Brunswick, an' he jus' start yellin' at me fuh no reason. Well, dat ain't right. He do have a reason. Grandma, Miss Elouise, and Miss Lizbeth played a trick on him to get Grandma her freedom. You've heard dat story. He seem to hold dat 'ginst me. You too, I reckon."

Rachel frowned, quiet for a moment. "He prolly gon have more to worry 'bout dan me and you." She nodded back to her right. "Dere's water in dat pitchuh obuh dere. Go wash up. He ain't gon whip you. He come heah and start whippin' people for nuttin, dere gon be a price tuh pay. I hope folks won't put up wid dis mess." She shook her head slowly. "Course it look like Thomas done los' 'is mind."

Etta washed her face, drying it on a rag next to the old dark brown ceramic pitcher. *I feel some better. Still a knot in my stomach. How could Mister Wilson do what he done?* "Mama, I ain't gon never have no respect for Thomas Wilson ever again."

Rachel hung her head and, in a moment, a tear slid out. "Hard tuh make sense uh things, ain't it?"

The fire in the stove popped. "Yeah, Mama, it sure is. You got to feed de foremen today?"

"No, thank goodness. Dey being fed up at de Main House." Rachel shook her head. "Reward fuh all dat good whippin', I reckon."

Etta gave a weak smile and shrug to her mother. "Food prolly better down heah."

168

Rachel turned and gave a twisted smile back, but then frowned. "We need to tell Anna all you know 'bout dis man. Guess we all in fuh it fuh a spell. He hate Medina? Well, Abraham is her daddy. He needs tuh know."

"I see 'im on Sunday."

Rachel had turned back to the stove. "Anna'll get de word to 'im. You can go tell her all you know 'bout de Cap'n after you eat sumpin. Got plenty of food."

Rachel looked off. "I remember when Mama told me 'bout what happen, how she got her freedom, but I ain't thought nuttin 'bout it much since."

She spoke over her shoulder, "Dere's some fried chicken, greens, red peas, and cornbread heah on de stove. I'm steepin' yuh a cup uh Ebuhlastin' Tea. After you eat sumpin, go on over to Anna's, tell her ebuht'ing you know and walk on back to work wid her." Rachel poured the hot tea in a cup and added honey. "She'll get de word out. I'll go over to Mama Hester's and tell her bout you an' dis Cap'n. Tell me all yuh know 'bout 'im."

Etta ate a little as she talked to her mother, but drank all the tea. In a few minutes she walked down the porch steps, looked up and paused. A strong breeze stirred the water oaks next to the cabin. *Reckon I ought to be scared, but I ain't. Least for de time bein'. I'll try to stay out of trouble, but I ain't bowin' down to dat man.*

169

CHAPTER 18

The first of July was marked with stories from the women about how Cap'n Jack had taken the whip to a boy who was slow to help him with his horse and how he had tried to run a man down with his horse. There were new stories every day about Jack cursing and striking somebody.

Lazarus, the driver over the work in the barn and surrounding building, came into the greenhouse and shared new rules with the women. "Don' nobody look a white person in de face, but keep yoh head down. Don' speak unless you are ax'd to speak, an' if'ns you talk to a white person, yuh start wid 'Suh', an' yuh end wid 'Suh'. Yuh peoples unuhstan' dat?"

The women all nodded. "Yassuh, we unuhstan'."

Etta felt she could read the mood of the community by what these women had to say. She realized that at first the abuse frightened and cowed most everybody, but Etta began to hear more and more anger from the women in the greenhouses. There were an increasing number of small incidents as the slave population at Tabby Landing began to push back.

Charlene told Etta, "Las' night somebody open a whole section uh de corral and lets all de hawsses an' mules out. Dey found de mules dis moanin', eatin' young cotton plants right out heah 'hind de greenhouses."

Etta shook her head. "Reckon we'll have tuh replant 'em."

Charlene laughed. "Dey still ain't found some uh de hawsses."

Etta had seen Cap'n Jack on horseback riding through the fields looking at the crops or headed to different operations on the island. She kept her head down and looked busy whenever she saw him.

His office is right over heah in de main barn. Dat's a little too close fuh comfort.

A week later, Etta was cleaning and stacking wooden planting trays when Lazarus came into the building. "Etta! Etta!"

"Yassuh!" She turned and lowered her eyes.

"Cap'n Jack wants tuh see yuh in 'is office. Right now."

"Yassuh." Etta put down the trays, wiped her hands on a cloth and looked around for Anna, who was nowhere to be seen. Her fears trailed her as she followed Lazarus out of the greenhouse and nextdoor into the barn. *Stay calm now. Breathe slow. Don't provoke 'im.*

She walked toward the back where the office door was standing open. Etta had never been in this room that was stuck onto the back of the barn. She slowed outside the door and studied the room. There was a large desk against the wall, straight across from the door. To the left of the desk was a flat-topped, small, cast-iron wood heater with a kettle on top. Between the stove and the back left corner was a set of stove tools hanging on pegs in the

171

wall. To the right of the desk was a tall bookcase holding the Plantation's crop records. Cap'n Jack was standing in front of the desk with the top right drawer open. Etta lowered her eyes, stepped through the doorway and waited.

Holding a sheaf of papers in his right hand, Cap'n Jack turned and looked at her. "Well, look who's here. Ain't you got no pastry for me this morning?"

"Suh. Nawsuh." Eyes still down, she tried to keep any emotion off her face.

"Now, one thing I remember about you is they say you can read pretty good. Is that right?"

Etta nodded, still looking down. "Yassuh. I kin read, Suh."

"Alright, come over here. You see this paper?" He pointed to the top paper of the stack he had just put on the corner of the desk. "Read what it says."

Etta took the paper and looked it over. "Dis heah says invoice across de top. A bill from Landrum's Hardware, in Brunswick, for de amount of $4.50 for a hundred pounds of Number 20 nails."

Cap'n Jack stared at her for a moment. "Get all the papers in these desk drawers and put them in stacks according to what they are. Put the bills in one stack, letters in another stack, and then take each stack and put each piece in order by how old it is. Oldest on top. Think you can do that?"

"Yassuh." Etta looked at her toes.

Jack stared at her, frowning. "Don't take these papers out of this room, and keep your mouth shut about what you read, or I'll give you that whippin' I promised. Now get busy and let's see what you can do."

"Yassuh." Etta didn't look up.

Cap'n Jack walked out of the office.

She waited a moment or two, then picked up the stack of papers. *Let's see heah. Where do I start?* It took her about an hour to clean out the desk drawers and organize the contents. *I just knowed dat I was gon get dat beatin'. Guess he gon hold it over my head. Look at dis. Letters and bills just stuck in heah goin' back to before he come heah. Wonduh if he can read any? Does Mr. Wilson know Cap'n Jack can't read? He ain't gon be able to handle de paperwork by hisself. He sure enough knows who I is, but maybe if he really needs my help, he won't take nuttin' out on me. We'll see.*

Etta found herself called to the small office most days, sometimes several times a day, to read some correspondence, record information, or write a response. *Don't reckon Mr. Wilson can recognize my handwritin'? Sure can learn a lot readin' all dese notes and letters. I like doin' dis, but sure don't like bein' 'round dis man.*

Etta's 15th birthday was July the 11th. On the Wednesday before her birthday on Friday, she stepped out of the greenhouse at noon. She noticed a group of men unloading a wagon at the blacksmith shop but didn't look closely, turning toward her mother's cabin.

"Etta!"

She turned quickly around and stared at the man approaching her. There was a moment of silence. "Dan!" Etta put her hand over her mouth. She hurried to him, looking now to see who the other men were in the group. She spoke more quietly. "Let's don't 'rouse Cap'n Jack."

Dan frowned. "Who?"

Etta nodded to the other men and turned to Dan, speaking quietly and pointing. "You see dat big garden? When you finish heah, go way on de other side and wait for me."

Dan nodded and smiled broadly. "We be done shortly."

"Awright den. See yuh in a little while." She hurried off to the cabin. Rachel was putting bowls of food on the rough tables out under the pole barn. None of the foremen, drivers, or Cap'n Jack had arrived.

She went right to her mother and spoke quickly as a smile lit her face. "Mama, guess what? Guess who?"

"What are you talkin' 'bout?" Rachel looked up. "Well, I ain't seen dat face in a while. What's goin' on?"

"You remember dat boy I told yuh 'bout dat I met at church over in Brunswick?"

Her mother put the last bowl down. "Yeah, I 'membuh."

Etta looked around and moved closer. "Dan's heah. Looks like he brought a load of plows from Brunswick, and dey unloadin' 'em up at de blacksmith shop. I'm goin' to meet 'im."

Rachel knitted her brow. "Awright. I'll go get you two some food, wrap it up and bring it in de cabin. Take it and find someplace y'all can eat and talk."

Etta nodded and hurried to the cabin. She found a small blanket, filled a glass bottle with water from the pitcher and corked it.

Her mother came in and put the food in a small handmade basket. "Here you go, Honey. I just picked stuff you could handle. "Prolly better if you two ain't seen togeduh."

174

"Thank you, Mama. I'll be careful." Etta put the bottle in the basket, opened the door a crack, looked carefully and slipped out. She used what bushes and trees she could to shield herself from Cap'n Jack's path to dinner and slipped around to the east end of the garden. She didn't have to wait long.

"Dere yuh is, Etta. Cain't see yuh fuh de weeds." Dan pushed at some taller weeds with the back of his hand. Etta almost tackled him with her hug.

Dan hugged her back strongly, laughing. "I missed you, too."

Etta released him. "Come on. Let's get out'uh heah." Etta lead the way toward the beach. She spoke over her shoulder, "Almos' didn't know yuh, yuh gotten so big."

Dan followed, head down. "Well, dem Giles is sho stingy, but I do say dey feed me good."

He put out his hand. "Gimme dat basket. "Weh we goin'?

Etta turned it over. "Out to de beach."

Dan stopped and looked around. They were approaching the large dunes. "Nebuh been to de beach b'fo'."

Etta looked over her shoulder. "You lived close to it, didn't yuh?"

Dan nodded. "Yeah, but hit's mostly marsh down dere. Dere wuz a beach close, but I nebuh got to go."

Etta smiled. "Well, come on den! Let's fix dat!" She started running, letting the blanket flap in the wind.

Dan followed, moving slowly on the dunes. Etta waited for him on the top. She called down. "When you got to go back?"

Dan, struggling in the sand with his boots, looked up. "I gotuh be on de five o'clock ferry, and I got to get dem mules taken care of, but dat won't take long."

Etta frowned. "I got to go back to work in a bit, but come on. We got a little time."

Dan made it to the top. Etta started down the other side, but Dan hadn't moved. He stood, his mouth open, staring. "Lawd hab' mercy! Dis heah de prettiest place I ebuh seen in my life."

She led him down as he continued to look up and down the beach and out at the ocean. Etta smiled at him, led him to the dry sand above the waterline, and spread out the blanket. "Have a seat."

He continued to stand and stare. "Yuh see dem big birds out dere diving?"

She smiled up at him. "Yeah, I did. Dey're pelicans."

He sat down. "You come out heah ebuh day?"

She shook her head. "Naw. Ain't really had de time since I moved in wid Mama, but I do love it heah." She began to unwrap the food her mother had sent. "What you doin' out heah on Bonita?"

Dan poked his chest out and grinned at her. "I's a busy man. D'libuh'd a load uh plow stocks and still have one moh d'lib'ry tuh make."

She frowned deeply and tilted her head. "Delivery? What you got 'sides dem plow handles?"

He poked out his lips. "Oh, I got a special d'lib'ry for somebody obuh heah."

Etta opened the water bottle. "What you talkin' 'bout? Who to?"

Dan's eyebrows shot up. "It's a d'lib'ry for somebody havin' a birfday."

Etta's mouth flew open. "You jokin', ain't yuh?" She handed Dan a piece of fried chicken.

"Ain't no joke. Got a box on de wagon fuh Miss Etta frum her frien's in Brunswick." Dan reached for a piece of cornbread.

Etta grinned at him. "I'm gon have to wait 'til I get off dis afternoon. What we gon do wid de box 'til den?"

"It's unduh de wagon seat. I oughtuh take de wagon back to de dock and bring dem mules back to de barn. My mules is back at de Brunswick dock. Is dere sumuhs I could take de box?"

Etta frowned and was quiet. "Hmm, ain't got time tuh show you."

Dan spoke with a mouthful of chicken. "You get off 'bout three o'clock?"

Etta nodded.

"Come on obuh to de dock w'en you get off. De box ain't heavy. You kin carry hit widout any trubble."

She smiled and nodded. "Awright, dat sounds good."

"Tell yoh Mama dat I 'preciate de food. Supper gon be late."

Etta stared off for a moment. "I'm sorry, Dan, 'bout gettin' you in trouble at de store. I knowed better dan go in dere and try to see you. I didn't 'xpect Giles to be in dere."

Dan looked down. "Hit's awright. Sorry I didn't get tuh church. Had a big ol' scab obuh my eye. Didn't want nobody tuh see it."

Etta reached over and touched the scar. "I'm learnin' from my grandma how to heal cuts like dat."

177

He smiled at her. "I hope I'm gon be comin' obuh heah ebuh so of'n. Not sho."

Etta handed the bottle to Dan. They ate quickly.

Dan stared at Etta. "What's dat hanging 'round yoh neck?"

Etta took the fossil and held it out toward Dan. "It's a shark's tooth. It's very ol'. Belonged to my pawpaw."

He took it in his hand and looked at it carefully. "Yeah, hit's a sharp tooth awright."

Dan's head jerked up as he stared over her shoulder. "Hey! Somebody's comin' down dis way on a haws."

Etta looked around. "Prolly Edward."

Dan stirred as if to stand. "Duz we need tuh go?"

Etta turned and examined the figure closely. "Naw, I don't think so. I'm sure it's Edward."

Dan wiped his hands on his pants and settled back. "Who's dat?"

"He's a friend. He's de Massuh's youngest son. Come on, I want yuh to meet 'im. Den I got tuh get on back tuh work."

Dan stood up, frowning, as Etta folded up the blanket. "Yuh be frien's wid de massuh's son?"

"Dat's a long story. We growed up together at de Main House. Don't tell nobody dat we was wid 'im out heah."

She took Dan by the hand, and they walked toward Edward who jumped down easily from the horse. "Hey, Etta. They finally got Caliph back over to me. How do you like 'im?"

Dan spoke up. "Yassuh, dat's a fine lookin' haws, awright."

Edward grinned. "Fast, too."

178

Etta nodded. "Edward, dis heah is Dan, a friend of mine. His massuh has de dry goods store dere in Brunswick. Makin' a delivery over heah today."

Edward nodded. "You like horses?"

Dan rubbed the horse's neck. "Had moh 'xperience wid mules, but my las' massuh had a haws dat I gots tuh ride some."

Etta turned to Dan. "Oughtuh go. You find yoh way back?"

"Sho." He turned and took her arm.

She hugged him and kissed him on the cheek. "I'll see you shortly." Waving toward Edward, she called out, "Oughtuh go." She pointed at Dan. "You take care of dat box now, you hear?"

Dan grinned and nodded as he watched her take the basket and blanket and head for the dunes. He turned back to Edward and the horse.

Etta walked back on the field side of the garden. She was late and hoped that Cap'n Jack hadn't sent for her. There was no one around as she walked across the open area between the front of the garden and the greenhouses. Just before she got to the doorway, Lazarus came out, looked at her hard but said nothing. Etta forced herself to keep walking. Putting the basket and blanket away, she went back to work preparing syrup cane segments for planting.

The afternoon passed slowly, but when she thought it was safe, Etta ran across the road toward the dock. She went around the barn and warehouses to find Dan stretched out across the bed of his empty, muleless wagon parked in the shade, close to the dock. The ferry was tied to the right side of the dock, but no one was around.

179

Etta called out, "Hey, Dan. Makin' all dem deliveries must'uh wore you out."

Dan sat up and slipped down to the back of the wagon. "Still got one lef', but hit's jus' a little ol' box. Prolly don't 'mount tuh nuttin'."

Etta folded her arms and tilted her head. "Lots uh valuable things come in small boxes. Is it addressed to me?"

"Yassum, hit is." Dan hopped down. "Let me get hit fuh yuh." He walked around to the side of the wagon and slid a one-foot by two-foot cedar box out from under the seat. Etta came around, and he handed it over.

She held it in front of herself and examined it. "Think I'm gon need a knife to open dis thing."

Dan reached and got a small flat piece of metal. "I t'ought uh dat. Let me see hit." Dan set the box on the rear of the wagon, took the cultivator blade and pried the lid off the box.

Etta had put her hands over her face. "I can't believe it. I never 'xpected dem to get me anything for my birfday. Let me see." Folded tightly in the top of the box was a brand-new dress. "I know who made dat. Dat be from Grandma." Etta shook her head. "Send me a Sunday dress so I'll be sure an' go tuh church." She held it up in front of her and felt something in the pocket. She took off the safety pin that held it closed. "Look at dat." She found a little change purse and held up the 50-cent piece that had been inside. "Most money I ever had."

Dan leaned against the wagon, smiling.

She put the money and safety pin back, folded the dress over the side of the wagon and looked back into the box. There was a Harper's Weekly, Godey's Lady's Book, and an Atlanta newspaper, *The Daily Intelligencer*.

The Harper's had a note stuck behind the first page. *"Etta, I hope you enjoy these. There's some articles in this Harper's that I know you will like. It is hard now, I know, but I believe we will see the end of slavery in our time. Love you, Elizabeth."*

Etta stacked the magazines next to the box and looked back in. There was a large book down in the bottom; she pulled it out. *Wuthering Heights by Ellis Bell. Dere's a note.* "It's from Elouise."

Etta, Honey, we sure do miss you around here. It's not the same without you. I hope you enjoy this book as much as I did. I found out a secret about it. I'll tell you when I see you face to face. Look in the bottom of the box. Love, Elouise.'

She studied the bottom of the box. There was another note and a coin. She picked up the coin and showed Dan. "A quarter!"

His eyes got big. "Moh money."

Etta pulled out the note. It simply said, "Happy Birthday." Winnie had printed the greeting and added her name in cursive at the bottom. She had drawn hearts in the corners. Etta looked up at Dan. "Winnie signed her name in cursive. Grandma must be teachin' her to write some. She knew I'd like dat."

Dan had folded his arms. "Dat's good. Can you teach me to sign 'Dan'?"

She beamed at him. "Sure, I can."

Etta put her hands on her presents. "Dese are de best presents I ever got."

181

Dan reached back under the seat. "I belieb dere's one moh." He brought out a small present wrapped in wrinkled brown paper and roughly tied with a ribbon. Dey tell me dat yuh might be wurkin' outside a lot."

She nodded her head. "Looks like I'm 'bout to start." She took the present and opened it. It was a calico bonnet.

Etta hugged him. "How sweet and thoughtful. How'd you get hold of a bonnet an' ribbon?"

Dan raised his eyebrows. "Well, de papuh an' de ribbon wuz in de trash. An' de bonnet? Dey won't miss one bonnet. Sho won't blame me fuh no missin' bonnet." Dan grinned at her and shrugged.

Etta shook her head at him. " I knowed you was a bad man all along."

He shook his head back. "Fella's got tuh do whut he got tuh do. But tell me, don't a man get a kiss fuh such a nice present?"

Etta turned it in her hands. "Well, he would if'n he 'ad come by it in de right way."

"Well, de way hit got heah ain't as impot'ent as de fact dat it is right heah in yoh han's. Let's see hit on yuh. Gon be lack a picture frame 'round a pretty picture." Dan took it from her and put it on her head. Then he used the ties to pull Etta to him and kiss her on the lips. She kissed him back briefly but turned and looked around. "You've heard 'bout our new overseer, I reckon."

"Yeah, de mens in de blacksmith shop didn't seem tuh min' me hearin' 'em talk." He gave a short laugh. "I wuz t'inkin' dat you gon have it easy obuh heah. Sounds like I wuz wrong 'bout dat."

182

She pulled him away from the wagon and closer to the windowless walls of the warehouse. "Come over heah where we not so easy to see." She stood close to him and looked up, waiting for the next kiss.

Dan kissed her and held her to him. She kissed him back but then leaned back and looked around. "We need some place to go, like de beach, but we prolly ain't got time to go back over dere."

He pointed with his thumb over his shoulder. "Dere's dis barn ovuh heah. I ain't seen nobody 'round hit tuhday."

Etta nodded. "Dey use it in de early spring w'en we got more mules down heah. We use it for services. Let's go take a look. Might can go in dere."

They walked around the warehouse to the space behind the barn. Dan put up one hand. "Wait heah. Dey ain't gon do nuttin' to me." He walked around the barn corner like he was on a stroll.

She didn't wait but hurried over and peeked around after him. He had opened an end door to the barn and stuck his head in.

He turned and motioned to Etta. She hurried to him and into the doorway.

Dan grabbed her hand. "We got our own big ol' house."

"Yeah, but we ain't married yet." Etta leaned back against a post.

"Might be one day. Let's practice at it." He pulled her to him.

She laughed at him. "You don't need no practice. You prolly gettin' plenty of dat." They kissed for some time. Etta enjoyed holding him close.

There were voices. She pulled back and in a whisper said, "Who's dat?"

He frowned and listened. "Prolly de crew. Dammit, why dey back so early?"

Her head jerked up. "My presents is out dere."

Dan shook his head sadly. "Dey won't bodduh 'em, but I do oughtuh get dat wagon on boa'd."

Etta was already headed toward the door. "Come on."

At the wagon she carefully put her dress, book, and magazines back in the box. "We needed more time together. I hope you do get to deliver over heah. Maybe things will settle back down, an' we can be together."

She went on. "Thank you for bringing my presents. Got to go show 'em to Mama and Matthew."

She looked out at *The Clara*, then kissed and hugged him. "I sure hope I see you again soon."

Dan gave a deep sigh and smiled at her. "Me, too."

Chapter 19

Using a broom made from broom sage, Etta swept the tops of the rough tables that ran down the center length of the greenhouse. The cotton replanting had been completed two weeks earlier. Most of the women had been given a hoe and sent to the fields. *Charlene left yesterday. Sure gave me a look. I think she jealous of de work I been doin' for Cap'n Jack.*

Anna seemed concerned when I told her how Cap'n Jack was staying in his office when I worked, how he was puttin' his hands on me and standin' close. Afraid of what dat man gon do.

Etta put down the broom and looked for the rake she used for the dirt floor. *Since de beatin's, I ain't thought of Mr. Wilson like I used to. Make my stomach turn. He know peoples gon die jus' so he can make a little more money. He knows. Already 'ave all de money in de world.*

Lookin' out on dat crowd de other day, huge crowd of folks holdin'
hoes, dey jus' stood dere and took it. One day, slaves on some of dese farms
ain't gon take it no moh.

She stopped in her work for a moment, brow furrowed. *Hmm,*
everybody knows dat if we was to fight back, dey would bring out de real
weapons. Cut us down like red ribbon cane.

One morning Etta was working in Cap'n Jack's office while he was at
his desk. She sat at a small table on the left wall and opened mail. *Ain't*
much he can do at his desk if he can't read. Oh, he's sharpenin' de pencils.
Etta laughed to herself.

Capn' Jack turned to her. "I need for you to find that bill from the
folks that was supposed to sharpened our sawmill blades."

She looked through a stack and pulled out the invoice.

He stood up and started walking around, looking at the invoice like he
was reading it. "I want to send them a letter and tell them why we ain't
going to pay that bill. Listen to what I got to say and then write the letter.
Read it to me when you're done."

"Yassuh." Etta reached and got pencil and paper.

He was behind her as he began talking about sawmill blades that
hadn't been properly sharpened. He finished, and Etta wrote out the letter in
a clear long-hand, making each point. He walked behind her and shut the
door. Looking over her shoulder she finished writing and read it back to
him. As she finished, he put his hand on her neck.

"Uuuugh!" Etta jumped, leaning forward.

He pulled his hand back. "Ain't nothing to be scared of. Just never
noticed how pretty your neck is." He put his hand on her neck again.

186

She stared at her hands in her lap. *Why he got to pick on me?* Etta tried to turn herself to stone. He *ain't gon feel nuttin' comin' from me.*

He pressed himself against her back as he put his hand on the front of her dress and pulled her back to him. Etta gritted her teeth. *Ain't gon feel nuttin' from him neither. What can I do? Might could twist out from under 'im. What am I gon do den? Dis is a bad spot. He gon rape me right heah.*

"You just relax, Honey. Ain't nothing bad going to happen. Maybe something good'll happen." He rubbed her breast. "If we're really smart, ain't nobody going to get hurt."

The large bell outside the barn rang more loudly than usual, announcing the noon meal. Cap'n Jack raised up, frowned, turned slightly and released his grasp. "It ain't noon yet."

Go! Now! Etta jumped up, eluded his grasp, announced the letter complete and walked out the door. She spoke loudly to others in the barn even though no one was there.

When Anna came across the road to her cabin, Etta was leaning against the porch, arms crossed, head down and face grim. "You awright, Honey? Whut's wrong?"

Etta looked up, her face like stone. "He was gon rape me, Aunt Anna. I got lucky and got away." She shook her head. "But he ain't gon stop."

Anna, hands on her hips, nodded at her. "Naw, yuh right, he ain't gon stop. We got tuh stop 'im. Go tell yuh mama. I'll go down tuh Abraham's. Anna turned toward the road, then turned back. "Yuh sho yuh awright?" She walked back to Etta and put her hands on her shoulders.

Etta took a deep breath and looked up into Anna's eyes. "I'm awright. Thank you. That was close. Tell me sumpin, didn't de bell ring awful early today?"

"Naw." Anna gave a small snort. "I t'ink hit rang jus' 'bout right." She smiled at Etta. "I'm gwine on now." She turned and hurried off, shaking her head.

Etta went straight to the pole barn where a couple of foremen were already sitting. *Cap'n Jack will be heah soon. I can't tell her right now. She'd be upset. I'll go in de cabin and wait on her. She'll have to come to de stove. Prolly should wait 'til she through servin' to tell her, or she might do somethin' crazy.*

Etta sat down on the edge of the bed, leanin' forward, elbows on her knees and chin in her hands. *Wonduh how we gon stop 'im. What choices I got? What chaince I got?*

Rachel walked in with a bowl in her hand. "Hey dere, Honey. She turned her head, then looked back at Etta, staring. "What's wrong?"

Etta frowned and paused. "I'm fine, Mama." She paused again, searching for words. "I got a problem wid Cap'n Jack. You finish servin', and den I'll tell yuh 'bout it."

Rachel put down the bowl. Her eyes big, she turned to Etta. "You can tell me right now."

Etta stood up and shook her head at her mother. "No, I ain't gon tell you now. Don't mess things up. You go on back. I'm awright. I'll tell you when you done out dere." She turned away.

Rachel stood for a moment, then turned, filled the bowl and left.

188

Etta laid back on the bed, staring up at the pole rafters and rusty tin. *I hope PawPaw can help. Dere ain't much I can do by myself. Fish in a barrel.*

She closed her eyes and jousted with thoughts armed by her fears. *Take a deep breath now. Blow it out slow. Trust your folks and keep your wits 'bout you. Dey'll do what dey can.*

Her body relaxed some. Shortly, her mother opened the door, came over and sat on the edge of the bed. "What happened, Honey?"

Etta closed her eyes. "He put his hands on me, Mama."

Rachel bowed her head and clenched her fists in her lap.

"I didn't want to tell you while you was servin'. I was 'fraid you'd spill somethin' hot in 'is lap."

Rachel looked up, speaking slowly. "Yeah. I might do more dan dat."

Just barely, Etta heard her add, "Gut dat sum'bitch."

She sat up against the wall at the head of the bed. "De bell rung for dinner, an' I jumped up an' got out'uh dere. I think Aunt Anna had somethin' to do wid dat early bell."

Rachel nodded. "I t'ought it rang early, too."

"She went on down to tell PawPaw what happen, but now I got to go back. I'm 'fraid dey ain't nuttin' nobody can do to help."

Rachel frowned and nodded. "It's good dat you got word tuh Abraham. Don't know if he can do anything 'bout dis man." Her eyes narrowed, and she put her hand up to her chin. "Go on back to de greenhouses like nuttin' happened. I'll do what I can."

Etta, arms crossed over her chest, stared back. "What you gon do, Mama?"

189

Rachel frowned and shook her head. "I don't know right now, but I'll think of sumpin."

Etta stood up, still staring at her mother. "Don't do nuttin' crazy now, get yohse'f in a mess. Maybe he won't send for me."

"Awright, Honey. Stay out'uh 'is way if you can."

Later, Anna and Etta were able to speak quietly as they stacked the last of the wooden trays. Cap'n Jack walked in, frowned deeply, and spoke directly to Etta. "We ain't through. Got more work to do."

"Yassuh." Etta glanced at Anna and followed him back to his office.

He sat at the desk, and Etta stood in the middle of the little room. He swiveled around in his chair. "Come over here, Honey. I don't mean you no harm."

Etta stood still, looking down. "Suh. What work do you have for me, Suh?"

Cap'n Jack's eyes narrowed, and his tone changed. "The first work you have to do is come over here to me right now. You understand?"

"Yassuh." Still she didn't move, staring down. He got up, came to her and put his arms around her and tried to kiss her. She continued to look down. *Ain't gon kiss dis stinkin' man.*

BOOM! Suddenly a huge crash shook the small office. Cap'n Jack and Etta both lost their balance. It appeared for a moment that one wall of the office would collapse as it swayed outward.

"WHAT IN THE...!" Jack ducked his head and threw his hands up, then ran outside shouting. Etta went directly back to the greenhouses. Anna was there as well.

"Anna! whut happen to de barn?"

190

Anna looked at Etta and gave a big shrug. "I ain't had nuttin' tuh do wid hit."

Etta blinked. "What?"

Anna shook her head.

"What'd you do?

She leaned over to Etta and spoke quietly. "Hit was yoh mama, not me." She looked around carefully. "We wuz peekin' in de window dere from outside. De blacksmith leabe a team uh oxen tied to a corner support fuh de barn dere nex' to de office."

Anna put her hand over her face and looked around as she smirked. "We seen yuh wuz in trubble. Yoh mama looked 'round, found dat pitchfork leanin' dere 'ginst de back uh de barn, and she was chargin' dem bullies wid it b'fo' I knowed whut wuz gwine on. Last I seen 'em, dem oxen wuz draggin' dat big post, some boards, and part uh de roof out t'rough de cotton dat we jus' replanted." She laughed quietly. "Le's see whut he do now!"

Etta glanced at the door. 'Oh, Anna, dat was danejus. Somebody might'uh seen y'all."

Anna shook her head at Etta. "Ain't nobody gon say nuttin'. He done fin'ly made ebuhbody mad down heah. Maybe he leabe yuh 'lone now. We'll see."

Before noon the next day, the stablehands had retrieved the oxen and put the support back in place. They were nailing the shingles back on the roof when Cap'n Jack sent out word for everybody who worked in the blacksmith shop, barn, or greenhouses yesterday, to come to the barn before they left for lunch. Five men, plus Etta, Anna, and Lazarus made up the group.

191

Cap'n Jack, holding his short whip coiled in his right hand, stalked back and forth in front of everyone but Lazarus, who stood to one side. "I guess the word got out about the problem we had this afternoon." He gestured with the whip. "Somebody or something spooked a team of oxen, and they tore out one of the corner supports for the barn." He slowly surveyed the group. "I could'uh been killed."

The men shook their heads, looked down and muttered. "Sho 'nuf? Dat's turr'ble."

"Now, somebody had to see something!" Jack pointed to the blacksmith. "Marvin? You fellows in the blacksmith shop see anything? You was right there."

"Uh, Suh, nawsuh. I tied dem oxen tight; I did. I use a big ol' leather strap wid dem bully boys, but I didn't t'ink dey'd pull dat whole post down."

Jack gritted his teeth and moved toward the blacksmith.

Marvin continued, "Anyways, I 'ad jus' walked into de shop dere an' Kaboom! I didn't see nuttin'. I dropped down on my knees, closed my eyes tight and prayed to de Lawd." Etta noticed some of the young men cut their eyes as if to laugh. "Jus' knowed Jesus wuz comin'.

"Dem boys dere wuz out back."

Jack turned on Anna, sneering. "What about you? Where were you?"

Anna, looking down, shruggged. "I wuz dere in de greenhouses finishin' de cleanup w'en I heard it. Like Marvin, I t'ink hit wuz Jesus fuh sho. I call out, 'Praise de Lawd.'"

Jack gave a short, derisive laugh, got close and stared into her face. "What if I tell you that somebody say they saw you sneakin' 'round out there about the time this happened?"

Anna looked up, rolled her eyes and stared back down, shaking her head. "Dey hab' tuh be lyin', Suh. Must'uh been dem dat done hit, an' dey tryin' tuh blame me." She shrugged and glanced up, eyes wide. "Whut reason I got tuh do sumpin lack dat?"

Cap'n Jack's eyes narrowed, and he stared back at her. He opened his mouth but didn't speak. He looked over at two men standing together. "What did you boys see?"

"Nuttin', Suh. I mean, uh, Suh. Nuttin', Suh. We wuz out at de corral hookin' some mules to uh wagon w'en we heard de noise."

Jack looked over at the other man.

"We, uh-- I ain't seen nuttin', Suh." He shuffled his feet. "Suh, I did take a close look at dem oxen, an' one uh 'em been bleedin' on his rump pretty bad. Don't know whut cause hit 'xactly. Look like he been stuck wid sumpin."

Cap'n Jack looked back at Anna, who was still looking down.

Someone from the group volunteered. "Maybe hit wuz a bee or a wasp."

Cap'n Jack's head swiveled toward the man. He raised his whip and yelled at him. "Anybody ask you to talk?"

"Suh, well, you …"

"Wadn't no god-damned bee!" He paced around, frowning for several moments. "I ain't done with this. I'll be sending for some of you to come to my office and answer some more questions."

He glared around. "Now, one more thing. This ain't nobody else's business. Ain't no need for anybody to know nothin' about it. If I hear

193

about it from somebody else, this whole bunch gon be whipped." He shook the whip at the group. "You hear me?"

They nodded their heads, shuffled their feet, and spoke strongly. "Yassuh! Yassuh! We unuhstan'. Sho does."

Jack looked at everyone in turn except Etta, spun on his heel and stalked out.

The next morning Hester came by the greenhouse. "How is yuh doin' dis moanin', Honey? I jus' t'ink I'd come over heah an' see fuh mysef whut hit is yuh do all day."

Etta was raking the dirt floor of the greenhouse. "Grandma! Sure didn't 'xpect to see you dis morning." She kept raking. "I reckon dey gon send me out to de fields any day, but dat's awright."

Hester came over and hugged Etta, held her back and looked in her face. "How yuh doin'?"

Etta stood still and met her gaze. "I'm awright for de time bein', Grandma."

Cap'n Jack walked in quickly and looked at Etta. "I need you in my …" He stopped as he recognized Hester, frowning at her.

Hester released Etta and turned to face Cap'n Jack. She moved directly between he and Etta and raised her right hand toward Jack, palm out. She closed her fingers except for her forefinger. She wagged the long, crooked finger left and right as she stepped toward him, staring straight into his eyes.

He leaned back, turning red. "What …"

She took one more step, and Cap'n Jack bolted out a side door.

194

Hester dropped her hand and turned back to Etta. "I t'ink he got de message." Hester looked around the barn and smiled. "Let me know if'ns he boduhs yuh anymoh."

Etta blinked and nodded. "Yassum."

Hester walked out the same door that Jack had taken.

Etta stood with her mouth open. *I nebuh seen nuttin' like dat before in my life. Can't believe it, but he was scared. Wonduh if it'll last?*

Etta was not approached by Cap'n Jack the next day. The next week she was given a hoe and a section of the field that was her responsibility. She worked for 10 days chopping weeds from around the cotton plants and pulling soil around the plants for support against storms. *Dey say dis is de las' hoein' dis year. Bolls look like dey 'bout tuh bust open. Maybe it'll be cooler when we start picking.* Etta took out a red bandana and wiped her brow. *Already hot today an' ain't nowhere near noon.*

She looked down at her hands, her right one wrapped in a bloodstained cloth. *Didn't think I'd get blisters aftuh all de work I been doin'.*

She looked up. Who dat comin' dis way. Etta leaned on her hoe for a moment, staring. *Dat's Lazarus! Better get back to work.* Etta dropped her head and started hoeing.

In a few minutes, Lazarus walked up and came right to the point. "Cap'n Jack wants yuh tuh come tuh 'is office." He turned around and walked off.

Etta stomped her foot. *Damnation! I thought he might leave me alone. I know he needs somebody to read for 'im.* She slowly followed Lazarus back to the barn. *Maybe Grandma done put de fear of God or de fear of*

195

sumpin in 'im, and we can jus' do de work. Etta shook her head as she
moved her 'wooden' feet in a shuffle toward the barn.

Cap'n Jack was all business. That afternoon he told her to come by his
office every morning unless he told her otherwise. Things went fine for a
week, but then Jack began to stand close to Etta as she sat at the little table.
He hadn't touched her, and Etta had not mentioned it to Hester.

Early one afternoon, Etta was standing with Charlene and several other
women. They took turns with the ladle, drinking water that had been brought
out to them. Charlene was looking back toward the barn. "Here comes
Lazarus, Etta. Yuh might as well go on. Yuh know he's comin' fuh yuh."

Etta gave her head a strong shake. "Why don't you go fuh me today,
Charlene?"

Charlene started laughing. "Nooo, dat won't do. He don't t'ink I'm
pretty 'nuf for dat wurk. She pursed her lips. "Don't belieb anybody could
do dat wurk but you."

No one else spoke.

Lazarus had gotten close enough that he crooked his finger at Etta.

She lifted her head to him, then turned to Charlene. "You don' think I
rather be out heah hoein', den you is a crazy bird!"

Etta dragged herself off after Lazarus but not before hearing Charlene,
still laughing, say just loud enough for her to hear, "Dey gon be some moh
white babies runnin' 'round heah b'fo' long."

Etta clenched her teeth. *I ought to go back dere an' beat de tar out'uh
her fuh dat.* But she kept going. Glumly, she entered the barn and turned
toward the office. As she approached the interior door, she sniffed and

196

jerked her head up. *Dat smell like whiskey!* She stopped outside the doorway, but he had seen her movement.

Cap'n Jack was sitting at his desk examining a piece of paper. He looked around. "Come in and shut the door." He smiled broadly at Etta, showing his tobacco-stained teeth. "Wilson done give me a raise. He told me he was sending me a letter, raising my pay, and I think this is it." He held up a single sheet of paper. "Read it to me." He handed it over to Etta and leaned back in his chair, his hands behind his head.

Etta took the paper and read it back to him, giving the amount that Cap'n Jack would be paid. The last paragraph was, "I like the way things are going. Keep up the good work."

Jack stopped smiling and stared at Etta. "You keep your damn mouth shut about this now, you hear?"

"Yassuh. Is dat all, Suh?" Etta put the letter on the desk and turned just slightly toward the door.

Cap'n Jack picked up a glass, swirled the amber liquid and held it high. "Here, take this." He handed the glass to her. "What's your rush?" He poured a quantity of whiskey into another glass. "Don't be so quick to leave the party. You need to stay and help me celebrate."

Etta took the glass, holding it in front of her. She looked down into it, her mind working feverishly. "Yassuh." *Damn, I wish I had told Grandma he was botherin' me again.*

"Why so glum? I should share. You'd like a new dress, now wouldn't you?"

"Uhh, Nawsuh." She grimaced and bit her tongue.

He sat his drink down and stood up. His eyes narrowed, and he leaned toward her, his breath hard to take. "You sassin' me?"

Etta surveyed her bare toes. "Nawsuh!" She inched away from him to the left of the desk.

Cap'n Jack tossed back his head. "Come here!"

She didn't move. He gave an uncoordinated lunge at her, trying to grab her shoulder and pull her to him. She instinctively sprang back, and all he caught was the front of her dress, ripping the thin material, scratching her chest, and breaking the sinew holding her grandfather's relic.

Etta fell back heavily on the small wood heater, dropping the glass. Steadying herself and trying to stand, her right hand fell on the heaviest of the handmade stove tools. She covered herself with her left hand, feeling her neck.

He sneered at her. "Guess you'll need a dress after all. You know, I been thinking. We just can't have a slave as smart as you not raisin' any babies, now can we? Bad for business. That's some work we can take care of right now."

I'm trapped. What am I gon do? Think. There was the strong smell of whiskey on his breath as time stood still. There was a small puff of air in her face, and now a strong odor of the swamp filled her nose. Etta felt the heft of the stove tool in her right hand. She took a deep breath, and her mind settled. She looked up directly in Cap'n Jack's face. "I'll help wid de work, Suh. Jus' don't touch me, an' we'll get a lot done. Suh."

Etta watched as Cap'n Jack's face registered shock, then confusion. She watched him closely. *He know he got to have my help.*

198

His face turned deep red. "Ain't no god-damned nigger gal gon talk to me like that!" He lunged for her, both hands reaching for her neck. Etta stepped to her right and hit him solidly with the stove tool just above his left ear. He went down on his desk like a sack of feed. He lay on his side, his head against the back wall. Breath left his body in a long groan, and he rolled more onto his stomach, drooling from his open mouth, and blood dripping from his nose.

Etta stared down at him and took a deep breath. His head now hung off the back left edge of the desk, his bald spot obvious. She looked at the tool in her hand. It appeared to be an extra-long railroad spike bent into an "L" shape on one end. Looking back at him, she raised her arm again, paused, and tossed the heavy metal bar onto the desk next to Jack's body. *I think I done kilt 'im.*

She put her hand to her neck, again feeling it. She looked at Jack's hands, then the floor around the desk. She picked up the shark tooth and put it in her pocket. Looking down again at the lifeless form of Jack, her hand came to her mouth. *Dey gon kill me for sure. Ain't gon get no whippin' for dis. Gon be a hangin'.*

Chapter 20

Etta stepped into the barn, glad no one was there. She slipped out a side
door. Her pace quickened as she crossed the road and headed toward her
mother's cabin. *Slow down now! Walk natural! Don't give nobody no
reason for alarm.* Frowning, she looked back toward the barn, expecting an
outcry. Her brain kept screaming to her legs, "RUN," but she maintained her
pace.

She still heard no reaction as she approached the cabin, relieved to see
her mother still cleaning up from serving dinner. Etta looked around
carefully as she hurried up, still holding the top of the torn dress. "Mama, I
got to talk to you."

"Wai..,"

Etta took her mother's arm and pulled her toward the cabin. At the steps, she looked around carefully, then turned. "Mama, I done kilt Cap'n Jack."

Rachel jerked back, and her eyes and mouth flew open. "You done WHAT?"

"Be quiet, Mama." Etta looked around again.

Rachel noticed Etta trying to hold up the torn dress, and she saw the scratches that Cap'n Jack's fingernails had left on her neck and chest. "Oh, Gawd. Oh, Gawd." She put her hands on Etta's shoulders. "What did he do to you?"

Etta gave a quick headshake. "I stopped him, Mama. I stopped him good dis time."

Rachel burst out crying, hugging Etta. "Oh, Baby. Oh, Baby. What we gon do?"

Etta pushed her mother back. "I know where we can go. Be safe for a while."

Her mother looked wildly around. "You sure? I'll go to Thomas."

"No, I ain't gon do dat, but you do what you think's right. I got a chaince but got to get on de move."

Rachel stared off in space for a moment. "We got tuh go tuh PawPaw."

Etta shook her head. "Ain't nuttin' he can do 'bout dis. I know a place I can go. Help me get what I need."

Etta began moving around briskly. "Come on, Mama. Get dat bucket over dere. Wrap up all de food yuh got cooked. Get dat butcher knife. Put all dat in de bucket. Get dat lantern."

Folding up an oiled tablecloth and a dress she had taken off the clothesline, Etta looked up at her mother. "Didn't mean to get you and Matthew into dis mess. You do what you think is right, but I ain't waitin' 'round heah for de hangin' party." She took another knife and cut down the clothesline, balled it up and threw it in the bucket.

Rachel stood still and looked off, then back. She looked at Matthew and shook her head. "Awright, we comin' wid you. Tell me what we need to do."

Etta pointed under the cabin. "Get dem old sweet taters and some white taters, too. Grab some canned goods. Put 'em in dat croaker sack. Get dat box of matches and bag of meal. Dey can go in de sack."

Etta went in the cabin, got her Harper's and money and put them in the sack. Stepping outside, she restrung the fossil, kissed it, and tied it back around her neck. She grabbed up Matthew and his blanket and looked around at her mother. "Let's go."

Rachel looked at the cabin, shook her head and turned away slowly. "Where we goin'?"

Etta was already walking away. "I'll show you. Come on."

Rachel opened her mouth to ask more questions, but Etta was already headed into the fields and toward the beach.

Etta scanned the fields as she walked, moving fast. *Lord, I hope we can make it to de beach widout bein'seen.*

She looked over her shoulder. "Mama, don't be starin' back dere. Come on now, look at where you're walkin'. Stay in de path." *Hope she don't give up on me. Good. She keepin' up.*

As they were getting close to the beach, the paths between the fields began to give out. Just before the dunes, there was a thin row of hardwoods edged by stunted pines. "Come on, Mama. Etta led a straight line through the trees toward the dunes and the beach. At the top of the dunes, she and her mother leaned on each other, breathing deeply. Etta looked back, shaking her head. *I need to cover dem tracks. I hate to take de time, but dey sure a give-away.*

"Mama, put your stuff down and hold Matthew for a minute." She held him out, then went back down the dune. She broke off a pine limb and began rubbing out the footprints as she backed her way up the dune. At the top, she stood up and took Matthew back. "Go on, Mama. Go straight toward de water. I'm comin'."

As her mother left, Etta picked up the pine limb again and began brushing out their tracks on top of the dune. Suddenly, she stood up straight. *What was dat?* Etta heard a faint shout in the direction of Tabby Landing, then another.

She took only brief swipes at their tracks down the backside of the dune. She hurried to her mother, standing at the water's edge, and threw the limb into the ocean. "Good, it's low tide. Let's go."

Rachel blinked, not moving. "Go where?"

Etta pointed up the beach. "North. Dat way. No time to waste. Come on. Stay way down close to de water for right now." Etta moved quickly up the beach.

Her mother followed, calling out. "Yeah, but where we goin'?"

Etta stopped, looked behind them, waiting for Rachel to catch up. They continued walking side by side. "We're headed to Blackbeard Island." Etta shifted Matthew to her other side. "We got a long walk north."

She set a strong pace, and her mother kept up. She looked over at her daughter. "How we gon get over to Blackbeard?"

Etta glanced up. "Dere's a boat dere dat I know 'bout."

They strode on, heads down, a warm wind on their back. "Honey, tell me what happened."

Etta grimaced. "Aww, he was drunk. Mr. Thomas gib' 'im a raise, for God's sake, an' he wanted to celebrate by carryin' on wid me. Wanted me to drink wid 'im. Said he was gon see to it dat I 'ad 'is baby." She raised her eyebrows at her mother. "I jus' warn't gon go long wid dat. I tol' 'im dat to 'is face. He didn't take it too good. Tried to choke me. Hadn't been for de whiskey, he mighta had de good sense to jus' leave me alone. Jus' take 'is raise and go buy what he was lookin' for."

Etta looked back at her mother. "He went for my throat, an' I hit 'im up side de head wid a stove iron."

Rachel brought her hand to her mouth. "You sure you kilt 'im?"

"Looked dead to me." She shook her head. "Didn't see no breathin', but I didn't stay 'round long to check neither."

Rachel looked down, shook her head and spoke in a quiet, emotionless voice. "Dey gon string us up for sure." She looked back toward Tabby Landing and swallowed hard.

Etta shifted Matthew higher on her hip. "Let's keep movin'." They slipped past the cutoff to the Main House, continuing north. Weighed down

204

by fear, Matthew, and their meager supplies, they trudged up the endless beach.

Etta looked around. "We gettin' close to de creek. I believe dat's it up ahead." The tide was rising.

"Come up to de woods heah, Mama." Etta's eyes frantically searched the edge of the trees. "Thank God. Dere it is." Etta lay Matthew down, and they wrestled the long, narrow, dugout canoe out of the brush, across the short beach, and into the edge of the water.

Etta looked around the area where the boat had been turned upside down. She handed her mother a homemade paddle and took another. She picked up the large bamboo pole for pushing the boat in shallow water, and a smaller, cane fishing pole. Putting those items in the boat, she went into the clearing and grabbed some things they had used to play house.

Etta, Matthew on her hip, stood in the edge of the water, holding the boat as her mother got in and kneeled in the front.

Etta handed Matthew over, took a long look down the empty beach, shoved the canoe firmly into the current and jumped in. She picked up a paddle and began to use it strongly. It was now about a hundred yards straight across to Blackbeard, but she allowed the current to push them to the left, toward the mainland.

Kneeling, Rachel held Matthew in one arm and clutched the side of the canoe with the other. She looked back at her daughter. "What can I do, Honey?"

"You're fine, Mama. I can do dis." She aimed for the back of Blackbeard. Looking behind and to her left, she could see where the river came out of the mainland behind Bonita Island. *Anybody on de river could see us right now. Need to get to some cover.* As they slipped behind Blackbeard, the swamp closed in, and they were soon out of sight of the river and the mainland. The incoming tide now helped a great deal as they moved up a small creek. The water shallowed. Etta put down the paddle, picked up the pole and stood up. She poled their way toward the center of the mile-wide, five-mile-long island.

Rachel relaxed her grip on the side of the canoe and sat up a bit more normally. "When did you learn how to handle a boat?"

Etta continued to focus on the poling. "Dere was a lots of things I did dat you didn't know 'bout." As they continued, the channel became less and less obvious, and they were in a general swamp. There were large, light-colored trees with thin, cedar-like foliage growing right in the shallow parts of the black water. These trees had large cone bases that tapered sharply upward in the first 10 feet to create a more typical-looking trunk. The roots of the trees seem to have recoiled from the mud as if it were painful to touch, creating formidable protrusions or 'knees' rising from the water around the base of the trees. Etta followed a treeless curve in the swamp that defined the deeper water in the run of the creek. Sand hummocks began to appear on their right, the largest of these supporting palmetto and moss-draped hardwoods.

With a frightening croak and noisy wings, a huge, blue-tinted bird took flight. It frightened them so badly, they almost overturned the canoe. Etta retrieved the pole she dropped and continued their progress up the creek.

After coming around several large trees on their left, Rachel gave a muffled scream. A large alligator slipped from a hummock into the water in front of them. Rachel swiveled and looked at her daughter in terror. "You goin' right over 'im! He gon kill us an' eat us fuh sho!"

Etta's eyes were big, but she managed to stammer, "It's all right, Mama. It won't bother us." *We've seen 'em up heah lots, but I ain't never been right over de top of one like dis.* Rachel clutched Matthew to her and scanned the water for the coming attack. All was calm.

After a couple of turns and more work with the pole, Etta noticed a higher bank up ahead. Mud extended about halfway up the side of the bank, but the top was sandy and covered with leaves and limbs from the oaks and bays that grew there. Etta nodded toward the bank. "Dat's where we goin'. Dat place almos' an island in de middle of de swamp."

Her mother examined the area.

Etta slowed the canoe. "Dere's 'bout a hundred acres of land in heah, I reckon. A trail over dere." Etta pointed. "It goes all de way to de beach." She pushed them up against the bank to their right. Just in front of them, Rachel could see a current of water boiling up from the bottom of the swamp.

"Awright, Mama, we heah."

Rachel, still holding Matthew, struggled to get out.

"Wait a minute." Etta hopped out on the creek side of the canoe and held it firmly against the bank. "Put Matthew down in the boat; I'll get 'im." Etta steadied the canoe as she waded down to the front. She picked up Matthew and handed him up to their mother, who was standing on top of the bank. Etta pulled the end of the canoe up on a flat lip of soil, stepped out of the creek and began to remove what they had brought.

Rachel looked around at their new home. Turning and walking over to her right, she called out to her daughter. "What's dis over heah?"

Etta looked around. "Edward told me dat de Indians built it. From what Grandma Hester say, it was prolly Grandpa Chocu. He loved to come up heah to hunt an' fish. He still love it heah." The wind stirred in the large trees. She glanced up and smiled.

Rachel walked around and stared at the eight-by-eight-foot platform. Holding Matthew in one arm, she pushed on the boards of the flooring to see if they would hold any weight.

Etta stacked everything from the boat out on the sand bank and looked around. "It ain't a chikee 'xactly, but I reckon he could get dem boards from de sawmill. Must be cut from dis wood heah." She pointed over her shoulder with her thumb at one of the trees with the protruding roots. It don't rot."

Rachel frowned and stared at her daughter. "Weh you learn all dat stuff from? Edward tell you dat?"

Etta gave a weak smile and shook her head. "Naw. Grandma taught me 'bout cypress. Chikees, too."

She and her mother continued to examine the structure. It was built between some huge trees with a floor that was about two or three feet off the ground. The roof structure had fallen in.

Rachel cleared some debris from the floor and lay Matthew down on his back. He began kicking and fussing. "I got to feed 'im. Don't 'membuh when I fed' im las'." Carefully, Rachel sat down, took Matthew in her arms, pulled her dress off her left shoulder, offering him a swollen breast. Etta watched as Matthew began to kick, moving his face around in frantic joy, searching for the nipple. Soon he was drinking and cooing.

208

Rachel leaned over against one of the trees supporting the structure. "How'd you ever find dis place?"

Etta was bringing their supplies over to the shelter. "Edward came heah several times wid 'is daddy. He liked it so much dat he begged his daddy for dat boat. You know he got whatever he wanted." They both nodded their heads.

"After he got dat, we'd come over heah when we had time. You an' Miss Frances be gettin' ready for some to-do; me and Edward be up heah." She emptied the bucket and stepped back into the creek.

Rachel sat up. "Where you goin'? What you doin'? Dere's gators out dere."

Etta looked back at her mother. "Be right back. De bes' thing 'bout dis place is de boilin' spring. Give us all de fresh water we need. She waded out to where the current came up from the bottom of the creek. Dipping her bucket right down in that hole, she collected a gallon of fresh water. "You can do without food for a long time, but you can't go far without good water."

Wading back, she stepped up out of the creek and carried the bucket back to her mother. She filled two cups with water. "Here you go, Mama." They both drank their cups dry. Etta dipped them another.

Sitting her cup down, Etta pulled her wet, torn dress over her head and hung it over a dead limb. She slipped on the dry one. "Ooh, dat feels better."

Rachel looked over at Etta. "Who all knows 'bout dis place?"

209

Etta walked over and leaned against the structure next to her mother. "Well, s'pose dey a few, but Edward de only one dat knows dat I know 'bout it."

Etta looked around. "We like de Ebo, Mama. We can live heah 'til we find some place to go."

Her mother shook her head but said nothing.

Etta leaned back and folded her arms. "We're gon figure out something, Mama."

Rachel and Etta looked down at Matthew. He was sound asleep. His milk-encrusted chin quivered.

Etta took the tablecloth, folded and laid it on the ground. She took Matthew from her mother and laid him on the oilcloth.

They sat in the front of the structure, toes touching the ground. The light was fading on the day. Etta glanced at her mother. "I'm thinkin' of buildin' a fire."

"Why you gon do dat? Somebody might see it."

"I got a idea 'bout dat." She started digging a large hole on top of the bank. "I'm gon build it down in dis hole. We need some coals."

"What do we need coals for?"

Etta continued her work. "You hear dat hum?"

Rachel turned her head to the side. "Yeah. What is dat?"

"Dat's mosquitoes. Dey apt to be bad out heah after dark." Etta broke a quantity of small, dry twigs into the hole and stacked larger pieces over the twigs. She pulled a paper label off a can, stuck it under the twigs and lit it, adding more wood as the fire caught.

Rachel picked up Matthew, laid him on his back on their platform, and changed his diaper.

Etta took the dirty cotton rag, washed it in the creek and hung it on the dead limb next to her dress. She fed the fire, then let it burn.

Etta leaned against the chikee. "Mama, would you wash off a couple of dem sweet taters?" Her mother took the two largest and walked back down the creek. "You know dese are last year's taters."

Etta glanced up. "Watch out for cottonmoufs."

"What?" Her mother stepped back and looked around.

"Dey a lot uh cottonmouf moccasins out heah." Etta scooped up coals in a metal cup and stirred the fire. "Edward say dat dey won't boduh you if you don't boduh dem, but I was always 'fraid of steppin' on one."

"Dey stay close to de water, out on a low limb over de creek or laying on de bank. Dey short an' heavy for a snake. One time I walked up on one over dere." She pointed down the creek. "And he reared up like one of dem snakes in India dat dey keep in dem baskets. He open up an' show me his fangs an' dat white mouf of his.

"Edward say dey do dat to scare you. Sure worked on me. Just watch and don't get too close to one. If you in de boat, don't get under no low limbs. Edward say he got one in de boat wid 'im like dat one time."

Eyes big, looking around, Rachel carefully slipped down to the water's edge and washed off the potatoes. "You got any ideas 'bout where we can go from heah?"

Etta pulled several handfuls of the moss hanging from nearby trees and stuffed it down into the cup with the coals. She sat it on the upwind side of Matthew. "No, Mama, not really."

211

Rachel put the potatoes down and leaned against the platform, sipping her water. "We need to get word to Mama and see if she can help us, but I ain't sure how we gon do dat."

Etta took the potatoes and walked back to the fire. "Yassum, I been thinking dat, too. I figure our best hope is wait heah 'til de paddyrollers and de sheriff ain't out looking for us so hard. In a week or so, after dark, we might slip into town an' get to Grandma's. She may know a place we can be safe, at least 'til we can get up North somehow."

Etta took the potatoes, dug a hole in the hot coals with a stick and buried them. She and her mother slapped mosquitoes and nibbled on raw vegetables and fried chicken as they waited for the potatoes to cook. Etta made another little smoker and sat it on the floor of the structure.

The wind stirred the trees again. Etta looked up. "He's wid us, Mama."

Rachel gave a startled look around. "What you talkin' 'bout? Who's wid us?"

Etta rubbed the shark's tooth between her fingers. "Chocu's wid us. He's wid me lots. I hear 'im in de breeze. Sometimes he sings Indian songs to me jus' to make me feel better."

Her mother gave her a tight smile and a deep shrug. "I sure hope you is right 'bout dat."

Though full, they spent a restless night huddled in their shelter. The next morning, Etta got up and nibbled on some cold, fried cornbread. "Come on, Mama, we got to fix dis place up some. You know it's likely to rain dis afternoon dis time of year." Etta began cutting palmetto fronds and stacking them on the floor of the open-air structure.

212

"Would you go cut all de palmetto you can find? I'll be right back." Etta picked up the butcher knife. She pointed. "De other knife's over dere." She walked up a trail away from the creek, back through the large trees. *I think dey was back up in heah somuhs. Dere dey is. Hoping dey was still heah.* She walked over to a small canebrake where she and Edward had cut fishing poles years earlier. She cut two large canes and 10 or 12 smaller ones, trimming the small tufts of leaves off the side and cutting them all about 12 feet long. She dragged the large bundle back to camp.

She and her mother created a frame over the platform, using rope to secure the canes to the trees and then spacing the canes about a foot apart. With the frame complete, Etta began laying the palmetto fronds in rows, starting on the lower side. Her mother continued bringing more fronds. After some time, they both stood back and examined their work.

Rachel tilted her head. "Looks pretty good to me. Maybe it'll keep us dry. Where did you learn 'bout makin' a roof out'uh cane and palametuh?"

"Grandma told me 'bout her and Grandpa's 'chikee. I 'specially asked her 'bout de roof, what dey did 'bout rain. She told me how dey used palmetto, but it prolly ain't done 'xactly right." She walked around, looking closely. "Hope dem fronds don't blow off. We'll see."

Etta leaned against the platform and looked around. Shortly, she announced, "I'm gon try to catch us some dinner." She took a small pot they had brought and began looking under rotten vegetation for fish bait. After tearing apart a log, several large, white larvae rolled out. Etta grabbed them eagerly. Looking under a log in the mud, she found a salamander and several large energetic earthworms. Taking the fishing pole they had brought, Etta tied one end of the boat to a small bush. She then sat in the back of the boat and threw the baited hook in some of the deeper holes of water she could reach. Soon she called out, "I got one, Mama!"

Rachel, carrying Matthew, walked over to the creek bank. "How you gon cook it?"

"I'm not sure 'bout dat yet." Etta dropped the large bream in the bottom of the boat. It flopped around loudly. In a short time, Etta had caught two more bream and a large catfish. *Be careful. Dem spines are danejus.* She strung the fish through the gills on a green willow limb, slipped down the boat and stepped out.

Rachel reached out. "I'll take dose. You usin' palametuhs got me thinkin'. I 'membuh somethin' Mama would do sometime when we went fishin' to de creek."

Watching carefully for snakes, Rachel took the fish to a log on the creek bank. She began to scale the bream and gut them all. She looked around. "Honey, would you buil' me a fiuh in de pit dere?"

Etta built a fire. Rachel put the fish in a pan, and they waited for the fire to burn down.

"Wish I had some oil; wouldn't have to do dis. Hope I 'membuh an' do dis right. Go cut me 'bout four palametuhs."

She kneeled down next to the fire and, with a stick, began to spread the coals out on the bottom of the pit. She dug up a large double handful of sand and began to spread it about an inch deep over the coals. "Hand me dat cup." She took the cup and poured a small quantity of water onto the sand.

Etta put the fronds next to her. Rachel put one on top of the sand, then another. She took the fish, spread them on the fronds and then covered them with two more palmettos, followed by another layer of sand. Soon steam

214

was wafting through the sand. In a half hour or so, Rachel began to carefully rake the top layer of sand off and then slip the palmettos off the fish. She placed the steamed fish into a pan and took it over to the platform. They pulled the meat off the bones and ate it with their fingers.

Etta stared into the pan. "Didn't realize how hungry I was. Dis sure is good, Mama."

That night, Etta built a larger fire and used the bucket to boil water.

Her mother added vegetables and filleted out the fish Etta had caught that afternoon. She chopped up the fish and added it to the stew. After an hour's cooking, they served up two large bowls.

They sat on the platform and ate. "Dis ain't such a bad place now, is it, Mama? How long do you think we ought to wait before we try to get to Grandma's?"

Rachel shrugged. "Dem fish you catchin' hep a lot, but I reckon some hunter or uduh fisherman gon come up heah 'ventually."

Etta frowned and nodded slowly. "Yeah, it wouldn't surprise me none."

Rachel took some bones from her mouth and tossed them toward the creek. "I bet dey watchin' Mama's place, but dey ain't gon do dat long. If we could stay heah 10 days, prolly be a lot safer trying to slip into town."

On the afternoon of their third day, Etta was fishing from the bank, and Rachel was cleaning up Matthew when they heard a faint but melodious sound carrying across the water.

Etta dropped her pole and ran to her mother, taking her by the arms. "Mama, dat's de sound of a hound gettin' a scent! It ain't rained since we were over dere. Betcha dey done got our scent where we dragged de boat out'uh de woods."

Etta envisioned a hanging party, rope in hand, staring across the tidal creek toward Blackbeard Island. "Dey prolly ain't got no boat wid 'em. Let's get our things an' get out'uh heah."

Rachel clutched Matthew, her eyes wide. "Where we gon go?"

"We'll hide out somewhere 'til dark and try to get to Grandma's. Dey'll prolly search de beach first. Since we came in by boat, dey won't get our scent 'til dey find dis place. Can't risk stayin' heah long."

They began collecting their few possessions. Suddenly there was a loud squawk, and a large heron flew right over their camp. Rachel cried out, "Ohh, dat scared me."

Etta dropped her head, and tears flowed. "Dey got us, Mama. Dey comin' up de creek, or dat bird wouldn't flew toward us like dat." Etta spoke wearily. "Take Matthew and run to de beach. It's me dey after."

Rachel stared back at Etta. Her lips moved, but there were no words.

CHAPTER 21

"Etta! Etta!" She whirled around, staring back down the creek. She could see Dan in the front of a large, dugout canoe. He called out again and motioned to her. "Etta! Come on!" She could see Edward in the back, using a push pole.

Etta's heart soared. "Dan! Dan!" She ran to them.

Dan jumped out of the canoe and pulled it up on the creek bank. Edward scrambled forward and out of the boat. Dan turned to Etta as she bear-hugged him. "I jus' knew we was done for."

Rachel rushed up. "How did you know where we wuz?"

Edward looked around. "We'll talk on the way. We got to get y'all out'uh heah. Leave everything like it is. When they find this spot and that boat, they'll think you're still on Blackbeard. It'll take 'em a while to search this whole island. That'll give us some time."

217

Etta ran back to the camp, grabbed the shoulder sack and stuffed in a rag for Matthew. "Grab dat paddle, Mama."

Dan and Edward held the boat as they got in and sat in the middle. Dan pushed his end of the canoe into the current. It swung around as Edward controlled the rear.

Etta looked up at Dan. "How'd you know where we were?"

Dan began paddling forward and spoke over his shoulder. "Well, Edward de one dat figured dat out, but let me start hit frum de beginnin'."

Etta picked up her paddle and began to help. *Looks like Dan's learned to use a paddle pretty good.*

Dan glanced back. "Dis moanin' Miss Medina come by de sto, ax'd tuh talk tuh me. Dey let 'er take me aside. She tol' me whut happen. I ain't had no idea. Tol' me dat if I could get 'way frum de sto, tuh go fin' Edward, ax' 'im if'ns he'll hep fin' yuh an' hide yuh. I slipped 'way an' headed tuh Bonita."

Edward spoke up. "I was in Brunswick yesterday when I heard the news. I heard, Rachel, that it was you that nailed Ol' Jack. I went straight home, remembering that Daddy was up in Savannah. I made the afternoon ferry, rode down to Tabby Landing and talked to Anna. She told me the whole story.

"This morning I rode to the North End. I thought I knew where you had gone. I saw that you had taken the boat, so I knew for sure then where y'all were.

"When I got back to the Main House, Jack and a bunch of his friends..."

Rachel and Etta whirled around and spoke in unison, "WHAT?" Etta added, "Cap'n Jack ain't dead?"

218

Edward and Dan looked at each other. Edward responded, "No. They found him stumbling around, talking out of his head, and took him to the doctor in town. Man at the Main House told me they had wanted to keep him at the hospital there, but Jack walked out this morning and started getting a patrol together to search for you.

"Daddy isn't going to like it that he didn't wait for him to get there. Course, I'm not sure he has got the word even now."

Edward shook his head and gave her a tight smile. "Jack still got a big bandage on his head where you hit 'im. The patrol had just gotten to the Main House from the noon ferry. They had bloodhounds with 'em, and I figured we might not have much time. Y'all hear them dogs?"

Etta nodded. "Yeah. They know we over heah. Where you takin' us?"

Dan and Edward were quiet. Finally, Edward spoke. "We don't have a place really. I'm hoping that Medina's got an idea. I know it's dangerous, but that's where we're headed. Right after dark."

Etta furrowed her brow. *Maybe Grandma and dem women will come up wid somethin'.*

Edward put down the pole and picked up a paddle. "Had to push Caliph hard to get back down to Tabby Landing to catch the ferry back. Then as I was getting off the ferry, Dan was on the dock waiting. He had missed the noon ferry.

Dan looked back and smiled at Etta.

She returned his smile.

219

Edward continued. "We needed a boat, a big boat and some way to carry it. We went back to Gile's store. You better watch this one, Etta. He's got a silver tongue."

Dan grinned at him.

Edward paddled hard. "I stood outside and listened as he talked to Giles. Dan said something like, 'Howdy, Suh.'"

"I heard Giles say, 'Where you been, Boy?'"

"He said something like, 'Well, Suh, 'bout noon Mr. Simmons come down heah. You knows dat man whut buy dat big porcelin stove frum us? He lookin' fuh yuh, and we cain't fin' yuh nowehs.'"

"Giles say, 'What about 'im?'"

"He in a foul mood. Want us to come pick up dat stove."

"What?"

"Say he ain't happy wid hit. I knowed yuh won' lack dat. I went down dere and tried tuh hep 'em get hit tuh work. De stove pipe ain't done right. I'm gon be down dere fuh a while, head up in dat chimney, I reckon, 'less you want tuh go."

"Uh, naw. Naw."

"I'll be down dere hepin' 'im, if'n dat's awright wid yuh? Gon get some uh dis stove pipe heah."

"Yeah, alright. Go on back down there then. Take all the stove pipe you need."

Edward started laughing. "That Dan is something. He kept on. 'One moh t'ing, Massuh. Dat man Simmons made me promise to bring de wagon back down dere in case we cain' t fix dat stove, an' I have tuh bring hit back.'"

220

"'Well, alright then, take the wagon, but do whatever it takes to fix that stove.'"

Dan looked around smiling. "See, I know weh he go at dinner time. Lot uh days he go get de red light special down at Effie's, spen' time layin' 'round an' talkin' to de gals. He know I know whut's goin' on. Fact too, dat man wouldn't hit a lick at a snake."

Edward laughed. "Anyway, Dan got the wagon and picked me up at the end of the alley. I knew where there was a boat, and the man wouldn't miss it before we got it back."

They were out of the swamp and paddling north in the sound between Blackbeard and the mainland. Dan spoke in a low voice. "Let's be quiet now. Talk low. May be fishermen out heah."

Dan looked around at the group. "Maybe you two oughtuh lay down in de boat. Me and Massuh Wilson heah is jus' out fishin' our ownse'fs." He looked back at Edward. "We prolly need tuh slow down too, paddle slow, like we on a outin'."

Edward nodded and slowed his paddling.

Etta put down the paddle. She and her mother put Matthew between them and lay down below the gunnels of the boat.

Edward scanned up the mainland shore, northward. "The wagon is just south of Shellman's Bluff. We got a short stretch of open water where there will be some pretty good waves. There's a tarp spread above the beach, so we can see where to go. We thought we'd wait in the woods until dark before we go any further."

Etta lay on her side, Dan kneeling in front of her and Edward sitting in the back.

221

Edward looked around carefully. "Dan, let's start moving to the left, closer to the mainland, before we clear the back of Blackbeard." Past the end of Blackbeard, they began to get more wind and swells. "Stay outside the breakers for now."

Dan stared ahead. "I see the tarp. It's a ways up."

"Alright. We'll ride the waves in when we get straight out from the tarp."

Rachel looked up at him, then took Matthew back in her lap as the boat bucked. "Lord have mercy, I hope we don't turn obuh."

Etta reached out her arms, "Here Mama, let me have Matthew."

Rachel's eyes were big. "You know I cain't swim."

Dan glanced back at her. "Me neiduh."

Edward looked serious. "This boat is overloaded, but I think we'll be alright. If we do turn over or take in lots of water, grab the boat and hold on. The waves'll wash it into shallow water."

He was paddling hard. "When I give the word, Dan, we'll turn the boat toward the tarp. Paddle for all you're worth. The faster we're going, the better off we'll be."

Dan, looking grim, nodded.

They paddled a while longer. "All right. NOW!

As Etta watched, holding on to Matthew and the boat, they turned a sharp left, toward the beach. A swell caught them, lifting the rear and throwing the nose down, but it out ran the boat, and they fell back.

"Come on, paddle!" Edward urged.

Etta looked down at Matthew. *I ought to be paddlin', too.* The next swell lifted the boat and caught it in its crest as the wave broke. Etta watched as Dan paddled furiously, and Edward fought to keep the boat straight.

They gained speed. Rachel looked at Etta, who read the terror on her face. Water came over the gunnels, but the wave swept them all the way to ankle-deep water where the boat stuck in the sand.

Rachel's head dropped. "T'ank yuh, Jesus."

Dan and Edward scrambled out and pulled the boat further in toward the steep, narrow beach as other waves helped the effort.

Etta and Rachel struggled out.

Dan took the front, Edward the rear as they dragged the boat up on the beach, over the tarp and into the woods. They turned it upside down in the back of the wagon.

The stragglers followed.

Edward straightened up and put his hands on his hips. "Whew!" He slapped Dan on the back. "That was fun!"

Dan wiped his brow and shook his head slowly. "Well, den dat's 'bout all de fun I kin stan'."

Edward laughed at him.

Etta looked around. She could see tracks through the underbrush where they had driven the mules and wagon through the woods. Dan and Edward pulled the tarp back up behind the wagon. Dan sat up in the back, next to the canoe. Edward, Rachel, and Etta sat down on the tarp.

Etta looked up at Dan. "How we gon do dis?"

223

Dan blinked, leaned back and glanced toward Edward. "We been talkin' 'bout hit. See how we propped up de canoe heah wid two big blocks."

Edward added, "That's to give you a little more air."

Dan leaned forward. "We belieb dat yuh kin lay under dat boat an' be hid.

"I'll dribe de mules real slow out'uh dese woods." He glanced around for a moment. "Naw. We gon 'ave tuh unhook dis wagon an' back hit 'round our ownse'f tuh get out'uh heah."

Dan continued to look around. "I belibe dat yuh bettuh walk 'til we get tuh de road. Dis boat apt tuh shif' 'round, us bein' on de side uh de hill lack we is. Put de tarp obuh hit, tuh hep hol' hit in an' hide yuh bettuh."

Edward spoke quietly. "We'll pull up in Medina's backyard. She may want us to take you somewhere else. I don't know."

Etta nodded. "Awright."

She looked at Rachel, who also nodded, then looked down at Matthew in her lap. "You got a cloth for 'im, ain't you?"

Etta pulled out the rag she had brought.

Rachel lay Matthew down on his back. "I'm gon nurs' 'im. I'll jus' take dis wet one off." She took off the wet diaper and picked him back up. She turned away from the group, dropped one shoulder of her dress and allowed him to nurse. Dan, Edward, and Etta discussed their situation until Matthew was sleeping.

Dan looked at Edward. "Yuh want tuh go 'head an' turn de wagon 'round?"

Edward stood up, and they got busy unhooking the wagon and pushing it backward in a half circle around in the woods.

At dusk they were at the beginnings of the road. Etta and her mother fit themselves and Matthew under the boat on the blanket Dan had spread for them. They started off.

Etta could hear the mules' feet on the hard clay soil. She put a hand on the boat just to make sure it wasn't moving. She looked down. Her mother, holding Matthew, was curled at Etta's knees, close to the back of the wagon. She could feel her but couldn't see her very well. Etta whispered over the noise of the mules and wagon. "Be careful. Don't fall out de back."

Her mother patted her on the leg, and they rode without speaking.

Before they got into town, Edward leaned back and whispered, "Y'all doing all right back there?"

Etta cupped her mouth to the opening. "Yeah, we awright."

Dan drove the mules slowly into the edge of the small city of Brunswick. They made it without incident to Medina's house. There was a lighted lantern on the small front porch. Dan turned up the driveway into the backyard behind the house.

Edward got down, leaned over the wagon and whispered, "Y'all stay put. I'll talk to Medina." Dan stayed seated.

Etta held her breath as they waited.

Chapter 22

In a few minutes Edward came back and leaned over the edge of the wagon. "Me and Dan are coming to the back of the wagon, try to block any view while y'all slip out and get inside. Wait 'til we get back there."

Etta felt her body tighten. She heard Dan and Edward talking quietly as they took position beyond the end of the canoe.

Her mother called to her. "Ready?"

"Yassum."

"Le's go." Rachel slid out first and picked up Matthew. Etta followed, keeping her head below the level of the wagon and canoe. They ran to the house. The door opened as they got there.

"Oh, Bless de Lawd! Bless de Lawd! Come on in heah." Medina took them all into her arms.

Held tightly, standing in her old room, Etta could feel her grandmother's wet cheeks on hers. She felt Elouise put her arm around her back. Everyone hugged and cried, more or less quietly. Slowly, they released each other. Rachel, Matthew, and Etta came more fully into the room, walking around a pie safe pulled to the center of the floor.

Medina picked up a broom. With the handle, she pushed up hard on a portion of the ceiling out from the door to the kitchen. Rachel stared, and Etta's mouth dropped open as a small door swung down. "I didn't know 'bout dat."

Medina looked at her and smiled. "Ain't told nobody 'bouts hit 'til now. Yoh Grandpa Lonzo built dat in." She shook her head and gave a short laugh. "Tol' me I 'ad a place tuh put all my money."

Medina took Etta's arm. "No need tuh be hangin' 'round down heah. Go on, climb up dere. I'll bring yuh sumpin tuh eat."

Matthew fussed and started crying when Medina took him. Rachel followed Etta up into the attic, and Medina passed Matthew up to her.

Etta looked down at her grandmother, who she could barely make out in the dark as she spoke to them. "See, Honey, dat doh got a handle an' a latch on yoh side. Be sho an' close de latch w'en yuh up dere."

"Ain't no light up dere yet. 'Fraid hit would sho'. Yuh 'ave tuh feel yoh way 'round."

Etta felt the inside of the trap door and whispered back, "Yassum, I can tell how it work."

Medina walked over to the back door. "We'uns 'll get some food an' water up tuh yuh. Goin' out tuh de well."

227

Elouise pushed the pie safe back against the wall. Medina went outside, and Etta pulled the trap door shut and locked it.

It was pitch dark in the little room. Matthew was patting her leg. Etta rubbed his head and started feeling around.

Rachel whispered, "Ma's got a stack uh quilts obuh heah for us to lay on. Guess she figured we was comin'. Pitcher, bowl and towel over dere, but ain't no water. Slop jar heah if you need it."

"Awright, Mama." Etta crawled in that direction. She sat up and put her hand over her head. "Can we stand up?"

Rachel touched her shoulder. "No. You can get on your knees 'long as you back heah toward de kitchen. Dere's a wall heah dat we can lean back on, but de roof slope down to nuttin' toward de backyard."

Etta used the enameled jar, put the top on and slid it toward a low corner. She and her mother stretched out, containing Matthew between them. They talked quietly and rested for a while before there was a light tap on the floor.

Medina handed up large plates of field peas, corn on the cob and cornbread smeared with butter. There was a pork chop on each plate.

She whispered, "Give me dat pitchuh." She took it to the kitchen, filled it, and then handed it up along with two cups.

"Edward an' Dan be takin' de boat an' wagon back. Might see 'em 'gin tonight. Aftuh yuh get some rest, we'll get yuh down an' talk fuh a spell."

In a couple of hours, there was a light rap at the trap door. Etta opened it. Medina looked up. She pulled the pie safe out and helped Etta down. Etta took Matthew and handed him to Medina. Rachel followed.

228

Etta pushed the pie safe back.

"Won't light no lamp. Sit right down heah on de flo' an' le's talk. I want tuh heah whut happen."

Rachel and Etta sat down in front of Medina, who sat on the edge of the bed. "Edward came back by but lef' an' gone obuh to 'is school. Gon sleep in de barn dere, go back to Bonita in de moanin'." Medina continued. "Dan's hidin' outside heah, keepin' uh watch out."

Rachel took Matthew, who was being fussy. She spoke up. "Is dere a plan?"

Medina nodded. "Warn't sure w'en or if'ns yuh might get heah. I wuz hopin' dem boys fin' yuh b'fo' de paddyrollers did."

"Anyhow, we wurkin' on hit. Miss Elouise movin' somebody out'uh a cabin she got out by hitsef on one uh her farms. We t'ink we kin hide yuh out dere fuh a spell."

She shook her head. "Right now, dis is de only place we got. T'ank God dat Lonzo put in de trap do'. Nebuh t'ink I'd say hit 'bout Lonzo, but I belieb he wuz touched by God w'en he done dat. Knowed dat somebody gon hab' tuh hide up dere."

Rachel looked up at her. "Dey gon come heah aftuh dey know we ain't on Blackbeard or Bonita. Only place left." Etta leaned back against a piece of furniture. "We can't stay anywhere 'round heah fuh long. Somebody'll see sumpin and talk. We got to get up North."

Medina shook her head slowly, then paused. "Yeah. Cain't hide long 'round heah widout somebody gettin' wise. We'll figure out sumpin."

"Elouise's drivuh picked her up an' she gon tuh Lizbeth's tuh tell her dat yuh wuz safe. Dey boff comin' obuh in de moanin'. If hit looks safe, we'll get you down and talk."

Etta looked at her mother, who spoke to Medina. "Awright. Etta an' me'll be thinkin', too. May not have long to get 'way frum heah."

Medina spoke quietly. "Jesus got yuh heah safe. We'uns gon keep yuh dat way. Now tell me whut happen."

Etta looked up and shook her head. "It's a long story, Grandma."

Rachel spoke up. "All started when dat Cap'n Jack showed up but, Mama, I'd feel better if we talk some more 'bout what we gon do."

"Awright. W'en Elouise get heah tomorrow, we'll figure out how an' w'en tuh gets yuh out to her cabin. Dat's de main t'ing right now. You know dey'll bust right in heah.

"Cain't use Elouise' buggy, 'cause she don't drive, and we'uns don't want her drivuh tuh see yuh. We gon ax' Lizbeth tuh take yuh out dere."

Etta and Rachel looked at each other and nodded their heads. "Awright, Mama, dat's good. We was talkin' up dere. I think Etta's right dat we gots to get up North. She got a frien' on de ferry dat she thinks might can help."

Etta spoke up. "Maybe Dan could go see my friend Sam and ask 'im to talk to de crews on some of dese big ships dat dock dere. Dere are ships in dere ever day. Betchuh dere free African men on some uh dem ships. Sam could find out where dey goin' an' how de captain feel 'bout slavery. Don't know how we'd get de money, but he could see if we could buy passage up North. Find out what it would cost."

230

The bed creaked as Medina leaned forward and stood slowly. "Yuh sho yuh kin trust 'im?"

Etta shrugged. "Got tuh trust somebody."

"I'll go get Dan." Medina pointed to the kitchen. "Give me dat pitchuh."

Etta got up and retrieved it. Medina spoke quietly. "I'm goin' tuh de well and get some water, see if Dan still out dere."

Etta and Rachel played with Matthew as they waited.

Dan came in the room quickly, ahead of Medina. Even in the darkness, Etta knew he was grinning at her. "How yuh doin', Etta?"

She smiled back. "I'm fine, thanks to you and everbody else, but we trying to figure out where we can go from heah. Only place dat's gon be safe fuh us in de long run is up North. Can you get 'way from de store fuh a spell again tomorrow? If you could, dere's a way you might be a big help--again."

He sat on the floor next to Rachel. "Sho! Whut yuh need fuh me tuh do?"

Etta explained the plan. "Dere's a young man named Sam on de ferry crew. Tall fella. Wears a big cap. Jus' ask for Sam. Tell 'im I sent yuh and dat I need 'is help. Tell 'im dat I need for 'im to find me a ship what could take me, Mama, and Matthew someplace in de North. New York, Philadelphia, Boston. It's a long shot, I guess."

"Tell 'im dat if he find one, ask how much it would cost, an' help us figure w'en an' how we could get on boa'd widout bein' seen. Tell 'im, too, not tuh tell nobody he don't have to. You got all dat?"

"Yeah, I got hit."

Etta looked at her mother and then her grandmother. "Anything else we need to ask Sam?"

No one spoke.

Dan stood up. "Awright. I'm gon go on back tuh de sto. Don't t'ink yuh got no pro'lems tonight. I'll go out tuh de ferry landin' in de moanin'."

Etta shook her head at him as she stood. "Don't get yourself in no trouble, now."

"Let me worry 'bout dat." He moved toward her, and Rachel shifted to let him by. They hugged. Etta thought of kissing him, but didn't, in front of her grandmother. Dan let himself out.

Together, Rachel and Etta sat and told Medina the story of all that had happened to them since Cap'n Jack had come in as overseer.

Medina put her hands behind her as she leaned back on the bed. "Hmm, hmm, hmm. De Lawd sho been lookin' aftuh both uh yuh."

Rachel responded. "We sho grateful, too. Yes, we are. Grateful to de Lord an' fuh everbody dat's helped us."

Etta put her hand to her chest and touched the tooth.

Medina stood. "Ya'll need tuh get some rest."

Etta and her mother got up slowly. The little family slipped back up into their sanctuary. They rested and played with Matthew. Etta thought of asking for a lamp. She still had her Harper's. *Maybe later.*

The tin roof over Etta's room and the little attic where they lay sloped steeply down from the older part of the house. By ten o'clock the next morning, the room had been lit for several hours by narrow strips of light between the rafters on the lower edge of the roof. Etta realized that she could lie down and look out into an inviting backyard. She was fighting the feeling

232

of being confined. Matthew was getting fussy from the increasing heat. Etta looked over at her mother and smiled. "Done tired of dis place already."

Rachel, a few beads of sweat on her brow, leaned back against the wall between them and the kitchen. She smiled back. "Maybe we can get down in a little while."

Etta jumped at the sound of a horse and buggy being smartly wheeled into the driveway. Staring under the tin, she could see Elouise's buggy pull in behind the house and stop. As her driver helped Elouise down from the buggy, another pulled in above it. Etta grinned as she realized that Lizbeth had come alone, driving her own buggy. The two women approached the house together and tapped on the back door.

Etta held her tongue as they walked by, not three feet away. Medina let them in. She heard the greetings as they walked under her and into the kitchen. She crawled over and got on her knees in front of the kitchen wall and began feeling the unpainted, weathered boards. In a short time, she had found a knothole. She put her eye up to it. There was no ceiling in the rest of the house, so she could see down into and through the kitchen, all the way to the front door. "Dey standin' in de kitchen, Mama, talkin'. I sure wish I could hear 'em better. Etta put her ear up to the knothole.

Rachel leaned toward her. "Can you?"

Etta shook her head at her mother.

In a minute or two, Medina came back and tapped on the ceiling. Etta opened the trap door. Her grandmother cupped her mouth with one hand. "Honey, we gon fix a spot tuh talk. Den we get yuh down."

Etta shut the door and turned back to her mother. "You hear her? Dey'll get us down in a little while."

233

"Awright."

Soon there was a tap. Etta opened the trap door, and Medina looked up and spoke, "Ya'll come on down an' let's talk."

The women had blocked the kitchen window with a blanket, moved the table and set up what chairs and other seats they could find. Lizbeth came straight over and hugged her friend Rachel while putting her hand on Etta's arm. She turned and gave Etta a proper hug. She looked directly at her, holding her now by the arms. "You awright, Sweetie? I'm so proud of you." She shook her head. "I know that brute you're dealing with. Feel kind of like it's my fault for egging the man on in the first place, but you know why we did that. Anyway, you are a brave young woman to stand up to him like you did." She nodded. "We are going to keep you safe."

Elouise approached Etta. She touched the scabs on her neck, then brought her hand up to Etta's face and looked her in the eyes. "You did the right thing. I'm glad you stopped him." They had a long hug.

Elouise looked at Rachel. "We've been sick with worry about all of you."

Medina spoke up. "Y'all come on in heah an' sit down."

Etta watched as everyone took a seat. She sat on a stool in the circle.

Her grandmother spoke first. "I told de ladies 'bout us needin' to get yuh tuh a safuh place right away. I told 'em, too, whut we doin' tuh find a ship."

There was silence for a moment, and Elouise leaned toward Rachel and Etta. "We got a place for you to stay, but there are other people out on the farm. Y'all have to stay inside. I'll bring you food and water. It should give us a little time to work something out."

234

Lizbeth looked over at Rachel. "I am going to take you out there. We'll leave soon as it gets dark tonight.

"Don't worry about the money for the ship. We are all going to pitch in if we can find passage. I'm going to check with some people David knows that might can get y'all on a ship. So you think this Sam fellow may be able to help?"

Etta nodded. "Yeah. He works in a good spot."

Rachel looked around the group. "So de plan right now is dat Lizbeth, you gon come and pick us up tonight and take us out to dis farm where we stay for a time. Everbody gon be workin' on findin' passage to de North for us three. Y'all tell Elouise any news 'bout findin' a ship, and she can pass it on to us. Dat de plan?"

Etta looked around as Medina, Elouise, and Lizbeth all nodded.

Medina looked at Rachel. "All we got tuh do now is make hit tuh dark. We'd go ahead an' moves yuh now, but Elouise got tuh go gets some peoples out'uh dat cabin an' obuh tuh anuduh one."

Rachel smiled. "Gon be a warm afternoon, but we be awright. Bring us plenty of water an' some rags dat we can wet." She turned toward Lizbeth and Elouise. "Thank you both for hepin' me an' my babies."

Medina spoke up. "I know hit's hot up dere, but I don't like yuh bein' out in de house like dis. I'll get yuh some fresh water, and yuh kin get on back up dere." After more hugs, they climbed back into the attic.

Etta entertained herself at the knothole for a while, watching the women work together to move furniture back and create a nice lunch. Elouise took a stoppered, cut-glass bottle containing an amber liquid out of

235

her large purse and put it on the kitchen table. She poured herself a small glass from the bottle. Two plates of food were soon handed up.

Etta ate quickly. She tried to read for a while but couldn't maintain her attention on any of the articles. She went back to the knothole and looked at the women sitting around the table.

"Bang! Bang! Bang!"

Everyone jumped, and Etta fell over and lost her view of the room. She stared at her mother. "What was dat?"

Rachel blurted out in a loud whisper, "It's de paddyrollers!"

Etta found the knothole again and whispered, "Grandma's goin' to de door." *Lawdy, Miss Lizbeth snatched dat blanket off de window an' tossed it next to the stove.*

Her mother was kneeling next to her, hand on Etta's shoulder. She turned her ear to the hole as her grandmother said, "Hello, Sheriff."

Etta looked again and whispered to her mother, "It's de sheriff."

She could see him through the open door. The large man was dressed in work clothes but wore a star on his shirt.

"What brings yuh out heah?"

The sheriff spoke loudly. "We need to have a talk!" He tried to push past Medina into the house, but she held her ground, briefly. After a moment, she stepped back and spoke directly in his ear as he passed. "Sheriff, I got rights."

Etta turned to her mother. "He's coming in."

The sheriff stopped abruptly, and his mouth dropped open when he saw the two white women. Elouise turned in her chair and spoke to him

236

directly, harshly. "Hello, Sheriff! Getting close to election day. I will make sure that all my friends know how you treat the citizens of this town."

She frowned deeply. "Can't you knock like other folks? You like to have scared us to death!"

Rachel and Etta could both hear now. Etta continued to watch. The sheriff reached up and took off his small hat, holding it in front of him. "Sorry, ma'am. I had no idea you'd be here."

Elouise wasn't through. "Sheriff, this free woman is my friend. She is a pillar of the Brunswick Baptist Church. I would appreciate it if you would, in your dealings here, afford her the respect she's due."

Etta watched as the sheriff shuffled his feet and nodded. "Yessum. I didn't mean to startle you ladies."

Lizbeth spoke up. "Well, Sheriff, I thought you might be coming to our meeting of the Church Temperance Committee."

The sheriff dipped his head toward Lizbeth. "Uh, no, Ma'am. Here on serious business."

Lizbeth cocked her head at the sheriff. "This is serious business, Sheriff. You of all people should be aware of the dangers of strong drink."

"Yes, Ma'am, I sure am. I see it every day."

Etta's eyes got big as she watched Elouise slip sideways in her chair to block the sheriff's view of the bottle and glass sitting on the table.

Etta turned and sat by her mother, who was nursing Matthew. They heard her grandmother. "Whut brings yuh heah, Sheriff?"

"I came by to tell you that I got a report of a serious crime that has been committed by your grandaughter against a white man. First case like this we've had since I been sheriff. Slave attack their overseer. Never heard

237

of such a thing 'round here. People are going to be riled up. Guess you done heard all about it."

There was silence. The sheriff paused, nodded and continued, "You know what's going to happen if those patrols catch her. Her mama and that baby, too, most likely. I imagine they'll catch 'em over there somewhere. I just want to tell you that if she makes it to you, send for me, and I'll try to keep 'em safe, least for the time being. I'll talk to Thomas Wilson and see what he wants us to do. The fact the man that got hit worked for him might give him some say. I don't know. Have to talk to the judge. Slave owners 'round here are going to be mighty upset. They going to want justice."

Etta slipped back up the wall and watched again. The sheriff was looking around the room.

Lizbeth looked up at him. "Well, Sheriff, that's terrible. There must be some mistake. I know that girl personally; she has worked for me. I trust her completely. I'm sure it was self defense."

The sheriff blinked and sputtered, "Ma,am, slave can't …"

Elouise cut in. "Anyway, Sheriff, that's terrible news. That girl needs to be saved from those people. You need to go stop 'em."

Medina frowned at Lizbeth and looked back at the sheriff. "Awright, Sheriff. T'ank yuh. I 'xpect dey already up Norf by now, but I 'preciates yuh comin' by. I'll t'ink 'bout whut yuh says. If I heah frum 'em, I'll let yuh know." She held the door open for him. He put on his hat and walked out.

Etta watched as the circle of women stared at each other, shocked looks on their faces. Etta turned and sat back down next to her mother.

238

Rachel put her hand on Etta's leg. "We'd be crazy tuh turn ourselves over to dat man."

Etta put her hand on her mother's. "If Mr. Thomas help you, you would get off wid a whippin', but I think dey'd hang me anyways. I got to get up North."

There were footsteps under her. Etta dropped down and looked out under the tin. Elouise briskly exited the house, climbed in the back of her buggy and spoke to her driver. More fast steps and Lizbeth, too, was gone.

They drank large amounts of water and used wet rags on themselves and Matthew. In the early afternoon, there was a tap at the back door. Etta heard Medina moving below her. Soon there was a tap on the trap door.

Etta opened it. Medina looked up. "Dat wuz Dan. He say dat dere some men gatherin' up in de street, stoppin' people and searchin' wagons an' buggies. Dan be heah tonight an' try tuh hep yuh gets by 'em."

Etta frowned and shook her head. "Sounds danejus." She rubbed the shark's tooth between her fingers. "Did he find Sam?"

Medina nodded. "He spoke tuh Sam dis moanin' at de dock. He gon try tuh hep."

Darkness was settling in. Etta was finding it hard to sit still in their little cell. She had been hearing noises from the street for some time. There was the soft crunch of wheels in the backyard. Etta leaned over and looked. She whispered loudly, "It's a horse and buggy." Rachel sat up.

In a moment, there was a tap at the ceiling. Etta opened the little door, and Medina motioned them down. She took Matthew as his mother and sister slipped through the opening down to the pie safe and the floor. Etta had her shoulder sack. Medina began stuffing in rags for Matthew, and food

239

wrapped in newspapers. "Dan wuz able to get Lizbeth's buggy through de woods in the vacant lot behind the house. "Dey stoppin' an' lookin' in ebuh buggy out front.

"Y'all ready? Dey gon take yuh out through de woods behin' de house." There was a tap on the back door.

Medina opened it, and Dan stuck his head in. "Ready to go?"

They nodded.

Dan put his finger to his lips. "Be real quiet. Dey still gatherin' up down dere. Make hit quick."

Etta and Rachel followed him out and dove into the buggy. From the driver's seat, Lizbeth looked around into the floor of the buggy and nodded toward the back. "Get under that quilt."

Dan took the bridle of the horse and began leading him back through the trees and bushes in the empty lot straight behind the house.

They could hear the brush going under the buggy and rubbing against the outside as they moved along slowly. Etta peeked out from under the quilt. *We'll be out tuh Pine Street shortly.*

Suddenly the buggy stopped, and Dan stuck his head in. "Get out."

Etta stared back. "What?"

"Dere voices comin' dis way. I see some light. Get out! Use de buggy tracks an' run on back tuh de house. We tryin' tuh get turned 'round b'fo' dey see us. Might pick yuh back up. We'll stall 'em if'ns we 'ave to."

Rachel and Matthew left the buggy first. The horses lunged as Dan turned the buggy too sharply to the left. Etta fell back and became tangled in the quilt. It took her several moments to free herself and jump from the lurching buggy. Panicked, she ran through the bushes too fast, tripping over

240

dead limbs. She scrambled up and looked around. *Where de tracks? Ran off and left Mama and Matthew. What was I thinkin'?* Etta listened for the buggy, then picked what she hoped was the right direction back toward the house.

There were voices. *Uh-oh, who's dat?* She saw flickering lights heading toward her and to her left. She found a large tree and got behind it. Squirrel-like, she watched as the men came even with her. Two of the four were holding flaming, fat-lightered torches. "Alright. We ought to be close. Jack just wanted to make sure that that gal don't run this way when they go to burn the house down."

Oh, no. I got to warn them.

"We s'pose tuh douse the torches, spread out, listen and watch. Stay in the edge of the woods. Alright? House can't be too much further."

Etta bit her lip for a moment, then felt around on the forest floor. Picking up a short, heavy limb, she tossed it some distance behind the men. They whirled around, and she moved quietly in the direction they were headed, finding the buggy tracks with her toes.

She hid in the sweet myrtle bushes surrounding the backyard. *Dere's de buggy. Believe it's empty.* She heard the men behind her. *Dey might see if I try to cross dat yard.* Etta eased down the strip of myrtle on the east side of the house. *Ain't no way to get in over heah.* She was even with the front porch and could see some of the people milling around the front yard and down in the street. *Can't stay heah.* She looked down the street, then toward the woods behind the house. She ran quickly and slipped under the front porch. She crawled up to the front steps and looked under one to see a throng in the yard in front of the house.

241

Etta's mouth dropped open. "Lord have mercy on me." She recoiled back under the porch. *Look at dat mob. Dey after me?*

She looked around. *Hope dey ain't no snakes under heah.* She lay there, aware of her beating heart.

Suddenly, a voice that she knew, "Alright in there, come out!"

Etta jumped and looked around. *He talkin' to me?*

She heard the floor creak when Medina opened the front door and walked to the edge of the porch, right above her. "What do you people want?"

Etta looked under the top step again. At first she could see only legs and boots, but got lower. There was Jack, no hat, a bloodstained bandage on the left side of his head. *Looks like eight or ten men wid 'im, crowd behind dem.*

He had turned toward the crowd. *He's waving to people. Look back dere. Dere's some women and children. I know some of dem people. Dere's de neighbors' kids, runnin' 'round, jumpin'. What dey so happy 'bout?*

Three of the patrol members were holding torches. Faces in the crowd were, in turn, frozen and extingushed by the wax and wane of the yellow flames: Lithographs of hate scratched onto Etta's heart. She cried quietly, grieving something for which she had no name.

Etta lifted her head and looked out again. Jack seemed to be trying to excite the crowd, waving his arms, yelling something. He turned back to Medina. "I'll tell you what we want, Woman. We want your granddaughter, Etta; your daughter, Rachel, who's been helping her, and that baby, too, and we want them now."

242

Medina used a strong, slow tone. "Well, dey ain't heah! An' yuh might bettuh talk tuh de fahduh uh dat baby b'fo' yuh go grabbin' at dat one. My daughter, too. You de one gon be in trubble. Yuh need to back off, talk to de sheriff. He's on de way. Yeah. Better go talk to yoh boss b'fo' yuh do sumpin you gon regret. I hear he'll be back tomorruh."

One of the patrol members was tapping Jack on the shoulder. Etta watched as Jack turned and got in an argument with his men. His face turned bright red.

Medina called out to someone she saw in the crowd. "Hey, Billy! Been missin' yuh in church lately. Looks like you foun' a dif'nt crowd tuh hang out wid."

A teenager on the edge of the patrol began to put some distance between himself and the group.

"Yoh mama sho didn't look good w'en I went by tuh check on her de uduh day. I hope she doin' bettuh. Yeah, dat's good. Yuh bettuh run home an' check on her."

Etta watched as Billy turned his back and was gone. Some in the patrol were startin' to mill around, and the crowd spread out some. She watched as Jack turned and sneered. "Etta is the one I want. Now give her to me, or my boys here going to have to light up a little bonfire, make sure she ain't in there."

The crowd surged forward. There were hoots and calls. "Burn it down!"

Her grandmother spoke, "I tol' yuh she ain't heah! You need tuh be careful wid dat fire dere. W'en's de las' time hit rained 'round heah. You burn my house, you gon get de whole neighborhood.

243

"Hey, dere, Johnny. You belieb how dis win' blowin'?" The wind roared in the trees. "I t'ink hits blowin' right tow'ds yoh place."

Etta noticed a buzz in the crowd. A knot of men were around Jack, but the group as a whole had fallen back a step.

Jack walked up to the porch and stared at Medina. "Alright then, we'll start by coming in and taking a look." He turned to the men right behind him. "Get them axes out of the wagon, boys. We are going to make sure there ain't no place to hide in this house."

Etta put her hands over her head and cowered as Jack took one of the axes and headed straight toward her. He stomped up the steps.

A deep voice called out, "Hold up! What's going on here?"

Etta bent over and looked to her right, under the edge of the porch. In the driveway, next to the little house, was a horse and buggy. *I believe dat's Lizbeth's buggy.* She couldn't see his face but realized that the sheriff had stepped down as the buggy moved on into the backyard.

Jack was right above her. "Hello, Sheriff. This is the regular Brunswick patrol. We're here to search this house for runaway slaves from Bonita. What are you doing here? This ain't none of your concern."

Etta could hear the wind stirring the trees. The sheriff spoke. "Yeah, I heard about that gal hittin' you in the head, Jack. That's a crime in this county. Dealing with crime is my job.

"Are you alright? I heard you were hurt real bad. You prolly need for me to deal with this, and you go get some rest."

"Naw, Sheriff. Can't let this one get away. I'm gon watch that young one swing, nice and slow-like." Jack laughed. "Ain't gon tie her feet. Hang around for the dance, Sheriff. It'll be fun."

244

Etta could see dry leaves blowing in large circles, some coming under the porch. Sparks flew from the torches.

The sheriff looked over at the group of men. "You boys need to put out a couple of them torches. You're going to start a fire.

"And look here, Jack, ain't no need for axes. There's a white woman in there from a prominent family. Don't neither of us need that kind of trouble."

"Yeah, I seen her. I know who she is."

"You stand down now, and I'll go take a look. If those gals are in there, I'll find them."

There was a pause. In quieter tones, Etta heard the sheriff add, "I'll take the mama and baby. You can have that gal that hit you."

Terror gripped Etta's throat, and she couldn't breathe. She heard the boards creek above her as Jack shifted his weight.

Medina spoke up. "Awright Sheriff, come on in."

The boards groaned as the sheriff climbed onto the porch. Etta looked up. *Dat floor might fall in, right on top of me.*

The door was slammed shut above her. *Lord, I hope he don't find Mama.* Etta peeked back through the steps. *Look back dere behind de crowd. Dere's Edward and Dan. Dan got his mouth up to Edward's ear.*

She watched as Edward walked up close to a patrol member toward the back of the group. They spoke for a moment. The man looked startled and came forward, toward Jack.

Etta watched as Edward went up to another man and spoke to him. He stared back at Edward for a moment, then moved toward the porch and the growing knot of men around Jack. Edward watched, turned and rejoined

245

Dan. They huddled, watched for a moment longer, then turned and ran across the street, into the deep shadows.

The first man had walked up to Jack, who was standing not far from the steps. Etta backed away toward the base of the chimney but not before she heard them. "Yeah. He says he's Thomas Wilson's boy, Edward. Said he had to go but wanted to come by and tell us that they just caught all three of them runaways over on Bonita."

Someone called out to the crowd, "They caught 'em on Bonita!" Some of the crowd cheered.

She could hear Jack's voice above the crowd, "Wait a minute. Where's that boy? Where did he go? Let me talk to him."

The voices faded and the boots moved away. Etta slipped up further under the house, toward the chimney. She kissed the shark's tooth. *Please, oh, please help us, Grandpa.* Crouched in a hole next to the chimney, she rocked back and forth and prayed to anyone she thought might hear.

There was movement above her. She heard the front door open and close. There were heavy footsteps across the porch and down the steps. She heard the sheriff. "Hey, Fred! Let me see that torch for a minute."

Etta's eyes got big and she scrambled around behind the base of the chimney as the sheriff bent over and used the torch to light the underside of the house. Lurid shadows danced with the light. She drew her hands and feet inward and held her breath. *Help me, Grandpa.* A deep shadow settled over her like a blanket.

The Sheriff moved around with the light, looking closely. He stepped back and stood up. "All right, Boys. They ain't here."

246

There was a voice she didn't know, "We just got word, Sheriff. They caught 'em over on Bonita."

"Yeah, that's what I figured. I'll go over on the morning ferry and check on that."

Etta was trying to get a full breath.

"You boys go on home and get some sleep."

He called out loudly, "Hey, where you going, Jack?"

"See if I can get a boat."

Etta waited an hour or so before she crawled back down to the steps and looked around. It was quiet. On her stomach she looked out from under the end of the porch. *Don't get caught now. Better go out de other side.* She crawled out from under the side of the porch where she had entered and ran back into the myrtle bushes. She slipped up behind a large tree and peered into the backyard. *Wonder if dem men still out in de woods watching.* There was movement close to the tree where she hid, a shape she recognized. "Grandma!"

Her grandmother came around the tree, and Etta buried her face in her bosom, breathing her essence. "Dem men still out dere?"

"No, Honey, dey gon."

Surrounded by Lizbeth and Dan, Etta shook uncontrollably, her legs weak. Her grandmother had to hold her up.

Medina hugged her again and looked up. "T'ank yuh, Lawd." She put her arm around Etta. "Let's get yuh inside."

247

Chapter 23

It took Etta hours to shake her terror, relax some, and go off to an unsettled sleep. Well before daylight there was a tap on their little door. Etta was groggy as she came down and sat on the floor. Her attention was taken by the aroma of baking pies. *Sure have missed dat smell.* A kerosene lamp in the kitchen threw a little light into the room.

Medina took a seat on the bed, nodded toward her daughter and looked over at Etta. "I'm 'fraid we may've missed our chaince. We wuz gon go ahead an' move yuh late las' night, but Lizbeth's husband David came and took her and de buggy home. He wuz pretty upset."

Etta mumbled, "Yeah, me too."

Rachel spoke quietly, "Scared us all."

Etta took a deep breath and let it out slowly.

Medina looked at Rachel, then Etta. "She could be heah anytime, but if she don't come soon, hit'll be too late tuh move yuh. W'en dat ferry lands obuh heah dis moanin', folks gettin' off will tell ebuhbody dat dere warn't no capture on Bonita or Blackbeard. We might hab' 'til noon if Cap'n Jack go on tuh Bonita an' don' send some uh 'is buddies right back obuh heah."

Rachel grunted, and Matthew bobbed up and down in her lap.

Medina continued, "Las' night I wuz t'inkin' 'bout whut we kin do if'n dey start searchin' wagons and buggies 'gin. If dey show up heah b'fo' Lizbeth can get yuh out, den we gots a pro'lem.

"We need some way fuh yuh tuh be ables tuh walk 'way frum heah. If yuh look on de street out dere, whut yuh see is black men and white men walkin' up and down, 'specially on a Sat'd'y, like today. I t'ink we kin cut up some thick quilts, make you some vest an' leggins fuh yuh tuh wear unduh some men's clothes. Make men's out'uh yuh. Get some big ol' floppy hats, pull down obuh yoh face. If we could get yuh out tuh de street, might blend in. Walk right off."

Etta was quiet. *Dat might work. De pro'lem be gettin' down to de street widout bein' looked at too close. Dat and de pro'lem of where we go from dere..*

Rachel bounced Matthew. "What 'bout dis 'un? I ain't leavin' 'im behind."

Medina nodded. "I t'ought 'bout dat. I kin make 'im a little harness. You kin hol' 'im on yoh tummy. Put a big ol' man's shirt on yuh and cobuh 'im up. If'ns he be quiet and still, he make yuh look fat like mos' uh de men 'round heah."

Rachel snorted. She looked at her mother. "If we try it, I'll make sure he hungry, and den I'll nurse 'im. He sleep sound den."

Etta looked at her grandmother. Even if we is able to get out to Elouise' farm and get a ship, we gon hab' tuh gets de money together."

Medina leaned toward her. "Let me worry 'bout dat. I've talked to Lonzo since all dis started. You know yoh Grandpa Lonzo make a little money on de weekends. He want tuh hep. You heard Lizbeth 'bout de money. I'll talk to her an' Elouise 'bout dat if'ns we kin fin' a ship."

Medina got up, walked into the kitchen and peeked in the stove. She turned, picked up a pie that had already cooled and brought it to Etta. "Here, take one uh dese pies up dere wid yuh. Dat's gon be breakfast tuhday."

She stood in the doorway to the kitchen. "We got anuduh pro'lem. Winnie gon be heah in a little while. I lub' her, but she talk too much. While she heah, y'all gon hab' tuh be real quiet. She don't need tuh know whut's goin' on. I'll get her out'uh heah quick as I kin."

Etta, Rachel, and Matthew returned to their nest and finished off the whole peach pie. Etta was thrilled to hear a buggy turn into the yard. Her grandmother went to the door, and Etta could hear voices. She reached for the latch but didn't open it. There were more voices below her. She sat back, frowned, and shook her head toward her mother, even though she couldn't see her in the darkness.

Etta went to the knothole. There was no one at first, but then Winnie walked into view, talking. "Oh, Miss Medina, I is so worried 'bout Etta. Sho glad dem mens didn't get her. Weh you reckon she is? I hope she up Norf by now."

"Yeah, Winnie. I t'ink she already up dere."

250

Matthew, who had been stirring, began crying. Etta turned toward him as she heard her grandmother begin singing a hymn loudly.

Rachel picked Matthew up, and Etta went back to the knothole. She could see the whites of Winnie's eyes. She hadn't stopped talking, "Well, I sho …"

Etta heard her grandmother, "Winnie, I got tuh to go out heah and talk tuh Lizbeth. Go ahead an' git dat las' batch uh pies out'uh de stove. Start loadin' dem uduhs. I be right back." Etta heard the outside door open and close. In a few moments the buggy turned around in the backyard and went back down the driveway.

A little later, Etta heard conversation in the kitchen. Looking through the knothole, she saw Lizbeth along with Winnie and her grandmother. They were packing Winnie's big backpack with pies and pastries. Medina was giving Winnie instructions. "Aftuh yuh make dese 'liveries, go obuh tuh de hardware and tell Lonzo. You know Lonzo?"

Winnie nodded. "Miss Medina, I belieb dese pies still too hot."

"Dey'll be awright. He's dere today. Tell 'im dat I need tuh see 'im right away. Soon as he kin get heah."

Winnie was putting on the huge canvas backpack.

"Bring de backpack wid yuh Monday moanin'. No need fuh yuh to come back heah tuhday. Don't need hit b'fo' den."

Sometime later there was a tap at the trap door. Lizbeth and Medina helped them down. There were hugs from Lizbeth. "I'm sorry I couldn't come back and get you last night. David wouldn't allow me to leave. Thought it was too dangerous." Lizbeth shook her head. "He drove me over.

251

Wouldn't let me have the buggy." She should her head. "I could have gotten you out of here, but he wouldn't hear of it."

Rachel looked down and shook her head. Etta played with Matthew on the floor, and the other two women sat on the bed. Medina nodded toward Lizbeth. "I told Lizbeth heah 'bout de uduh plan we talked 'bout. She t'inks we kin make hit wurk."

Lizbeth stood up. "Let's get started. Where is your tape measure and scissors, Medina? It'll be like making costumes for a play"

As they finished measuring Etta and Rachel, there was a tap on the back door. Medina went and let Dan in. He went directly to Etta and took her hands. "We got it! We got it!"

Medina stared at him, hands on her hips. "Got what?"

Dan's eyes got even bigger. "We got a ship! Sails tonight!"

Etta leaned back, her mouth open. She looked at her grandmother. "Can we do it, Grandma?"

"Lawdy, Lawdy. De quickuh, de bettuh, I reckon. Hit won't take long to make whut we gon make."

Etta frowned. "How we gon get de money dat fas'?" She looked at Dan. "How much is hit?"

He announced to the group, "Twenty dolluhs each. Baby is free."

Etta watched her grandmother look at Lizbeth, who looked back and nodded.

Lizbeth spoke. "We got work to do. Medina, get me your thickest quilts, and I'll start marking and cutting. I need your heavy scissors."

Dan was still holding Etta's hands. She looked up. "How we gon get on dis ship?"

252

Everyone paused and looked at Dan. He dropped Etta's hands, stepped back and looked around. "De ship gon stop in deep watuh off Harris Neck. We got tuh get a boat an' get yuh out to dat ship jus' b'fo' sundown."

The group listened quietly. Dan continued. "I seen Jack an' some uh 'is buddies at de ferry. Dey awready talkin' 'bout how we tricked 'em. He went on obuh tuh Bonita. I ran back, but some of dem men be heah anytime. If yuh needs foh me to, I could catch de ferry, go gets Edward an' we'uns could see 'bout a boat."

There was silence. Etta noticed her grandmother, hand on her chin, her brow furrowed. "De nex' ferry be noontime. Come talk to us b'fo' yuh tries tuh get on hit. I'm 'xpectin' Lonzo anytime. He knows lots uh people. May have a way tuh gets y'all out dere. I 'membuh w'en he built a cabin fuh 'is massuh out at Harris Neck. Wurked out dere fuh a long spell. Maybe he kin hep."

Medina jerked her head up toward the attic. "Awright, let's get yuh back up dere b'fo' dere too many eyes 'round heah."

Dan hugged Etta, and they shared an excited kiss. "I oughtuh get back to de sto'. I'll be obuh heah b'fo' noon." They hugged again and Dan slipped out.

Etta and Rachel climbed back into the attic. They were aware of movement in and out and conversations below them. At one point they heard Lonzo's voice. Etta watched through the knothole while Lonzo, Lizbeth, and Medina had a long talk. Noon came and went.

About three o'clock, there was a tap on their trap door, and Medina motioned them down. "We got tuh gets yuh dressed. Lizbeth, make sho all de curtins closed good."

253

She and Lizbeth began fitting them with the heavy quilt undergarments they were using to add bulk to the slim women's frames, including a sling with leg holes for Matthew. Lizbeth looked up at Rachel. "These quilts are going to be mighty hot. I hope y'all can stand it long enough to get out of town. We're going to try it first without the leggins. The pants are heavy. They may be enough."

Rachel looked at her mother. "Could you reach me some moh water?"

Medina was sewing pads on the shoulders of Etta's quilt vest. "Awright, jus' a minute. Lonzo gon be heah shortly. We got tuh have yuh ready."

"He's gon walk wid yuh. Dere's a big rowboat out at 'is massuh's cabin at Harris Neck. Lonzo say de family ain't out at de cabin dis weekend. He gon row yuh out tuh de ship in dere boat. Pretty good walk tuh gets dere. We got tuh get goin'."

Medina looked around at her daughter. "Elouise say dey stopped her an' searched her buggy 'gin w'en she try an' turn in heah.

"Lonzo t'ink our bes' chaince is tuh distract de men down on de street long 'nuf fuh y'all tuh walk out'uh heah. He and Dan been talkin' 'bout some way tuh do dat."

Matthew crawled around on the floor as Etta and Rachel began to put on the two sets of men's clothes that Lonzo had delivered. Lizbeth fitted the sling around Rachel's neck and helped her with the baggy shirt and the denim pants. Each had a pair of worn men's boots. Rachel loosely tucked in the shirt and tied the pants with with an old piece of rope. She picked up the big hat and put it on.

Lizbeth stepped back and smiled at her. "Let's try Matthew in his sling and see how it's going to work.

Rachel called Matthew softly. He looked up at his mother. His face showed shock, then alarm. He started squalling. Rachel snatched off the hat and bent down to him. "Hush, Honey. It's me."

Etta bent down and Matthew examined her closely through his tears. She smiled at him. "Well, it worked on you, Matthew."

After they were dressed, except for the hats, Etta and Rachel played with Matthew on the floor, hoping to wear him out. Etta heard someone talking to Medina at the back door. "Mama, I think dat's Grandpa."

Etta walked through the kitchen to see her grandfather. *Didn't hardly know 'im before I came over heah. It's been nice havin' Sunday breakfast wid 'im every week. He's a smart man. Feel better dat he's helpin' us.* "Hey, Grandpa. Thank you for all your help."

Lonzo, a tall, solidly-built black man, hugged his granddaughter. "Well, look at yuh. Yuh knows I got tuh take care uh de only granddaughter I got." He smiled at her. "We gon get yuh out'uh heah."

Lonzo stepped back. "Let me see how yuh look?"

"Let me get my hat." Etta walked through the kitchen and came back in with the hat pulled low and her hands in her pant's pockets. She looked up and smiled.

He folded his arms. "Le's see yuh walk." Etta walked back and forth through the kitchen. He shook his head. "Umm. Go get yoh Mama and le's try dis some moh. Yuh need tuh take bigger steps, swing yoh arms."

They practiced walking like men. The shirt sleeves worked to cover their hands.

255

Medina and Lizbeth added large, strapped tool bags to the outfit to hold diapers and clean dresses, underwear and shoes, as well as a meal and water for all of them.

Rachel turned to her father. "Paw, Yuh 'bout ready foh us?"

He nodded. "Yeah."

I need tuh go nurse 'im real quick so he'll sleep."

Lonzo nodded. "Hurry up."

Soon Medina, Etta, the 'fat' Rachel, and Lonzo were huddled by the door in the small back room. Lizbeth was standing in the kitchen. Medina called for prayer. "Le's bow our heads. Thank you, Lawd, fuh keeping our chilren safe. We call on yuh 'gin tuh guide and potect 'em. Hold 'em close, Lawd. Dey yoh 'bedient servants and look tuh yuh, Lawd, fuh yoh strength and guidance. Amen."

"Amen," replied Etta and Rachel. Lonzo led as they slipped out the back door, went around the back and down the side of the house shielded from town. They waited, plastered against the wall. Lonzo peeked out at the front of the house, then leaned back and waved at someone down the street.

He looked back at them and jerked his head toward the street in front of the house. "Yuh see dat man right 'cross de street, leanin' 'gainst dat post?"

They leaned out, looked and nodded.

"He a paddyroller. Dere's anuduh one down de street to de right. Watch 'im now. Dis one heah gon walk 'way in a minute."

A wagon came up the street from their left. Etta looked close and spoke in a loud whisper, "Dat's Dan!"

256

"Yep, but watch dis man right heah. We go w'en he go." The wagon went by in front of the house. In a couple of minutes, there was a shout from the street. "What the hell you doin', Boy!?" More shouts and curses. The man leaning against the post looked down the street and walked in that direction.

They all left together, headed up the street in the opposite direction. Etta looked to her right, and there was Dan, holding the bridle of the mules, calming them. It appeared to Etta that he had tried to turn around in the street. It looked like both wheels on one side were off and that the wagon had turned on its side, dumping a load of old boards. With traffic blocked in both directions, Dan was getting it from all sides.

De paddyroller still got his back to us. Jus' a little further to de street.

Lonzo looked over at Etta. "Psst! Look dis way!"

Etta tried to focus her attention on her feet. *One moh step. One moh step. One moh step.* She held her breath and looked over at her mother. *It's workin'. We gon make it.*

"LONZO!"

Etta jumped and looked up at a man approaching them on horseback. *Look down!*

Lonzo was at her side, "Take yoh mama's arm an' keep walkin'. Keep goin'. I'll catch yuh."

Lonzo stopped and Etta kept walking. She brushed by her mother and whispered, "We got to keep goin'. He'll catch up."

Behind her, Etta heard the man's angry voice, "Where have you been? I expected you down at my house site today. You told me that you would be there early this morning."

257

"Yassuh. I sho did, Suh. But I 'ad a pro'lem dat I 'ad tuh fix at dis uduh place b'fo' I could get started." Etta looked around. Lonzo was holding his hat in his hand and dipping his head." They threaded their way up the busy street, heads down.

The crowd thinned, and they were finally on the outskirts of town, walking side-by-side and sweating profusely. Etta found herself trying to tamp down her anxiety. *Can't be late.* She turned and looked back for Lonzo. *Don't know where to go widout 'im. Wish he'd come on.* She looked back toward town again. "Dere he is, Mama. I think dat's 'im." They stood in the shade and waited as Lonzo, walking fast, caught up with them.

He shook his head. "Sorry. Had tuh deal wid dat fool. Let's get uh move on."

Etta just followed Lonzo as they made several twists and turns. After some time, she could smell the saltwater and then make out a small house down the hillside. Lonzo slowed, then stopped. "Y'all stan' obuh heah in de edge of dese woods. I'm gon walk down dere. Make sho ain't nobody heah."

Rachel and Etta took the opportunity to take off the sweaty vests. Rachel smiled. "Worked pretty good."

Etta smiled back. Matthew was stirring. She held out her hands. "Let me take 'im."

Rachel began getting him out of his sling. "Oh, yeah. Dat's a good idea. My back is killin' me. We need tuh change him, too."

Etta took one of the vests and spread it on the pinestraw and leaves. She pulled out a rag from her bag and quickly changed him. She picked him

258

up, put him on her hip and looked around. Her mother had her hands behind her back.

Etta watched the house. "Grandpa motioned fuh us. What we gon do wid dese vests?"

Rachel bent over. "I got 'em."

They went down the steep driveway to the house. Lonzo led them around the cabin and down to a small dock. A sailboat was tied to the end. Tied to the right side was a large rowboat, bobbing gently. Etta looked out from the dock. *Ain't no surf heah. Why not?*

Oh, dis house sit back in a cove. Dat spit of land catch de waves. Dis ought to be easier dan de other day.

Lonzo stopped in front of the boat and turned around. "I'm gon row y'all out dere. Wait right heah." He walked out as far as he could and looked carefully at the ocean horizon. He walked back. "Hit ain't out dere yet."

He stood facing them both. "Rachel, dis envelope wid de 40 on hit has de money fuh yoh passage. De uduh two is tuh hep y'all get a start."

Rachel gave Etta's envelope to her. "Thank you, Grandpa."

Etta put hers down in her bag.

Lonzo put one arm around Rachel and the other around Etta. "We all hep'd. Now, don't get up dere havin' a big ol' time an' fuhget 'bout us po' folks down heah. We lub' yuh and pray tuh God dat we gon see yuh 'gin in dis life. Soon."

Etta and Rachel hugged him strongly. He turned toward the boat. *Let's get on out dere. I can't see de sun tuh have any idea whut time hit is. Let me have dem vests.* He walked back and stuffed them under the dock.

259

He came right back and steadied the boat as Rachel got in first. She sat on the large rear board seat, and Etta handed over Matthew. Her grandfather untied the boat. She then scrambled into the front. Lonzo got in and sat on the middle seat. He lifted the oars and slipped them into the locks. "Push de nose out if yuh kin, Etta."

She pushed hard on the dock, and they were underway.

Lonzo's back and arms spread like wings, urging them toward the open ocean. He called out, "Gon get a little rough w'en we gets pass dat point."

Etta looked at her mother, who had grabbed a side of the boat. *I should'uh stayed back dere wid her. Can't do it now.* She turned back toward the front of the boat.

As they cleared the end of the little bay, the wind died and the ocean went calm. Lonzo stopped rowing and looked around over his shoulder. "Lawdy, I ain't nebuh seen dat b'fo'." He pointed. "Dere's wind obuh dere, but calm heah." He shook his head, shrugged deeply and went back to rowing. Etta touched the tooth on her chest, looked back and smiled at her mother.

In a few more minutes, Etta called out. "Dere's a ship comin'. Lonzo turned the rowboat so he could look closely. "Dat's got tuh be hit. I'm gon need tuh get fuduh out. Hold on."

In a few minutes Etta pointed to their right, toward Blackbeard. "Who's dat, Grandpa." A small sailboat had come out from behind Blackbeard and was heading in their direction. Lonzo turned and watched it for a moment, then began rowing faster. "Dem paddyrollers may hab' a boat. I ain't fuh sho, bu hit look like hit got uh li'l cannon on de front."

Rachel and Etta stared at each other. *Lawd, don't tell me we come dis close an' gon get caught.* She watched the boat, trying to judge how fast it was moving. She then looked back at the larger ship. *Dat is big. How we gon get up de side of dat thing.*

Lonzo rowed hard. In a few minutes he stopped rowing and looked around. He turned the rowboat to the right and rowed directly toward the ship. The ship suddenly reduced sail, dropped its bow anchor and slowly started to swing around with its stern leeward and pointing to shore. Lonzo approached the ship's north side.

Etta could see two crew members working on a lifeboat that hung in the riggings on the side of the ship. *What dey doin'? Dey lowerin' dat lifeboat. Dey gon pull us up in dat, I reckon.*

Lonzo rested his oars, watched the smaller sailboat closely and waited. Etta's view of the sailboat was blocked by the large ship. There was a noise of pulleys, and the lifeboat dropped quickly, splashing in the water. Lonzo dug hard on the oars, pulling the rowboat alongside the larger lifeboat. "Grab it!" he yelled out. He pulled one oar in as Etta grabbed the rolling lifeboat. Rachel and Lonzo helped. Soon the boats were rising and falling more or less together.

Still holding on with his left hand, Lonzo put away the second oar, leaned over and took Matthew from Rachel with his free arm. He pulled the lifeboat closer. Rachel threw a leg over the side and rolled onto her back in the bottom of the lifeboat. Etta watched her mother as she looked up into the faces of the crewmen crowded along the railing. She sat up in her old man clothes, took off her hat and waved it. The men responded by waving their own and calling out, "Hurrah!"

261

Etta took her hat off, waved it and went over the side of the lifeboat. "HURRAH!" All of the men cheered.

Etta looked back at her grandfather. "I love you, Grandpa. Thank you for savin' us."

"I love you, too, Honey. Yuh be sho an' write us. So glad dat yuh gon be safe. Write yoh grandma now."

They began ratcheting up the lifeboat. Etta and her mother waved to Lonzo, who was already rowing hard for the shore. Etta stood and looked for the sailboat. Soon the gunnel was even with the ship railing. Ten or twelve crew members were lined around the deck. A sailor brought a stool. He bowed and offered a hand to Rachel. "Madam?" Etta held Matthew as her mother climbed over and stepped down. She handed him back.

A young man abou her age approached. With his help, Etta tried to make a graceful exit of the lifeboat.

Someone that, by his hat at least, appeared to be the captain, strode up, removed the hat and bowed deeply. Rachel offered her hand.

How she know to do dat?

Etta 's head was spinning as the captain turned to her. "Madamoiselle." He bowed and kissed her hand. She thought to close her mouth.

"Welcome." He bowed again.

"Captain, may I ask a question?" Etta pointed toward the shore. "Is that other ship tryin' to stop us?"

The Captain smiled, turned, and took out a small telescope. Extending it, he examined the sailboat. "Too bad if they are. They're dead in the water. They've hit a windless pocket out there, I guess, or a sandbar." He shook his head, put away the telescope and glanced at the flags above him. "Don't worry about them."

He turned to the crew. "Let's get underway, Men. Next stop, Philadelphia."

The Captain offered his arm to Rachel and showed her to her quarters. The young man that had helped Etta from the boat walked up to her. "May I show you to your cabin, Mademoiselle?"

Etta smiled. "I see where dey goin'."

The young man bowed. "No, Madamoiselle. Your cabin is there." He pointed to a different doorway.

Got my own cabin. She looked at the young man. "Would you come back in a little while? I need to catch my breath out heah on the deck." Etta looked up at the many colorful flags, joyful in the wind. "I want to watch us get underway."

He smiled and bowed. "Certainly. I'll be back shortly."

Etta walked toward the stern as the men raised anchor and sail. She felt the tug of the wind on the ship and was concious of the men's work. She watched as Blackbeard and Bonita began to slip away. She looked up at the sails, now full. The flags on the tops of the two masts were dancing in circles. Etta shook her head. The tooth on her chest became warm. She took it and held it against her cheek. *You comin' wid us, ain't yuh, Grandpa?*

Etta knew the answer before she had finished the question.

Well, I know. We both be tied tuh dis place. I be back, claim what's mine, Grandpa, jus' like you say. We be together den.

Etta felt a warm peace spread outward from her chest. She looked back at Bonita and made a vow. "I'll always be Geechee, and you'll always

263

be home." She looked down at her scarred, calloused palms, then back up and took the young man's arm. He escorted her to her cabin and to her new life.

63005726R00148

Made in the USA
Columbia, SC
07 July 2019